HER
BROKEN
WINGS

BOOKS BY D.K. HOOD

Don't Tell a Soul
Bring Me Flowers
Follow Me Home
The Crying Season
Where Angels Fear
Whisper in the Night
Break the Silence

D.K. HOOD

HER BROKEN WINGS

bookouture

Published by Bookouture in 2020

An imprint of Storyfire Ltd.
Carmelite House
50 Victoria Embankment
London EC4Y 0DZ

www.bookouture.com

ISBN: 978-1-78681-901-7
eBook ISBN: 978-1-78681-902-4

To Michelle, Jasmine, Savannah, Cooper, Zack, Jake, Wesley, and Gary

PROLOGUE

Twenty years ago

Dark clouds rolled across the sky, starving the endless night, with no hope of illumination from the waning moon. Outside the wind whined through the trees and buffeted the house in wild gusts. She lay very still, not making a sound in the alcohol-soaked air. The door to the bedroom hung open, and the ticking of the hundred-year-old grandfather clock in the hallway stripped away the hours and minutes until dawn. Her head pounded and the cut on her lip tasted like metal, but she'd made plans to get away and it was now or never. Heart hammering, she slid silently from the bed and headed for the door, stepping with care to avoid the creaky wooden floorboards. She'd hidden her clothes in the bathroom laundry basket and quickly dressed before moving along the hallway like a ghost to her boys' bedroom.

Tousled but anxious for the secret adventure to begin, they shrugged into their coats, pulled on their boots, and snuck down the hallway to the stairs. Dizzy with fear, she crept past her bedroom door and pressing a finger to her lips urged them forward.

In a grind of familiar machinery, the grandfather clock struck the hour and she froze, mid-stride. *Gong, gong, gong, gong, gong, gong.*

The sound echoed through the house like an intruder alarm, but as the vibration of the last chime dissipated, not a sound came from her bedroom. She followed the boys downstairs and they slipped out the door in silence. She grabbed their hands and ran to the old battered sedan parked out front. With her boys safely inside, she climbed behind the wheel. Parked on the sloping driveway, she'd planned to roll the vehicle some ways away from the house before starting the engine and heading for the reservation. She could hide there and he'd never find her.

After fumbling the key into the ignition, she took one last furtive glance at the house. Light spilled from the bedroom and she gasped in terror at the face twisted with rage at the window. *He knows. He'll never let us leave.* She turned the key. The old car shivered and shuddered but refused to start. She banged her fists on the steering wheel. "Come on, come on."

After pumping the gas, she tried again and the engine spluttered into life. Wasting no time, she headed down the isolated dirt road, bouncing over tree roots and the sunken tire tracks left in the mud after last winter's melt. Tall, foreboding trees lined the driveway like sentries to form the dark tunnel to her prison. As she burst through the gate on the other side, the sun was no more than a light haze on the horizon. Not much further now, and the moment she turned onto the highway, she'd be free.

The old mining road stretched out before her, the grasslands like a sea of turbulent water under the swirling morning mist. Fear cramped her stomach with every glance into the rear-view mirror. She'd tried to escape before but each time he'd found her and dragged her back. His drinking had gotten so bad he'd kill her soon enough, and she refused to allow a monster to raise her sons. As the wall of pines lining Stanton Road came into view, she stared at the long winding blacktop that would take her to safety and floored the gas pedal.

"Daddy's coming." One of her sons had twisted around in his seat and was staring out the back window. "He's going to be angry again."

Panic gripped her by the throat and sweat coated her flesh at the sight of bobbing headlights, but she forced her voice to remain calm. "We'll be on the highway soon and he won't be able to catch us."

She took the bend onto Stanton Road at an angle, sending dirt and gravel flying up in a gray cloud. The old tires gripped the blacktop and she pushed the gas pedal to the floor. Five miles to the on-ramp and she'd be on the highway, and then only a few more miles to the private road deep in the forest that would take her home. As a Native American, once inside the reservation she and her sons would vanish like smoke. She glanced in the mirror and swallowed hard. The truck's headlights lit up the road and it was coming fast. The empty road ahead of her filled her with terror. She'd hoped by leaving early, a delivery truck or someone would be traveling into Black Rock Falls at this hour. If he caught up with her again, she'd be defenseless.

She let out a cry of anguish when the car's engine spluttered and steam crept out from under the hood, but she pushed on. Trees flashed by in a sea of green and black but her gaze remained fixed on the yellow line down the middle of the blacktop.

Bright lights hit her mirror, blinding her, and then she heard the roar of a powerful engine. Terrified, she willed the car to go faster and moved out to straddle the yellow line; if he couldn't overtake her, he couldn't push her off the road. The next moment the car's engine squealed in a metal-on-metal shriek and shuddered. Clouds of smoke poured from under the hood, obstructing her view of the road. Fumes filled the car and, choking, she wound down the window. A blast of freezing air slapped her in the face but the lights behind her had gotten closer. She gasped in distress and pressed the accelerator but the engine made one last moan and stopped running. The momentum took her some distance but he was almost on her, the bright lights from his truck filling the car's interior and burning her eyes.

With seconds to spare, she pulled off the road and sprang from the car, flinging open the back door. "Grab your backpacks and run that way." She pointed into the forest. "Don't look back."

To hide them from the enraged lunatic getting slowly from his truck with a shovel in one hand, she headed in the opposite direction to lure him away.

"Mommy, don't leave us here." A plaintive wail came from behind her.

She stopped and looked around as her tormentor crashed into the forest. She gaped in horror as he scooped up his son and then threw him to the ground like garbage. Blood trickled from the young boy's nose as he lay unmoving. She ran at her husband and pounded his chest with her fists. "What have you done?"

His laugh raised the hairs on her flesh as he tossed her aside and then swung the shovel like a baseball bat. The clang inside her head vibrated into her eyes. As she fell, the ground came up fast and pine needles prickled her cheek. She hoped her other son had gotten away but she would never know. As she reached out to touch the outstretched hand of her little boy, the smell of the woodlands filled her head as if to soothe her. She'd missed the pine-scented mountain air. Her sight blurred and then cleared for a few seconds, allowing her to see the sky. The storm clouds parted and the rising sunbeams pierced the branches like a halo of gold around them. High above a murder of crows circled and then filled the trees as if welcoming her home.

CHAPTER ONE

Monday afternoon

Heart pounding, Sheriff Jenna Alton edged her way inside the drugstore, keeping a line of shelves between her and the young guy in a ski mask aiming a gun at the pharmacist. The man's finger was on the trigger and his hands shook so bad, she'd have to use all her powers of negotiation to prevent him from shooting the pharmacist at close range. The voice of her second in command and close friend, Deputy David Kane, came through her earbud.

"Locked on target."

Jenna tapped her speaker twice, indicating, she'd received his message. Having a six-five, ex-military sniper as backup in situations like these sure made life easier, and if she gave the order, he'd splatter the young man's brains all over the store. Pulse thumping in her ears, she moved with stealth past the cosmetics. A myriad of perfumes from the products cramming the shelves accosted her. To her right a coffee machine suddenly hummed into action, startling her. Taking a steadying breath, she peeked around the corner and met the pharmacist's terrified gaze. She lifted her weapon to take aim, edging closer, and then held one finger to her lips, motioning with her Glock for him to move away from the man with the gun.

"Don't just stand there gawking at me." The young man lifted the pistol and aimed between the pharmacist's eyes. "How many times have I got to tell you? Pain meds, the stronger the better. Fill up this bag." He thrust a backpack across the counter. "Do it now, unless you want to die."

Jenna gave the pharmacist a curt nod. The gunman had given him an excuse to move away from immediate danger.

"Sure, just take your finger off the trigger, son." The pharmacist lifted his chin. "I'd rather give you what you want than risk the chance of not seeing my wife and kids one more time." He took the bag and turned away, moving behind a partition.

Jenna scanned her position; with the pharmacist out of the line of fire, she had to make a move. The flimsy shelving lined with cans of baby formula wouldn't stop a bullet, but it might slow it down some. Not wanting to startle the man into a gunfight, she aimed her Glock between the cans and kept her voice low. "Sheriff's department. Lower your weapon and we can talk about this before someone gets hurt."

"Listen, Sheriff, I don't want to hurt anyone. Just let me walk out with the drugs." The man's eyes locked on hers and he trained his weapon at her.

"Jenna, give me the word." Kane sounded insistent in her ear.

Her gaze moved over the young man's trembling body and she decided reasoning with him might work. "Unless you drop your weapon now, you won't leave here alive." She held her weapon in both hands and aimed at his chest. "You're surrounded and I have a sniper outside aiming at your head—and he never misses. Now lower your weapon and we'll talk. If you need help, this isn't the way to go about it."

"You don't understand." The gunman dropped his gun to his side and his voice came out in an anguished sob. "I've been fired and now I don't have money for my mom's pain meds. She's dying and I stayed home a few days to care for her. She can't go another night without pills." He lifted his weapon again and aimed at her. "I walk out with the meds or I'm killing you and the pharmacist."

Wrong answer. Jenna heard a zing as a bullet embedded in the man's shoulder. Kane had made the shot, not to kill but to disarm. As the young man cried out, his gun clattered across the tiles and he slid down the counter to sit on the floor. Moaning, he rocked back and forth, gripping his arm. Jenna dashed out from the aisle and kicked his pistol out of reach and then, aiming her Glock at his head, stared down at him. "Remove the ski mask. What's your name?"

"Dirk Grainger." He dragged off the mask with a bloody hand and then lifted his pain-filled eyes to her. "If I go to jail, my mom will die alone in agony. Please, Sheriff, do what you want with me but you gotta help her."

"You threatened to kill me." Jenna glared at him. "You're lucky you live in Black Rock Falls or you'd be dead." She bent to examine his wound. "It's a through and through. You'll be fine."

"Paramedics are on their way." Kane pushed into the store with Deputy Jake Rowley close behind. His gaze moved over Jenna and then he pulled on a surgical glove and bent to pick up the weapon. "It's not loaded."

"I know this boy." The pharmacist came out from behind the counter, unwrapping a wad of cotton. He bent down and held the dressing against the wound. "Press this against it, son." He stood and turned to Jenna. "He's telling you the truth. The nursing home turned out his mother a few weeks ago, and Dirk here stayed home to care for her. He had some vacation time due but the plant let him go." His brow wrinkled into a frown. "It's getting late, and if you arrest Dirk, who'll look after his mom tonight?"

Jenna frowned. She'd heard rumors about conditions at a local nursing home. "Was she out at Glen Park Palliative Care?"

"Yeah." Dirk's face was sheet-white. "When they took our money, they said she'd receive the best of care until she died. Three months she was there, and then they called me to go get her, said she wasn't dying." He looked up at her. "Doc Brown and two others told me she's terminal."

Jenna exchanged a look with Kane and he shrugged. She looked down at Dirk. "I'll see what I can do."

"Thank you, ma'am." Dirk looked panic-stricken. "I can't leave my mom alone for long. It will be dark soon and someone needs to be with her."

Jenna nodded. "Okay. Give me your address, and I'll need your house key." She took down the details and they waited for the paramedics to take him to the free clinic. "Go with him, Rowley. I'll call you."

As the paramedics wheeled Dirk out on a gurney, she turned to Kane. "We'll need to get help for his mom and then try and sort out this mess."

"I won't press charges against him." The pharmacist adjusted his spectacles. "I've known that boy since he was a baby. He must've been pushed to the limit to commit a crime."

Jenna straightened. "Obviously." She turned to Kane. "Outside."

She stepped outside, inhaling the fresh pine scent wafting on a cool breeze from Stanton Forest, and watched as the ambulance merged into the traffic. She had a responsibility as sheriff to bring criminals to justice, but she also had the discretion to charge someone or not. She'd been staring into space for some moments when Kane's voice broke through her thoughts.

"So, what are you planning on doing, Jenna?" Kane walked to his truck and leaned against the door. "He was playing with fire aiming a gun at you. How could I possibly have known it wasn't loaded?"

Jenna looked out to the snowcapped mountains and shrugged. "I trusted your judgment. You usually disable rather than kill." She moved her attention back to him.

"I figured he was shaking so much, he wouldn't have been able to hit the side of a barn, and you'd taken cover, but if you'd given the word, I would've killed him." Kane shook his head.

"But you didn't. You used sound judgment and disarmed him." She considered the situation and made the call. "If he comes up clean, I'm not charging him. It was extenuating circumstances and his weapon wasn't loaded. I don't believe he intended to hurt anyone and was obviously out of his mind with worry. I'll give him a warning and let him go. The gunshot wound to his shoulder is enough punishment." She sighed. "If it goes to court, without the pharmacist pressing charges, he'll only get a fine. He doesn't have money or a job and will end up turning to a life of crime."

"I'll check him out." Kane used his phone to run Grainger's name through the records. "Nope, not so much as a parking ticket."

"Okay, call Rowley. Tell him when the doctors are through with Grainger to give him a warning and a ride home. We're done here." Jenna thought for a few seconds and held up a finger to Kane. "Just give me a minute." She pulled out her cellphone and called Doc Brown's surgery. After a few minutes' wait, the old doctor's voice came through the speaker.

"What can I do for you, Sheriff?"

"I have a situation." Jenna glanced at Kane. "I'm not asking you to divulge information about a patient, but I need immediate care for Mrs. Grainger. The nursing home discharged her some weeks ago and her son tried to hold up the drugstore to get her meds. I need a place to care for her this afternoon; she's alone."

"I'll make some calls. I'm happy to treat her, and the free clinic will take care of her meds. I'll see if Sunnybrook will take her. They have a few places for uninsured patients. I'll pull a few strings and get back to you without delay."

Jenna heaved a sigh of relief. "Thanks. It's urgent. We're heading over there now but we can't care for her overnight."

"Dirk should have come to me for help." Doc Brown sighed. *"I'll find her a place."*

"Thank you. I'll look forward to hearing from you soon." She disconnected. "I guess we'd better get over to the house and wait with her until her ride arrives. Problem is, we don't have any pain meds to offer her."

"Maybe Wolfe can help." Kane opened the door of his truck and slid behind the wheel.

Jenna climbed into the passenger seat and stared at him in disbelief. Shane Wolfe, ex-marine turned local medical examiner, was the last person she would've called. "Don't you think calling in the ME before the poor woman has died is a bit premature?"

"Nope." Kane started the engine and headed down Main Street. "He's licensed to administer drugs. He became a medical doctor well before he studied forensics. Before that, he was a field medic. As we don't have anyone on hand and it's an emergency, he's the best choice we have." He entered Grainger's address into the GPS.

Since arriving in Black Rock Falls in the witness protection program, with a new name and face, Jenna hadn't been involved with the elderly or infirm. Her previous life, as DEA Agent Avril Parker, hadn't offered her any useful insight into the running of nursing homes either. She shrugged. "Okay, I'll call him. I hope he's not busy."

"Unlikely—no one has died around here lately." He glanced at the GPS and then headed through town.

A number of murders had occurred since she'd become sheriff, and she'd been enjoying a normal life for a change. Jenna shot him a glance. "Did you have to tempt fate?"

"Well, apart from today's adrenalin rush, my last case was chasing down a crate of dog food stolen from out back of the 7-Eleven." He grinned at her. "Don't worry. I figure the serial killers have holed up for winter."

Jenna laughed. "Don't be so sure. With our luck, they'll come out for Halloween."

CHAPTER TWO

Darkness crept into the room, a blackness so unforgiving that Carol couldn't see across the bedroom to the large picture windows. Not one moonbeam came through the glass to penetrate the night. She'd lain awake for hours listening to the old house creaking in the wind. The trees outside, once so beautiful dressed in their summer green, now resembled blackened skeletons intent on scratching their branches down the walls like nails on a chalkboard. Snow was late in coming this year, but bad weather was on its way and the old house complained as if its bones ached. Her heart pounded. The strange noises from the buffeting wind sounded like someone mounting the stairs, and even the comforting scent and warmth of her husband sleeping beside her failed to ease the intense feeling of foreboding.

Eventually, she snuggled under the blankets. Eyelids heavy, she had almost grasped sleep when the floorboards outside her door creaked in a familiar whine. The doorknob rattled. Panic had her by the throat and she poked her husband. "Lucas, wake up. Someone's in the house."

She forced her eyes wide open. The door sweeping across the carpet sounded so loud in the silence. "Lucas."

The next moment a blinding light flooded the room. She squinted at the dark figure filling the doorway.

Putt, putt, putt.

The light vanished, plunging her back into inky blackness. She slipped her hand toward Lucas, and her fingers brushed over the unmistakable shape of a feather floating in a pool of warm, sticky fluid. The liquid spread across the sheets, seeping through her nightgown. Petrified, she rolled off the bed and sprawled on the carpet, trembling with fear. Red spots danced in her vision, blinding her. She had to get away.

Her fingers swept the edge of the bed and she crawled into the narrow space below and made herself as small as possible. Her gasps seemed to echo around the room and she shoved one fist into her mouth, too scared to breathe. Sick to her stomach, she heard the brush of shoes on the carpet as the intruder left the room. Seconds dragged on like hours as she hugged her knees too afraid to breathe. The house shuddered and moaned as if crying out in distress and then the wind dropped, but all she could hear was the *drip, drip, drip* of blood as her husband's life flowed away.

CHAPTER THREE

Tuesday morning

Deputy Jake Rowley, had spent all his working life as deputy to Sheriff Alton, she'd trained him well and he enjoyed taking the extra responsibilities. When he'd received the garbled call from a woman, convinced someone was in her house, he'd acted immediately. Although, since the wind had picked up, the calls from people hearing things at night had increased. Of late, if anything happened in the middle of the night, and it was his turn for the callouts, it seemed he found himself in a dark sinister house, in a moonless night. He had to admit driving up the long dark winding driveway to the Robinson's isolated house, knowing a prowler could be close by had his adrenalin pumping. He aimed his cruiser at the front door and left his lights blazing. Surrounded by pines and leafless blackened trees that spread long shadows and moaned with every puff of wind. The modern style home stood open to the elements. The howling gusts had spread leaves across the front porch and through the open door to litter the polished wooden floor. Jake scanned the area, pulled on surgical gloves, and weapon drawn, approached the silent, dark hallway. "Sheriff's department. Are you there, Mrs. Robinson?"

His stomach clenched the moment his Maglite picked out blood droplets on the stairs and the red ribbon smeared along the wall as if someone had used it for support. He paused for a beat—if he followed protocol, he should hightail it back to his vehicle to radio for backup. He squared his shoulders. The frantic woman who'd called him for help might be in trouble. He yelled out again but only the whine of the house answered him. Only a fool walked into a dark house alone, and using the beam of his flashlight, he found a panel of switches and flicked them on. The ground floor of the house flooded with light, and only a few dark rooms led off the hallway. Alert and heart pounding, he moved into the room on his right and found the light switch. After clearing the area, he shut the door and then moved on to the next until he arrived in the kitchen. It was empty and led to a mudroom at the back, and from there a door led outside. He checked the back door and found it locked.

The moaning sounds from the house set his attention to high. The trees grew so close, the branches tapped at the windows and scraped the walls with each gust of wind. He moved out of the kitchen. "Mrs. Robinson, are you here?"

Nothing.

He swallowed hard at the implications of his unanswered call and moved back down the hallway. With the ground floor secured, he stared at the blood trail from the top of the staircase. Stepping with care to avoid destroying evidence, he followed a line of crimson droplets to one of the two doors set beneath the stairs. One had an open sliding bolt lock, which he assumed led to the cellar, and the other had blood smeared over the door handle. Not wanting to venture into a cellar without backup, he slid the bolt across. Heart pounding, he moved to the other door; with his back to the wall and weapon aimed, he eased it open.

An anguished sob came from inside, and turkey-peeking around the opening, he came face to face with a blood-soaked woman, hiding in a broom closet and dressed only in her PJs. "Carol Robinson?"

Instead of replying, she lashed out at him, babbling insanely. He kept his distance and tried to calm her. "Carol, I'm Deputy Rowley. You're safe now."

The hysterical woman gave a feral cry and, glaring at him, kept on coming, her eyes wild. He had no choice but to spin her around, cuff her, and then drag her screaming into the kitchen. She could be a killer and he wasn't taking any chances. He scanned the area for a suitable place and used flexicuffs to secure her to a sturdy towel rack attached to a center island. He pushed the trembling but now silent woman into a chair. "Sit there and I'll go check the rest of the house and find you a blanket."

He swallowed hard and headed back to the staircase. All above was in darkness, and the constant scraping and whining from the trees outside was distracting. He mounted the stairs and followed the bloody trail, turning on lights as he went, and paused at an open door. The warm stench of blood crawled up his nostrils; whatever was inside the room, it was real bad. He stood to one side. Not a sound came from within and he gathered his nerve to scan the room with his Maglite. The beam moved over a patch of blood on the cream carpet and onto the bed. His stomach lurched as the light flowed over a blood-covered body in pajamas. It was his worst nightmare. Beside the body, a pool of congealing crimson filled the once pristine white bedsheets. He hit the light switch and turned away to lean against the door, panting.

Pushing down the need to puke, he cleared the next three rooms and grabbed a blanket from the closet. He headed back downstairs, but even with the lights blazing in every room, he scanned the area constantly. If the killer had managed to elude him, he could be in danger. He went back inside the kitchen and draped the blanket around Mrs. Robinson. "You're safe now. There's nobody here. Do you want to tell me what happened?"

Apart from the initial 911 call and her cries of fear when he'd restrained her, she was silent, staring unnervingly into space. He cleared his throat. "I'm sorry for cuffing you but until I know what happened here, you're the prime suspect. I'm going to get you some help."

As he walked to the front door, he pulled out his phone and called the sheriff. He turned on the porch lights and returned to his cruiser to speak to the sheriff in private. He was surprised at how fast she picked up. It was way past two in the morning.

"Yeah, Rowley, what's happened?"

Rowley opened his notebook to relay the information. "Possible home invasion out on Riverside Drive, Majestic Rapids. I'm on scene. One deceased by the name of Lucas Robinson. Gunshot victim. Carol Robinson, his wife, called it in. I have a woman I assume is her but she's hysterical. I have her waiting in the kitchen."

"Did you check the victim's life signs?"

"Ah, no need. From the damage, it looks like the gunman used a hollow-point to the head." Rowley cleared his throat. "I went to the top of the stairs and could see from the door. It's not pretty."

"The wife may be the shooter." The sheriff sounded alarmed. *"Don't turn your back on her."*

"Copy that." Rowley sighed. As if he'd make that rookie mistake. "As there appears to be no sign of a break-in and nothing appears to be disturbed in the house, I came to the same conclusion and secured Mrs. Robinson. She's not happy but I've made her as comfortable as possible. I've cleared the house and all the lights are on, but I haven't checked out the cellar. I slid the bolt across the door but thought I'd wait for backup before heading down there alone."

"You followed procedure. Anything else I should know?"

He gave her a rundown of the situation. "This place is remote. The trees come right up to the walls and it's as if they intended to hide the house here—there's no lawn or garden just a twisty driveway. With the wind blowing the trees against the house, I'm hearing noises coming from all over."

"Does the kitchen have one door or does it have another leading out back?"

Rowley looked all around as he spoke. The shadows moving across the porch could conceal a killer. "The kitchen is at the back of the house. It has one door leading to a mudroom that leads outside. I made sure to check the lock on the back door and I'm staring at the front door. The other kitchen door leads to a hallway."

"Okay, call Wolfe. Go and stay in the kitchen with Mrs. Robinson. Turn on your com and I'll contact you again when I'm close. I'm on my way."

"Roger that." Rowley disconnected and called the ME, Shane Wolfe.

The ME would arrive shortly with the sheriff close behind. He heaved a sigh of relief and headed back to the house. Once inside the kitchen, he set about filling the coffee maker from the fixings on the counter. Carol Robinson was shaking so bad, he feared she might be going into shock. He tried to coax a few words from her and noticed she seemed to be settling a little. Once the coffee was ready, he released one of her hands and then slid her a cup, keeping well away in case she decided to hurl it at him.

Time seemed to move so slowly and every creak of the house had him on alert. He kept one hand on his weapon and sipped a cup of the strong coffee. Ten minutes had passed and at least she was drinking the coffee now and had stopped trembling.

He took a deep breath. "The sheriff is on her way. Is there a family member I can call for you, or your lawyer?"

The woman's bloodshot eyes lifted slowly to him and she regarded him for long moments as if considering her answer. The look she gave him unnerved him. Without moving her attention from his face, she gave an almost imperceptible shake of her head. To his relief, he heard a vehicle in the distance. He placed his cup on the counter and hurried to the front door to peer out the window, using the frame as cover. He had no idea if the killer was the woman inside or a maniac running loose in the grounds. When Wolfe's white van backed into the space beside his cruiser, he scanned the woods behind him, searching for any movement. The wind through the trees made the entire area seem alive. He opened the door as Wolfe ran up the front steps. "Did you see anyone on the way here?"

"Nah. What do we have?" Wolfe walked toward him carrying his forensics kit and tossed him a body bag. "We'll do a sweep of the crime scene first and then I'll come get the gurney for the body." He looked at Rowley's gloves. "Touch anything without gloves?"

Rowley shook his head. "Nope and I kept away from the blood." He followed Wolfe up the steps. "The wife, Carol Robinson, is in the kitchen. She's acting a little wacky, maybe you need to look at her first."

"If she was in the room when someone shot her husband, I'm not surprised." Wolfe stopped inside the door, looked at the stairs, and whistled. "Is she injured?"

Rowley followed his gaze to the blood-smeared wall beside the staircase and down the hallway to the bloody handprints on the broom closet door. "Not that I can tell. She's not saying much at all."

"Put the body bag down somewhere and I'll give you some booties to wear. We don't want to contaminate the scene any more than necessary." Wolfe placed his bag on a hall table, pulled out booties, and gave Rowley a pair before pulling on his own. "I'll check on Mrs. Robinson and then we'll start upstairs."

"I restrained her." Rowley led the way into the kitchen. "I believe she's okay."

"Carol? My name is Shane Wolfe, I'm the ME. I just want to check you for injuries and take a few swabs." At her complete lack of response, Wolfe exchanged a glance with Rowley. "Catatonic state after a shock is possible."

Rowley waited for Wolfe to check her over. As she still refused to speak, Wolfe sighed. "I'll call the paramedics; she needs to be assessed in a mental health facility."

"Is he dead? Lucas, my husband—is he dead?" Mrs. Robinson's voice came out in a soft quiver.

"I'm afraid so." Wolfe patted her on the back. "I'm sorry for your loss. Can you tell me what happened?"

"A man… with a gun." Her hands shook and she looked around wildly. "He's still here. I can feel him looking at me."

Rowley looked over his shoulder, checking the hallway again. The next moment, a loud bang came from the direction of the cellar, followed by a piercing howl.

CHAPTER FOUR

He'd forgotten how cold it was in Montana in October. Not that he minded. The icy chill seeping through his clothes only heightened his awareness. He loved the dark. The long shadows and black trees surrounding him added to his excitement. Wind gusts whistled through the pines and stirred up the fall leaves in great plumes of dust. The noise covered his progress back through the woods as he moved closer to the house. He wanted to be inside to watch the mystery unfold. The woman's sobbing screams still echoed in his ears and he wished the exquisite sound hadn't stopped. It was like the sweetest music and had tempered the missing part of his latest kill. He'd missed the begging and pleading he usually encountered the moment they knew they were going to die. Shooting a sleeping man had hardly whet his appetite but this was Black Rock Falls, and he owed it to the people of this fine county, the very best in murder and mayhem.

As he crouched behind a patch of dead undergrowth, it was as if the building had turned into a dollhouse, all lit up inside. The deputy who'd arrived first had turned on every light, giving him a grandstand view of the rooms facing the woods. In fact, he could see right down the hallway and into the kitchen. The wide staircase and the wall smeared with blood intrigued him. What had happened after he'd left? Had the wife rolled in her husband's remains before she ran screaming into the night? He stared at the wide-open door and wondered why the young deputy hadn't pulled the drapes. If he'd been inclined, he could easily shoot him through any of the windows at close range. For anyone inside the house looking out, the pitch darkness surrounding him would offer him maximum cover until it was too late.

He smothered a chuckle. The sheriff would arrive soon and he'd witness her expert crime-solving skills first-hand. He'd heard so much about her. In fact, she'd become almost a cult figure among men like him. Yeah, he had friends—no names, of course. In chat rooms buried so deep in the web nobody could find them, Sheriff Jenna Alton was a frequent topic of conversation, and outsmarting her was a fantasy for some. She'd become a challenge, and many creatures of the night, like him, would soon be rising for the bait.

CHAPTER FIVE

Jenna had sat bolt upright in bed at the sound of her cellphone. Her first thought went to Dirk Grainger's mother. She'd left the seriously ill woman tucked up safely in Sunnybrook Nursing Home under Doc Brown's care. However, the ringtone told her that Deputy Rowley, the young man she'd trained up from a rookie to become a first-class lawman, was calling her in the middle of the night. It was his turn to answer the 911 calls, and he wouldn't have disturbed her unless something bad had happened. The wind rattled the shutters on the windows as she turned on the bedside lamp and glanced at the clock. Oh yeah, at this time of the morning, someone had to be dead. She grabbed her pen and notepad and answered the call.

The moment she disconnected, Jenna pushed the hair from her eyes and called Kane. As usual he snapped awake in a second and was on his way.

Jenna dashed to the front door. By the time she'd fastened her duty belt around her waist and slipped into her coat, she could see Kane's headlights heading toward her. Having a deputy living in a cottage on her ranch had its benefits. She reset the alarm system and headed out the door into a dark, stormy night. An arctic blast hit her with force and cut through her thick jacket, raising goosebumps on her flesh. By the time she'd climbed inside Kane's truck, affectionately known as "the Beast," the cold had numbed her cheeks. "Drive fast. Rowley's alone out there."

"Roger that. I've had the engine idling since you called and there's no ice on the roads. I'll have us there in no time." The powerful engine roared and the truck's tires showered the fence with gravel as Kane pulled away from the house.

Jenna noticed that Duke, Kane's bloodhound, was missing from his usual place on the back seat. "I thought it would rain today but the storm clouds might bring the first snow. Is it too cold for Duke already?"

"Yeah. I left him asleep in his basket. There was no way he was coming out tonight." Kane sped along the driveway. "What did Rowley say?"

Jenna explained, entered the address into the GPS, and then turned in her seat to look at him. "We haven't had a home invasion before. Burglary, do you think?"

"I can't figure out why an intruder would use hollow-points in a burglary." Kane turned onto the highway leading into town. "They usually prefer to grab anything of value and get out fast. It will be interesting to examine the scene."

"I hope it's not a hit. I've seen a few execution-style murders involving the cartel." Jenna leaned back in her seat, trying to prevent bad memories from replaying like a movie in her head. "They wouldn't think twice about breaking into a house and killing a man in his sleep."

"Hmm, this town is spreading out so wide, anything could be happening out in the back country." Kane accelerated and the Beast purred as they flashed past the open grassland surrounding Jenna's ranch. The night was so dark, not one star peeked through the cloud cover. "What do we know about the victim?"

"I'll see what I can find." Jenna used her cellphone to access the records. "No priors. From what I can see, he's a financial advisor working in the local bank."

"Maybe he gave someone bad advice." Kane's gaze remained fixed on the road. "People have killed for less."

Jenna stared out the window. "I don't recall visiting Majestic Rapids. It must be the housing development close to the new White-Water Rapids Park."

"I believe it's between the park and the ski lodge." Kane glanced at her. "I'm looking forward to the snow this year. It's been a long time since I've had the chance to hit the slopes. Remember, as soon as the snow arrives and we have some downtime, you promised to come up there for a weekend to keep me company. It's no fun skiing on your lonesome."

Jenna laughed. "I wouldn't miss it. It'll be like taking a vacation." She pulled a knit hat from her jacket pocket and pulled it on. "Maybe Rowley will come with us and bring Sandy. I figure they're getting serious."

"We could ask him." Kane chuckled. "Maybe we should ask Wolfe and his girls along as well. I guess the town can get along without us for a couple of days."

"We do have Walters to fall back on." She considered her older deputy. "I mean, we'd only be a phone call away if the Four Horsemen of the Apocalypse rode into town."

Jenna chuckled as Kane turned onto Main Street and the headlights picked up the first Halloween decorations. The residents of Black Rock Falls went all out when it came to any festival, and Halloween was no exception. As they drove down Main and out to the suburbs, most of the homes would fit fine into the set of a horror movie. "Looking at our sweet little town, maybe the Four Horsemen have already arrived."

"Oh, I hope not."

Darkness seemed to close in around the truck as Jenna peered ahead for the entrance to the Robinsons' ranch. "I thought this area would have more houses. I've only seen two other driveways in the last mile."

"Maybe they're like you and want land to run horses." Kane slowed when the GPS told him the turn was coming up. "This looks like the place."

As the headlights picked out the name on the mailbox, Jenna nodded. "Yeah, this is it, and luckily, the gate's wide open."

Jenna glanced out the window as they negotiated the winding driveway, and an uneasy sensation crawled over her. The trees formed a dense wall each side of the road, and it was as if they tried to grab hold of the truck as they passed by. The long branches loomed out of the night like demons' claws from the surrounding blackness, only to become trees again in the beam from the headlights. With only the arc from their lights illuminating the turns in the road ahead, it was like driving into a tunnel. "I couldn't live out here. Can you imagine the wait for the snowplow to arrive during winter? I'm not so sure it would be able to make it around some of these tight bends."

"Most people aren't lucky enough to have the local snowplow driver living close by like you do, and they use their own." He flicked her a glance. "I'm getting one this year too."

Kane never ceased to amaze her. Jenna stared at him. "You want a snowplow now?"

"Yeah, it's neat. It attaches to the front of my truck. Rowley has a new one and showed it to me last time I dropped by. After last year's blizzards, I can't see the weather getting any better and we'll need it."

"Okay, but it's more work for you to do." Jenna searched ahead. "I don't see any lighting at all, and this driveway feels like we're driving around in circles."

"It's way too narrow. Too bad if another vehicle wanted to get by." Kane scanned the area and turned to her with one raised eyebrow. "I don't see any security either, and with the trees so close and all, they're asking for trouble. With this town's reputation, you'd figure they'd secure their ranch."

After another few minutes on the winding path, the glow from the house lights filtered through the trees. Jenna heaved a sigh of relief as they rounded the next bend and Rowley's cruiser and the ME's van came into view. "It looks like the gang's all here."

She attached her earbud and turned on the communications device attached to her belt. "Rowley, we're at the front of the house. I see the front door is open. What's your status?"

"We heard something just before, maybe coming from the cellar."

Jenna stiffened. "Okay, wait for backup."

"Copy that. There's blood everywhere. You'll need gloves and booties."

Jenna turned to Kane. "Stay alert. Rowley hasn't checked the cellar yet and it's a bloodbath so we'll need to suit up."

"I'll grab what we need from my kit." Kane slipped from the truck and opened the back door. "Here." He passed her a handful of equipment.

They moved up the front steps and Jenna caught sight of Wolfe and Rowley, weapons drawn and staring down a passageway. She pulled on her booties and then the gloves, and then shut the door behind them. "What is it?"

"Listen." Rowley motioned with his chin toward a door at the end of the hallway. "Sounds like someone or something is in the cellar."

The eerie shriek and thump sent an icy chill down Jenna's spine. *Why do I always get the creepy houses and dark cellars?*

CHAPTER SIX

The last thing Jenna wanted to do in the middle of the night after a brutal murder was to climb down a dark staircase into the unknown. She exchanged a glance with Kane and he shrugged. The remoteness of the Robinsons' home and the unusual noises had set her nerves on edge on arrival and the notion of opening the door to a cellar making noises straight from hell was sending her imagination into overdrive. She glanced at Rowley's sheet-white face, pulled her weapon and walked past him. "Stay here and watch our backs. We'll go and look." She swallowed hard. "Wolfe would you mind watching Mrs. Robinson until we're done?"

"Sure." Wolfe holstered his weapon, turned and headed for the kitchen.

A loud whine and a thump came from behind the cellar door. She turned to Kane trying to ignore the apprehension cramping in her stomach. "Not the Four Horsemen at least."

"Nah, maybe a hellhound or two." Kane's mouth twitched up at the corners. "Or an injured bear, whatever it is, men don't make that kind of noise."

Trust Kane to make light of the situation. "It's just as well you don't believe in ghosts or we'd be standing here all night. The door opens inward—pick a side." She ignored the fight or flight response making her heart pound in her chest and took a deep breath. "Ready?"

"Sure." Kane pulled his weapon, slid back the bolt, and glanced inside the pitch black. His voice boomed out in the dark space. "Sheriff's department, is anyone down there?"

The whine and bump came again. Jenna repeated the question, and when no response came, she edged closer to the opening. The freezing air smelled of wet cement, as if the owner had only finished it recently, and it didn't have the musty odor she usually associated with cellars. With the comforting warmth of her Glock in her palm, she eased one hand around the doorframe feeling for the light switch. She flicked it back and forth but nothing happened. Of course, the light didn't work; it was almost as if she expected it. An awful sense of foreboding crept over her. They could be walking into a trap, and if they stood at the top of the steps, they'd make clear targets. She flattened against the wall outside the door and turned to Kane. "Why is it every time we go into a cellar the lights are out?"

She reached for her Maglite and it came on in a brilliant white stream. Aiming it around the door and into the cellar, she moved the light down a flight of stairs and over an open bag of cement with a shovel beside it, leaning against the wall. Long shadows seemed to fill every corner and she didn't move until she'd checked out each one. Of course, the room was L-shaped and she couldn't see around the corner. *Never go into a dark cellar.* The warning rattled around in her subconscious. "It's as if it's daring us to walk into the unknown."

"At least the stairs are wide." Kane's flashlight came on beside her, and they stood side by side and scanned the area. "It looks empty but I guess we'd better take a look at what's around the corner."

The whine and bang came again, and the hairs on the back of Jenna's neck prickled. "There it goes again. Where is it coming from?"

"Furnace maybe?" Kane slipped down the steps and moved along the wall with his flashlight aimed along his weapon.

The sound came again as he disappeared around the corner.

"Shit!" Kane barked a strangled laugh. "Now that scared the hell out of me."

Heart pounding, Jenna rushed to his side. The darkness crept in behind her and an icy breeze seeped through her jeans. As she turned the corner, Kane's wide shoulders blocked her view. "What is it?"

"It looks like they're into taxidermy." Kane's light moved over a full-grown grizzly. Its glass eyes reflected the light back at them. "Funny place to keep it, down here in the damp."

Knowing the bear was long dead didn't prevent a rush of terror gripping Jenna as her light moved over the gaping mouth and outstretched paws. She took a step back and pushed down the need to run. After flicking her Maglite around the rest of the area, she sighed. "It's empty."

"It is apart from the bear and furnace but that's not what's making the noise." He moved his flashlight to a window on ground level. "It's that."

Jenna stared up at a window propped open with a stick. The unfastened shutters whined and bumped against the side of the house with each gust of wind. She moved her flashlight to the floor. Leaves had fallen inside making a small pile and she made out indistinct footprints leading away. "I think we've found the point of entry."

She moved closer to examine the window. "We'll leave that for now and come back when it's light to check for fingerprints and any footprints outside."

"Sure." Kane holstered his weapon. "I'll get a few shots of the scene." He pulled out his cellphone and took the pictures.

Jenna blinked from the flash but she turned and searched the floor. In one corner was a patch of drying cement. "Get a shot of that as well. I hope they're not burying bodies in here."

Once he'd finished, she headed back up the steps with Kane close behind. After locking the cellar door, she looked at Rowley's anxious face. "Just an open window. The noise was the shutters. It looks like our point of entry. We'll come back and check it out in daylight. Oh, and there's a stuffed bear down there." She smiled at him. "Go and take over from Wolfe. I'll view the crime scene and then interview Mrs. Robinson if she's talking. Does she have anyone she can stay with tonight?"

"No, ma'am." Rowley frowned. "I already asked her."

"Well, she can't stay here." Jenna frowned. "Call the hospital and make arrangements for her to be placed in our secure wing. I want her checked out by a doctor, and have them do a psych evaluation on her too. She'll be safe locked in the ward but make sure hospital security keeps an eye on her until we can arrange for someone to stay with her. I'll pack a bag for her as soon as Wolfe has cleared the crime scene."

"Copy that." Rowley turned and headed to the kitchen.

Jenna waited for Wolfe to return and they followed him single file up the stairs, avoiding the blood spatter on the carpet. The bedroom was off a landing at the top and its door stood wide open. Blood smeared the glossy white finish and frame as if someone had stumbled against it. The sight inside the room made Jenna gag. She'd witnessed many crimes from mutilated bodies to burn victims, but the smell of fresh blood seemed to surround her and crawl up her nose. Wanting to look away wasn't an option, and she took the face mask Kane pushed into her hand and placed it over her nose. What she discovered here could be crucial to identifying the killer, and no matter how disturbing, it was her responsibility to find justice for the victim.

The ME took the lead in a crime scene, and Jenna listened to Wolfe's running commentary. All around her, the house whined and moaned. She'd never experienced such wild weather since her arrival in Black Rock Falls, and as if seeing a blood-soaked victim wasn't bad enough, the rattling windows made her glance over her shoulder more than once. She glanced at Kane, who had his usual mask of professionalism fixed in place. He had the unique ability, like Wolfe, to turn off his emotional side and concentrate on the crime scene as a whole. She could blank out emotion to some degree, due to her own training, but to see Wolfe and Kane in action was awe-inspiring. "What do we have, Shane?"

"The victim is male but that's all I have so far, and I found a black feather in the bed. It might mean nothing but I've bagged it." Wolfe took several photographs of the scene, moving around the room and aiming his camera at every possible angle before pulling back the blood-soaked sheets. "From the metal fragments embedded in the wall and mattress, I'd say two maybe three shots to the head, and Rowley was right, this damage is from hollow-points." He sighed. "One would've sufficed, and two or three is way in excess. It's the same as a stabbing in some ways: people can use one thrust to kill, but in anger they stab a person multiple times. From this, and considering no one has disturbed anything in the house, I'd say this is a crime of passion."

"Or maybe a hit." Jenna looked at Kane. "This is your field of expertise, what do you think?"

"Possible." Kane leaned over the bed to examine the bullet fragments. "Using hollow-points tells me the intent to kill was there from the get-go. It's a sure thing, and whoever did this hit his target without injuring this man's wife."

"Or the shooter is the wife." Jenna pushed down nausea and moved to his side to examine the body. "It looks well planned. I didn't see any signs of forced entry but we'll have a better idea in the morning. We assume, he came in via the cellar and gained access through a conveniently unlocked door and then straight here, two maybe three shots before he walks out the front door leaving it open."

"Yeah." Kane straightened and turned to Jenna. "If they'd left the window open to maybe dry the patch of wet cement, I would've thought they'd have secured the shutters."

Jenna nodded. "And locked the cellar door." She shuddered. "I mean a bear could get through that opening. Why did they leave the door unlocked? I believe I need to have a chat with Mrs. Robinson." She looked at Wolfe. "Rowley said she wasn't talking. Did you coax anything out of her?"

"She told me someone shot her husband. I've collected samples and taken photographs of the blood spatter on her. It will prove where she was at the time of the shooting, and if she was involved, I'd expect to see gunshot residue." Wolfe continued to collect pieces of metal from around the victim. "Take it easy with her, she's fragile."

"Fragile or a good actor?" Jenna turned away and headed to the door. "The open window and unlocked door seem like more than a coincidence. I wonder if she paid someone to kill her husband—and if so, why?"

CHAPTER SEVEN

Jenna walked into the kitchen and sat at the table. She pulled out her notebook and looked at the bedraggled woman sitting opposite. She was in her late forties, petite, and blood had matted her blonde hair into red dreadlocks. A cellphone covered with crimson fingerprints sat on the table beside her. "I'm Sheriff Alton. Can you tell me your name?"

"Carol, Carol Robinson." The woman turned an empty cup in her hand. "I'd like another cup of coffee if that's okay?" She pushed the cup away and picked at the dried mess on her hands. "You have one too."

Relieved the woman was at least communicating, Jenna glanced at Rowley and nodded. "Sure." She leaned on the table and looked at Carol. "Do you feel up to telling me what happened here?"

She waited for long moments as Mrs. Robinson gathered herself. "Okay, let's start with you in bed. Did something wake you?"

"No, I'd been awake for hours. We haven't been here through winter yet and I didn't expect the house to be so noisy. The wind was making the house whine. Sometimes it was like a howling, the shutters shook, and it sounded like someone was trying to force them open. I thought I heard the floorboards creak out on the landing and tried to wake Lucas to tell him someone was in the house." Mrs. Robinson looked at Jenna and her hands trembled.

Jenna nodded. "You're doing really well. Did Lucas wake up?"

"No, he didn't stir, and then the light came on. It blinded me and I couldn't see more than a shadow in the doorway. I heard three bangs, not loud like a gunshot, but then it was dark again. I called out to Lucas but he didn't answer and then I felt his blood all over me." Mrs. Robinson stared into space and shook as if reliving the scene. "I didn't go and help him. I know I should've but I was so afraid. I hid under the bed and waited for a long time."

"So, when did you call us?" Jenna frowned. "Where was your cellphone?"

"My phone was on the bedside table. I crawled out to get it and then called 911." Mrs. Robinson swallowed hard and screwed up her eyes. "The light from the screen... I could see the blood dripping onto the carpet. There was so much blood... I just had to get away. I found my way downstairs and hid in the broom closet." She lifted the coffee to her lips, spilling it over her trembling hands. "I didn't go back and help Lucas. He's dead because of me, isn't he?" She let out a wailing sob. "I killed him."

Jenna shook her head and kept her voice low and with a concerned tone. "No, he died instantly. You couldn't have saved him, Carol." She sipped the coffee, grateful for a hot drink. "Do you remember opening the window in the cellar, or leaving the cellar door unlocked?"

"No." Mrs. Robinson looked confused. "Lucas was down there finishing up the floor before dinner. It was a small repair. Maybe he left it open. I don't know for sure. I was busy cooking dinner."

"Okay." Jenna pushed on. "Do you mind if we search the house and remove any evidence that might give us information about who killed your husband?"

"No, please do." Mrs. Robinson looked at her wide-eyed. "I want you to catch the person who did this to Lucas."

Jenna noted she had said "the person," which was unusual. "Does your husband have any enemies—anyone he owes money to perhaps?"

"Lucas? Enemies?" Mrs. Robinson shook her head. "No, he was liked by everyone."

Jenna frowned. "Did he ever hit you?"

"No, we were very happily married. He was a perfect husband."

With Mrs. Robinson being the last person to see the victim alive, Jenna needed more information, and Mrs. Robinson seemed to be more lucid by the minute. Keeping her talking was easing the shock. "What about the people at his work?"

"I don't think so." Mrs. Robinson met her gaze and then shrugged. "He did say he couldn't please all of the people all of the time but he did his best."

"Okay, I'll speak to his boss in the morning. Where does he work?" Jenna made notes and then lifted her attention back to the woman. "We didn't find a gun. Do you have any weapons in the house?"

"Yes." Mrs. Robinson's gaze moved to the passageway. "There's a gun safe in the den. The keys are hanging over there." She pointed to a small line of hooks beside the door to the mudroom.

Jenna looked up at Rowley. "Go check it out and see what ammo they use."

As Rowley slipped out the door, she turned back to Mrs. Robinson. "Have you argued with your husband lately?"

"No." Mrs. Robinson yanked on the flexicuffs. "You don't think I killed him, do you?"

Jenna kept her face neutral. "I'm sorry if I've upset you but we have to ask these questions when someone is killed. I'm looking for the reason someone shot your husband. I couldn't see any signs of a burglary. Do you have any valuables in the house?"

"No, nothing."

"Okay." Jenna nodded. "When you're up to it, we'll do a walk-through and check to make sure nothing's missing."

"If the TV is still there, that's the only valuable down here. We have a safe upstairs and I know for sure whoever shot Lucas didn't come far into the room." Mrs. Robinson's face was pale and eyes forlorn. "I'd have heard them. The safe is at the back of the closet and the sliding door makes a noise."

Jenna glanced up as Rowley came back into the room. He held out his cellphone with images of the weapons. She scrolled through the photographs and found a couple of hunting rifles and a Glock, with regular ammunition. "Thanks."

Jenna heard the siren of an ambulance close by. She met Mrs. Robinson's red-rimmed eyes. "I'm sending you to the hospital to get cleaned up, and I'd like you to see a doctor for a psychiatric evaluation. If you agree, the hospital will have some papers for you to sign. It won't cost you anything."

"Okay." Mrs. Robinson nodded slowly.

Jenna glanced up from her notes. "Do you have any medication you need to take with you?"

"No." Mrs. Robinson stared at her bloody nightgown and then shivered. "I'll need a change of clothes and some toiletries if I'm staying for a while."

"Sure. I'll go and pack you a bag. I'd like you to stay until we've finished our investigation and had the place cleaned." Jenna turned to Rowley. "Keep the paramedics outside. I don't want them tramping through the house. I'll be back in a few minutes." She headed out the kitchen and made her way along the hallway.

A couple of things played on her mind. If the shooter had used a hollow-point bullet, the first shot would've killed the victim, but if the killer pumped three shots in at close range, the victim's blood spatter would be all over them. Or if Mrs. Robinson had been lying in bed, Jenna assumed the blood spatter would be consistent with what she could see on her. Either way, she could be the shooter. When Rowley initially searched the house, he was looking for an intruder, not a weapon. She wondered if Mrs. Robinson had stashed a gun in the broom closet. From the blood trail, it was the only possible place unless it was under the couple's bed upstairs. The way Mrs. Robinson seemed to gather herself so fast after witnessing a horrific murder concerned her. She'd seen so many strange things in her life, it wouldn't surprise her if Mrs. Robinson had shot her husband from the doorway, stashed the gun somewhere, called 911, and then gone upstairs and rolled in her husband's blood. She could've staged the entire scene.

She used her Maglite to search the broom closet and found no trace of a weapon, but she did find a pair of boots with cement traces on the soles. *Maybe Lucas Robinson opened the cellar window after all.*

The murder wasn't the most gruesome Kane had worked on during his time in Black Rock Falls, but it came close to the top of his list. With a laser measurer in one hand, he moved around the room, calling out measurements for Wolfe. He stood just inside the door. "I figure the shooter stood here."

"That makes sense." Jenna walked up behind him, pulling on a face mask. "Mrs. Robinson said the light came on, there were three soft shots, and the light went off."

The angle didn't seem right and Kane frowned. "From the blood spatter, how tall was the shooter? The angle seems too high from my point of view."

"I'll take the reading from the head—well, what's left of it and take the measurement from there." Wolfe held out his hand for the device and then pointed it toward the door. "Okay, from the readings, I'd say close to six feet tall. Of course, this depends on if he aimed the weapon with one hand or two. Some people take a bent knee stance when shooting with two hands. What would you do, Kane?"

"If it went down like Jenna described, I'd turn on the light with one hand, shoot with the other, and then switch off the light and leave." Kane turned to examine the wall and then looked at Jenna. "Well, that's interesting."

"What is?" Jenna raised her eyebrows.

Kane re-enacted the shooter's moves and then smiled at her. "Okay, one thing we know for sure: the killer's left-handed."

"How so?" Jenna frowned.

"Timing. If the shooter was right-handed there'd have been a pause between turning on the light, aiming and shooting. The light switches are always on the right, so if I turn on the light, shoot, and then turn it off, I'd have to waste time changing my weapon from one hand to the other or twist around to use the switch and then aim. In that time, she would have had time to see the killer." Kane demonstrated a right-handed shoot and then switched to his left hand. "See, if the shooting happened instantaneously as Mrs. Robinson stated, the shooter has to be left-handed."

"Why not ambidextrous?" Jenna narrowed her gaze at him. "I've seen you shoot just as well with both hands."

"True." Kane shrugged. "But this has all the signs of a hit, so we're figuring a professional. A hit must be clean and fast. He's coming out of the dark and would've taken into account the sudden brightness maybe blinding him for a second. The weaker hand is usually less accurate and he wouldn't have risked it."

"Well, that's a start, the killer is around six foot and left-handed." Jenna looked at Wolfe. "The paramedics are close by. Okay if I get a change of clothes for Mrs. Robinson? Oh, and she mentioned a safe at the back of the closet. Kane, will you check it out and make sure no one's turned the place over? We don't need a search warrant. Mrs. Robinson gave me verbal permission."

"You're good to go." Wolfe looked at Jenna over the top of his mask. "I'm finished here. I'll go and get the gurney."

Kane walked to the closet that took up one complete wall and slid open the door. The runners made a distinctive grinding noise as if needing oiling. He pushed a line of suits and shirts to one side and found the safe. After dusting it for prints, he scanned them and found a match for the victim. The safe appeared to be undisturbed. He turned to look at Jenna. "The prints on the safe haven't been smudged. I doubt it's been touched since the victim last opened it."

"Mrs. Robinson mentioned the door made a noise, and she didn't hear anyone enter the room or open the closet door." Jenna filled a suitcase with items and then walked into the bathroom. "That's all I need." Her voice seemed to echo from the small room.

Kane stuck his head around the closet door. "How long are you planning on keeping Mrs. Robinson locked up in the secure ward?"

"I'm not sure." Jenna came out carrying a makeup bag and dumped an armful of items into the suitcase. "She doesn't have anyone, so maybe a few days held under psychiatric assessment will give Wolfe time to come up with a few results." She clicked the suitcase shut and then looked up at him. "You both believe this is a hit, but I want you to run another possibility through your mind. She shoots her husband from the door—she's a tall woman, maybe five-ten—and then wants to get up close and personal to make sure he's dead and pumps another couple of rounds in what's left of his head. She staggers downstairs covered in blood and hides in the broom closet to wait for Rowley. The front door was open. She could've opened it before she went upstairs to kill her husband, come down, and thrown the weapon outside in the bushes. The blood trail goes out far enough."

Kane nodded slowly. "Hmm, possible, so what's your take on the point of entry?"

"I'd say the victim opened the window to dry the cement. He came upstairs, forgot to lock the door, maybe he intended to go back later. I found his boots in the broom closet." Jenna frowned. "We'll have to wait until daylight to do a complete search of the area and check if there are footprints outside the cellar window or a weapon."

"Okay." Kane took the suitcase from her. "The paramedics are here."

"Good, I'd rather she didn't see Wolfe remove the body." Jenna hurried down the stairs.

Kane stared after her. To him the scene was a typical hit, but Jenna rarely accepted the obvious and considered every angle in a case. Voices drifted up from the hallway and he hustled downstairs to hand over the suitcase. Moments later Jenna came from the kitchen with Mrs. Robinson.

"Are you left-handed by any chance?" Jenna led her to the paramedic's gurney.

"Yes, how did you know?" Mrs. Robinson gave her a puzzled look.

"Oh, just a hunch." Jenna cast a meaningful look at Kane and then turned her attention back to Mrs. Robinson. "Try to get some rest and we'll drop by to talk to you in the morning." She nodded to the paramedics to take her away.

Kane looked at her and raised an eyebrow. "A hunch, huh?"

"Wasn't it you who once told me that the last person to see a murder victim alive is the killer?" Jenna smiled. "Sometimes the answer is just staring us in the face."

CHAPTER EIGHT

Before dawn Wednesday morning

The morning frost sat in the corners of the windshield of Parker Louis' truck as he waited for his friend, Tim Addams, to slip out to meet him. It was the darkest before dawn, and only a sliver of light escaped from the front door before Tim was in the seat beside him. Parker looked at Tim and grinned. "We should be able to get in and out before the first shift arrives for work."

"Yeah, but we don't want to be noticed driving around so early." Tim chucked his backpack onto the back seat and then turned to look at him. "Drive nice and slow." He looked around. "Good you left your rifle behind. If the boss shows early and catches us, we don't want the cops saying we were armed." A puff of steam came out of his mouth, surrounding him like cigarette smoke. "It's freezing in here. Can I turn up the heat?"

"Sure." Parker moved his truck away from the curb and drove away in stealth.

Excitement welled up inside him. The idea of sneaking onto a building site and stealing appliances before the installers arrived for work had been pure genius. The site boss left the cabins unlocked rather than risk giving the casual labor a set of keys. This lack of judgment made it easier for someone to rob them, and they'd be able to outfit their own places for nothing.

In the early morning, the blacktop glistened with small patches of ice reflecting in the headlights. Once out of town, Parker took the forest road and accelerated. He headed in the direction of the on-ramp to the highway. If the roads stayed clear, they'd make it to the new ski resort cabins within twenty minutes.

Ahead an old truck chugged along, the exhaust blowing a stream of smoke into the pristine alpine air. He passed it, honking his horn and giving the finger to the driver. The vehicle slowed and then pulled to one side. "He's scared of us. Let's have some fun."

Parker drove for a few moments before taking his foot off the gas and coasting down to thirty miles per hour. He glanced in the mirror, waiting for the truck to pull out and pass him. He chuckled. He loved this game and allowed the vehicle to come alongside before he sped. The old truck accelerated and Parker floored the gas pedal. He whooped with excitement. "Man, look at the old fool, he's figuring on racing us."

Laughing at the sight of an oncoming eighteen-wheeler, he met the old truck's speed, trapping the vehicle beside him. Air horns blared and the other driver braked hard. Parker looked in his mirror as the truck fishtailed and plumes of smoke poured from the tires as it tucked in behind him, narrowly missing the oncoming vehicle.

"Oh man, I figured the eighteen-wheeler would spread him all over the highway." Tim laughed and turned around in his seat. "What a clown. He was determined to pass when all he needed to do was slow down."

Parker peered in the mirror and slowed down again. "Here he comes. Do you think he'll try to pass us again?" He gave Tim a slow grin. "Or is he chicken?"

"Forget him or we won't get to the ski resort before the workers arrive—that was the plan, right?" Tim glanced over one shoulder. "I don't think he's gonna try passing us again."

D.K. Hood

"I'll make him." Parker slowed his vehicle to a crawl and then waited for the truck to attempt to pass before speeding up again. Rather than play his game, the other driver dropped back. "Ha, told you he was chicken. Man, I think I saw smoke coming out his ears."

"Maybe not, he's coming fast. Step on the gas." Tim hung onto the back of the seat. "Shit! He's not gonna stop."

A jolt from behind and the grinding of metal shot Parker forward. His seatbelt pulled him up and came close to strangling him as his truck slid across the blacktop. "What the hell?"

He jammed his foot down on the gas pedal and his truck jumped forward with a roar but fishtailed on a patch of ice. He wrestled with the steering wheel and tried to accelerate out of the slide. The old truck slammed into them again and like a battering ram pushed them off the road. As his vehicle bounced over the dead undergrowth, Parker aimed his truck between two tall pines. He let out a breath in a puff of steam as his prized possession came to a jarring halt in the dim light. He glanced in the mirror and gaped in terror.

The truck's headlights lit up the highway with its twin beams. As the driver stepped from his truck, an eerie mist rose up and drifted across the blacktop, swirling like dancing ghosts. Dressed all in black, the stranger walked into the light, but his cowboy hat pulled low concealed his face. He carried a powerful hunting rifle in one hand and headed purposely toward them. Parker cursed under his breath. "Dammit, I left my rifle at home."

They were defenseless. Parker stared in horror as the man slowly raised the rifle to his shoulder. Panic shuddered through him. "He's not mad, he's batshit crazy, and I'm not taking a bullet." He pushed Tim hard on one shoulder. "Get out. He'll never find us in the forest."

He switched off the interior light then dropped out the door and, keeping low to the ground, headed between the tall pines, jumping blindly over the dry winter undergrowth. Behind him, Tim was breathing heavily. It was so dark, he collided with a tree and Tim crashed into him. Pain shot through his knee as he collided with a log and sprawled, tangled with Tim, on the ground. Under him, pine needles covering the forest floor dug into his jeans like shards of glass. He reached up for a low bough and dragged up his aching body to stand on one leg. Biting down in agony, he pushed on into the darkness. Low branches slashed at his bare cheeks, flinging icy water down his neck, but he kept moving.

"Slow down, you're making too much noise." Tim pulled on the back of his jacket. "Hide behind a tree and wait; he may have had his fun and be on his way."

Trembling with fear, Parker stood with his back against the rough trunk of a pine and bent over, hands on knees, trying to suck the freezing air into his lungs. He could just make out Tim beside him, staring back the way they'd come. He lowered his voice to a whisper. "See anything?"

"No. Listen." Tim's pale face turned to him. "He's coming after us."

Parker shivered and every hair on his body stood to attention. The steady footsteps of the stranger crunched through the forest, and then a shape with green glowing eyes loomed out of the darkness. "Shit, he's wearing night-vision goggles. Run!"

As he turned, a shot, earsplittingly loud in the quiet, connected with his left shoulder, red-hot pain searing in a thunderbolt of agony. He fell to his knees just as a second shot exploded in his head, and his sight blinked out like a candle in the wind.

CHAPTER NINE

The wind had kept up all night and by morning had brought with it a rush of sleet to wet Kane's cheeks as he dashed to his truck. He'd fallen into bed a couple of hours ago but hadn't slept, his mind wouldn't allow him to let go of the murder scene. He'd gotten up and went about his chores making sure the horses were comfortable. They'd be remaining in the barn today and would be fine inside. Working with the horses helped him clear his head. As a military sniper in his last life, the scene last night at the Robinsons' house was much the same as he'd left behind after hitting a target. It brought back memories of people he'd seen through his scope more times than he'd care to remember. He had little doubt in his mind Lucas Robinson had been the victim of a hit. Although Jenna was convinced, the victim's wife, Carol was responsible he had his doubts. The shooting did point to her. The wife was the only other person in the house the night of the murder. They'd found no other fingerprints, and the footprints in the dust under the cellar window could've been from the victim as he'd worked down there before his death. He hoisted Duke, his bloodhound, into the back seat, secured his harness, and then climbed behind the wheel. He pulled out his cellphone and called Wolfe. "Hey, morning, Shane. Did you do a gunshot residue test on Mrs. Robinson last night?"

"Yeah, it came up negative. She didn't kill her husband. At the hospital, I checked through her hair too—she had fragments of his skull in her hair. She was beside him, as she said, when the shooting occurred."

Kane cleared his throat. "Okay, thanks, I'll let Jenna know."

"I'm doing the autopsy on Lucas Robinson this morning around eleven if you're planning on dropping by. Although cause of death seems apparent, I need to be sure." Wolfe yawned. *"I need some sleep. Can you keep the crime rate down for the rest of the week, do you think?"*

Kane chuckled. "I'll do my best. We're heading for the office now, catch you later." He disconnected, backed out of the garage, and headed down the driveway to Jenna's front porch.

As usual, the moment he drove up, she came out the door and hurried to get inside. "Morning."

"I noticed you left out the 'good,' and from the dark circles under your eyes, you didn't sleep either." She handed him two to-go cups of coffee in a holder. "I think I'll need this in a drip if I'm going to make it through today."

Kane placed the coffee in the console and waited for her to buckle up before heading for the highway. "Yeah, seeing a crime scene like that triggers a flight or fight response and it takes a while for our bodies to come down from the adrenalin boost."

"Yeah and then we feel like this." She pulled an exhausted expression and then laughed. "Hey, you figure Duke feels like this all the time?"

"Maybe, everything seems an effort for him of late." Kane turned onto the highway, the wiper blades swishing back and forth pushing the ice particles across the windshield. "It might be the cold weather."

"You've had him checked out by the vet, what did he say?" Jenna turned in her seat to peer at the dog. "He's okay, isn't he?"

Behind them, Duke let out a mournful howl and buried his nose in the blanket.

"What was that for, Duke?" Jenna leaned over the seat to rub the dog's ears.

Kane glanced at her. "You'll have to spell the word 'v-e-t'. It gets the same panic reaction as 'b-a-t-h'." He snorted. "I can't believe I have to spell words in front of him. I didn't know dogs understood language and it was more of a hand gesture type of communication. Anyway, he's fine. A little overweight but nothing to worry about and its usual for this breed to conserve energy so they can keep going when we need them." He grinned at her. "You should have seen him at the 'v-e-t-s'. I couldn't get him to walk through the door. He sat down and refused to move and I ended up carrying him inside. Soon as he saw the poor guy load the vaccination, he let out this blood-curdling howl and tried to escape."

"He was okay when we took him the first time. What's happened since?" Jenna gave him a concerned look. "The v-e-t didn't hurt him, did he?"

Kane chuckled. "Nope. The first time he was so ill, he'd just about given up apart from being skin and bones. He had an ear infection and the animal practitioner clipped his claws. He had a ton of needles that day and remembers the v-e-t hurting him, I guess." He glanced at her. "He has a very good memory." He turned onto the highway and stared into the bleak morning. "I spoke to Wolfe before. The gunshot residue test on Mrs. Robinson came back negative."

"So, we're back to square one." Jenna sighed. "My gut tells me she's involved." She shivered. "Mind if I turn up the heat?"

Kane smiled at her. "Go right ahead, it's going to be a long, cold day."

"It sure is." Jenna remained quiet for the rest of the trip to the sheriff's office, sipping her coffee and staring out the window.

Kane pulled into his parking space next to Rowley's cruiser and slid out the door. He opened the back door and lifted the very reluctant Duke onto the sidewalk. Without a backward glance, the bloodhound scampered up the steps and nosed his way inside the glass doors. Kane collected his coffee and waited for Jenna. "You're quiet this morning. Something on your mind?"

"Yeah." She headed up the steps and inside the warm building. "We'll go back to the Robinsons' house this morning and hunt down points of entry." Handing him her coffee, she pulled off her gloves and then turned to greet the receptionist. "Hey, Maggie, anything urgent this morning?"

"Not so far." Maggie gave her a bright smile. "Maybe we'll have an early day and be able to get home in front of the fire."

"That sounds good to me." Jenna turned to Kane, took back her coffee, and then headed for her office. "Grab Rowley and we'll go over the Robinson case."

Kane cleared his throat. "Yes, ma'am."

"What?" Jenna paused in the doorway to stare at him. "I miss eating breakfast with you for one morning and we're back to you calling me 'ma'am'?" She narrowed her gaze. "Or do you have something on your mind?"

"Me?" Kane shrugged. "Nope. Only the case, it's a strange one for sure."

"Okay." Jenna shook her head and disappeared into her office.

Kane placed his coffee on the desk, removed his coat, and looked at Rowley. "Morning." He indicated with his chin toward the office door. "She wants us for a meeting."

"I guessed as much." Rowley smiled and slapped him on the back. "Another day in paradise."

Kane picked up his to-go cup, led the way into Jenna's office, and sat down. "Is there something we missed last night?"

"No, we did a thorough crime scene investigation, and from Wolfe's preliminary verbal report on scene and the gunshot residue test coming up negative, it seems clear now this murder was a home invasion or a planned hit." She glanced at Rowley. "I've read your report and I'm surprised Mrs. Robinson was uncooperative when you arrived on scene. When I spoke to her, she appeared to be quite lucid. Are you sure she didn't say anything?"

"I figured she was in shock or had just murdered her husband." Rowley frowned. "When she called, maybe the realization of what had happened hadn't hit her yet. I'm not a doctor but I guess shock can creep up on a person."

"Did you hear or see anything at all around the house, another vehicle, anything?" Jenna folded her hands on the table. "You didn't pass anyone on the highway?"

"Nope, I didn't see anyone, but if someone was thumping around the house, I wouldn't have been able to hear them with the wind blowing and all." Rowley swallowed hard, making his Adam's apple bob up and down. "I couldn't see more than a few yards in the dark, leaves blowing up all around, tree branches scraping the windows. I was expecting someone to jump me at any moment."

Kane chuckled. "Oh boy, as soon as we get close to Halloween, everyone gets the jitters."

"Yeah, well, when I caught sight of the victim, I wished I'd called for backup at the get-go." Rowley looked at Jenna. "But I searched the house and found Mrs. Robinson."

"Okay. From our initial walk-through, I couldn't find anything disturbed, so I'm going to rule out robbery as a motive." Jenna glanced down at her notes and then looked at Kane. "I agree it was a hit."

Kane nodded. "Yeah, it's too neat." He sipped his coffee and peered at her over the rim.

"So, we have a professional hitman in town?" Jenna pushed both hands through her hair. "Life just gets better by the second."

CHAPTER TEN

A blast of wind splattered icy rain against the window like buckshot and Jenna shivered at the thought of venturing out into the cold again. She looked at her deputies. How easy it would be to delegate and stay inside in the warm, but that was not her way. She bit back a smile at the idea and turned her mind back to the case. "Okay, so if it was a hit, the question burning on my lips is why anyone would want to murder a financial advisor?"

"Maybe he cheated someone?" Rowley shrugged. "Or gave them bad advice and they lost their money."

"Not likely." Kane shifted in his chair. "A professional hitman is not only hard to find but getting one to travel here would be expensive."

Jenna drummed her fingers on the desk, thinking. "Then we dig into the couple's lives. If Lucas Robinson mixes with the rich and famous, maybe he upset the wrong man. Rowley, I want you to look for any dirt on the man, where he went, what he was doing and with whom. If he was having an affair with a rich man's wife for instance." She made notes listing what she needed to do and then lifted her gaze. "Search the society pages for events and question his co-workers. People in offices often gossip, so speak to everyone he knew."

"Okay." Rowley scribbled in his notebook. "And the wife, same with her?"

Jenna nodded. "Yeah, find out what you can on them. There must be something dirty in their backgrounds. I mean, why live in practical isolation if you have nothing to hide?"

"Sure." Rowley glanced at her. "I guess you're heading out in the cold."

Jenna frowned at him. "Yeah, we'll be checking out the crime scene again and visiting Mrs. Robinson at the hospital. If we get time, we'll drop by the morgue to attend the autopsy on Mr. Robinson." She narrowed her gaze. "Would you rather swap duties?"

"No, ma'am." Rowley stood abruptly. "I'll get on this right away." He headed out the door.

Jenna turned her attention to Kane, folded her notepad, and stood. "Ready to go? We have a crime to solve."

"Sure." Kane gave her a slow smile and then pushed to his feet. "I'll grab my gear." He turned and strolled out the door.

In the daylight, the Robinsons' house didn't appear any less intimidating than the previous night. As they drove up the twisting driveway and the house came into view, Jenna scanned the area and shook her head. "Robinson must have been crazy building the home so close to the trees. If a fire broke out, they'd have no chance of escape."

"It would've been a nightmare trying to sleep." Kane pulled up outside the front steps and turned to look at her. "The trees have grown so close to the walls, the noise inside is disturbing. Last night I was waiting for a branch to come through one of the windows."

"Maybe that's why Robinson didn't hear the intruder?" Jenna zipped up her jacket. "He was probably used to all the creaks and whines. Anyone could've broken in and he'd have slept through it." She pulled her hood over her woolen hat and braced herself for the cold.

"Well, he slept through getting his brains spread all over the wall." Kane shook his head. "I wonder if his wife heard anything unusual before the shooting."

Jenna reached for the door handle. "She heard the floorboards creak is all. We'll ask her if she remembers anything else later."

The moment Jenna slid from her seat a blast of sleet smacked her in the face. "Ugh! I wish it would just snow already." She bent her head and dashed up the steps. Pulling off one glove, she removed the crime scene tape across the door and reached inside her coat. She fumbled in a pocket, surprised when the keys felt warm to the touch, and lifted them to the door.

As the door opened, the waft of death coming from inside the house greeted them. Jenna shook her head. "We'll stick together. The killer could be lurking around, and if he's a professional, he'd pick us off in seconds." She pushed the door wide open. "Maybe let some fresh air inside, to clear the stink." She glanced at Kane. "Remind me to ask Mrs. Robinson about a clean-up crew. She'll need one before she returns." She headed back down the front steps. "That's if she returns. I'm not sure I'd want to live here alone after what's happened."

"It would sure be a pretty place." Kane scanned the area. "This is prime real estate but after this no one will want to buy it."

Jenna noticed the look on his face. "You'd buy it, wouldn't you?"

"Once, maybe." He gave her a crooked smile. "The fact someone was murdered here doesn't worry me. The right security is the key, but I'm not planning on moving out of my cottage until my landlord decides to kick me to the curb."

The sad expression Kane gave her made her chuckle. "That's not going to happen. Come on we have a job to do." With the wind blasting ice into her face, she headed down the side of the house, weaving through the trees in search of the open cellar window and stopped dead and stared. "That can't be good."

The closed shutters over the cellar window made her turn and scan the dense trees. A prickle of apprehension crawled up her spine. Beside her, Kane tensed and they both instinctively moved behind the protection of a dripping wet trunk. Could someone be in the forest watching and waiting for their return to murder them as well? Jenna lowered her voice to just above a whisper. "See anyone?"

"No, but that doesn't mean a thing. With the wind and the low visibility, we can't hear or see anyone hiding in the forest." Kane turned and peered at the ground. "Someone has been here since it started sleeting. Those tracks are fresh." He moved off, following the footprints, and then turned back to her. "Meter reader. Likely, he knew nobody was home, noticed the rain getting inside, and closed the shutters. It would be a neighborly thing to do around here."

Jenna huffed out a frustrated cloud of steam. "Yeah, and he obliterated any signs of a break-in while he was at it." She bent over to peer at the shutters. "No sign of forced entry." She tried to open the shutters. "These appear to be locked. Maybe someone else broke in again and shut them from the inside?"

"I guess we'll have to go into the cellar and take a look." Kane narrowed his gaze. "I locked the cellar door when we left last night, so if someone went through this window they'd still be in the cellar."

An icy trickle of rain ran down the collar of Jenna's jacket and she shivered. "Oh, this day just gets better by the second."

Keeping a watchful eye all around, Jenna led the way inside the house. They both paused in the entrance to pull on surgical gloves and then she closed the front door. "We'll clear the rooms, just in case."

"Roger that." Kane tipped his head to the left of the entrance. "Do you want to split up?"

Jenna allowed her last visit to run through her mind. All the rooms on the lower level were spacious and had minimal furniture. It would be difficult for an intruder to hide anywhere. "Yeah, but first we'll see if the cellar is locked."

"Okay." Kane led the way to the hallway. "It's locked. I can see the bolt across the door."

"Good, then we'll split up. You check the study and upstairs, I'll go right. Call out as we go." Jenna headed back to the family room and, keeping her back to the wall, turned the knob and pushed the door open. She peeked around the room and, seeing it empty, closed the door. "Family room, clear."

As she moved toward the kitchen, she could hear Kane calling out as he cleared the rooms upstairs, and they met up at the kitchen door. She turkey-peeked around the door and then entered. After checking out the mudroom and back door, she turned to Kane. "No one has been here. They'd track dirt inside, and the mat outside was dry before we used it."

"Cellar next?" Kane turned to leave.

"Hold up." Jenna frowned. "We'll open the door and call out. If someone is down there, they'll want to come out rather than die of starvation." She sighed. "I'm more interested in searching for clues to discover why someone wanted to murder Lucas Robinson."

She waited for Kane to unbolt the cellar door. When he waved his flashlight around and called out, no response came. He looked at Jenna and shrugged. "There's no one down there. Want me to go check?"

Jenna shook her head. The idea of going into a dark cellar again chilled her to the bone. "It's not necessary. We have everything we need. I'll grab the pair of boots I found in the broom closet and take them to Wolfe for a comparison to the footprints under the window."

"I'll go and get the hard drive out of his computer. Did you notice a laptop anywhere?" Kane turned to the office doorway.

"No, but there was a briefcase resting on a chair in the bedroom." Jenna swallowed hard at the thought of viewing the bloody crime scene again. "I'll go get it."

Without waiting for a reply, she pulled a face mask from her pocket and dashed up the stairs, avoiding the blood trail. Inside the master bedroom, she averted her gaze from the congealed blood pools around the bed and collected the briefcase. As she slipped down the stairs, she heard tires on gravel. A car door slammed, and moments later, someone knocked on the front door. As Kane emerged from the office and went to her side, she looked at him. "It seems we have a visitor."

"Hmm, and one who isn't too worried about crime scene tape." Kane headed for the door, reaching for his weapon.

CHAPTER ELEVEN

Kane peered through the window. An old man dripping with water stood on the porch. He had wrinkled cheeks, and a tuft of gray hair poked out of the front of his fur-lined trapper hat. Brown eyes looked at him through black-rimmed eyeglasses. He'd bundled up against the weather, and Kane couldn't make out if the visitor carried a weapon. He opened the front door a few inches and looked at him, watching his body language for any signs of aggression. "Is there a problem?"

"Maybe." The man indicated behind him with his thumb. "Seen a truck in the bushes back a ways on Stanton Road. I stopped to take a look and the air thereabouts has a stink like roadkill. I figured it was a wreck, so I called 911. The dispatcher said the sheriff was at this address, and she said as I was close by, I should drop by and take you to where I found the wreck."

As the man finished speaking, Jenna's cellphone chimed. Kane could hear her speaking to Maggie and frowned. "I see." He edged onto the porch, blocking the door to avoid the visitor viewing the bloody walls inside the house. He pulled out his notebook. "Did you go and see if anyone was injured?"

"No, with the smell and all, I thought it would be better to call 911." The stranger shuffled his feet. "I didn't really want to get involved."

"You did the right thing." Kane met the man's dark gaze. "I'll need your details. What brings you out in this weather?"

"Tom Dickson, I'm out of Saddle Creek. I own a cabin up there and was heading into town looking for work." Dickson frowned. "I got myself laid off for the winter. I've not been at the plant long enough for paid vacation time."

Kane relaxed a little. Saddle Creek was an isolated area in the foothills of Stanton Forest. In his time in Black Rock Falls, he'd come to realize many people lived off the grid in the small cabins all over the forest. "There's no one hiring around here at the moment. Maybe try some of the ranches farther out. They'll have livestock that needs tending during winter." He heard Jenna disconnect and come toward the door.

"Yeah, I was thinking of the produce store maybe." Dickson rubbed his hands together. "It's warmer inside."

Kane turned as Jenna came out of the house, briefcase in hand. "Sheriff, this is Tom Dickson. He found a wreck on Stanton Road."

"Yeah, Maggie called and said he was on his way. We'll check it out." Jenna closed the door behind her and then gave Dickson a long, considering stare. "Do you have provisions for winter? You'll be snowed in before long."

"Well, yes, ma'am I did until a bear tore down my shed. It came back with a few of its friends and ate everything." Dickson sighed. "Then the plant laid me off, last on, first off they said, so I'm looking for work."

"We need someone to stack boxes in the cellar." Jenna raised one eyebrow. "It will take a day and it's nice and warm down there. Will that help?"

"It sure would, ma'am. Thank you kindly." Dickson frowned. "Do you want me to lead the way to the wreck?"

"Yeah." Jenna followed him down the steps. "Then head into the sheriff's department and speak to Maggie at the front counter. I'll call her and she'll show you what I need. She might know of other people around town who need odd jobs doing as well."

Kane watched Dickson walk away with a distinct limp. Whatever his age, he appeared to be struggling. "Do you work with horses?"

"Sure do." Dickson's mouth twitched into a smile. "It was my gelding who alerted me to the bear. Darn nuisance. By the time I got outside the damage was done." He swung into his truck. "Turn right at the end of the drive. It's about a quarter mile along the highway on the left."

Kane removed his latex gloves and pulled on his thick leather pair before placing the evidence bag containing the hard drive into the back of his truck. He turned to take the briefcase from Jenna. "You sure about allowing a total stranger into our basement?"

"What's he going to steal—the furnace?" She flashed him a grin. "The poor old man is destitute; would you rather I sent him to the soup kitchen?"

Kane closed the back door and opened the driver's side. "No, I guess Maggie will watch him."

"And Rowley. Walters will be in for a couple of days this week too. He'll make sure Dickson behaves himself." Jenna climbed into the passenger seat and turned to him. "The townsfolk look out for each other. Once the word gets out he needs help, he'll get work. A man like that won't take charity."

"I guess Maggie will have it all around town by the time we leave tonight." Kane started the engine and headed down the driveway. He glanced at Jenna. "If this is a wreck and it happened last night, I doubt anyone will have survived out in this weather."

"If it stinks like roadkill, it happened way before last night." She looked at Kane. "In this weather, decomposition would be slow."

Although sleet pelted the windshield and the driveway had vanished into a haze of gray, it didn't take Kane too long to catch up to the other driver. It was a cold, wet, miserable day, and as they turned onto Stanton Road, a thick mist made the tall majestic pines appear as if a bubbling lake surrounded them. Water dripped from the branches and disappeared into the swirling fog, whipped up by the continual howl of wind. He glanced at Jenna. "I'm wondering how he noticed a wreck in this weather. I can hardly make out the blacktop."

"Hmm, and it's gotten worse in the last hour or so." She tucked her hair under her hat and then pulled on gloves. "He's slowing down. I can't see anything from here." She sighed. "I have the awful feeling we're going to be here for some time." She indicated to the back of a truck wedged between two thick pines. "There it is."

"I see it." The truck had plowed through the undergrowth and come to rest between two trees. "The driver should've survived. I wonder what happened?" Only the tailgate was visible; the forest and heavy mist seemed to have swallowed up the rest of the vehicle. Kane pulled up behind Dickson's truck. As he opened the door, a sudden wave of unease rolled over him. He scanned the immediate area in all directions, the mist was so thick now, it was as if Dickson's truck was sitting in a cloud.

"Maybe he had a medical emergency." Jenna came around the hood and glanced at him.

"It's possible. Let's see if we can locate the driver and then we'll look for skid marks."

"Sure." Kane's gut was screaming at him something was terribly wrong with this scenario.

"I can't smell death. Let's be careful." Jenna's low voice came from close behind him, echoing his thoughts, and the sound of her weapon slipping from the holster appeared loud in the silence.

"Copy." Kane looked over at Dickson. He could see both his hands on the wheel. When the window buzzed down, he waved him away. "Thanks, we'll take it from here."

The old man gave them a nod and then drove away. As so many strange things happened in Black Rock Falls, walking into traps had become par for the course. He turned to look at her. "I can't smell anything either. If this is a trap, it's a great place. With the mist and constant sleet, it's hard to see anything. There could be a tripwire anywhere."

"I'll look down, you look up. I'm not seeing any footprints." Jenna was searching the ground with her Maglite. "I can't see any ground disturbance or tripwires."

Kane glanced up into the canopy and frowned. "Nothing above us apart from crows just sitting up there waiting. There must be something dead around here but I'm not sure why they're not on the ground."

"We can't stand here birdwatching all day." Jenna indicated toward the truck. "The body might be inside the vehicle, so the crows don't have access."

As they moved slowly between the soaked trees, underfoot the pine-needle-packed ground was like walking on blankets. All around was eerily silent. Stanton Forest was usually a hive of activity and home to a vast variety of wildlife. The silence was unusual and a warning something wasn't right. The truck seemed to emerge out of the mist; several dents covered the tailgate and both front doors hung open. Kane took photographs using his phone and then moved in slowly. He peered inside the cab: no sign of blood but he found the forest floor disturbed around both doors. "Looks like they were running away from something." He snapped more images and his gaze locked on something. A tingle of a warning raised the hairs on the back of his neck. "Oh, and this is unusual." He plucked two black feathers from the front seat and held them up. "Didn't Wolfe find a black feather beside Lucas Robinson?"

"Yeah, but it may not be connected." She pointed up. "They probably came from the crows. The wind could've blown them inside the truck."

"I'll bag them." He squinted in the unrelenting sleet. Even the tall pines didn't offer them much shelter. "There's no blood inside the truck. The logical place to go would be back to the highway."

"From the broken branches, they went this way." Jenna moved on ahead of him and then stopped dead. "Bobcat."

Kane moved to her side, raised his voice, and waved his arms around. "Get out of here." The cat raised its blood-soaked muzzle from the corpse of a man, snarled but backed away and bounded into the forest. "The cat was keeping the crows away."

"There's another body over here." Jenna turned to look at him and her face drained of color. "Headshots, both of them."

Kane crouched down beside the first victim. "This guy was running away and took a bullet in the shoulder; the headshot was last. From the damage, the shooter was packing for bear."

"Same with this one. He has a wound in the back, headshot to finish him." Jenna leaned against a tree and sighed. "Take as many images as possible. I'll call it in and get Wolfe on scene." She lifted her gaze to Kane. "Finding those feathers might be significant after all. I sure hope these murders and the hit aren't connected. The last thing we need over Halloween is another darn serial killer in town."

CHAPTER TWELVE

It was a miserable, gray day but the sight of the bright orange pumpkins piled up outside the grocery store made Shane Wolfe smile. It had become a tradition for him and his three girls to carve up a pumpkin for Halloween. It was one of the few remaining traditions left over from when they'd been a real family before his wife had died of cancer. After purchasing a suitable specimen, Wolfe stepped over the river of leaf-strewn muddy water hurtling down the gutter and slid the pumpkin inside the back of his SUV. These days he immersed himself in his work but his determination to give his daughters, Emily, Julie, and Anna, a normal life was paramount. All three took after him in coloring, with blonde hair and gray eyes, but thankfully they all had their mother's petite build and attitude to life. Emily was following in his footsteps and studying to become a medical examiner at Black Rock Falls College, Julie was in high school, and as bright as a button and his baby, Anna's priority in life was riding the paint pony Kane had given her for her last birthday. He grimaced when his phone rang and shook the rain from his hat before climbing into his vehicle. He fished the phone out of his top pocket. "Wolfe."

"It's Jenna. I'm afraid you'll have to postpone the autopsy on Robinson. We have a double homicide out on Stanton Road. Multiple gunshot victims. The killer chased them down and shot them in the back. We're on scene. I'll send you the coordinates."

"I'm in town. Emily and Webber are at my office. I'll go grab them and my van and be with you ASAP." Wolfe disconnected and started the engine.

He'd left his daughter Emily and his other intern, Colt Webber, a deputy who'd joined his staff to study forensic science, studying blood spatter from the Robinson case. Now he had more cases piling up to limit his precious family time. He sighed and headed through the mist-shrouded town, arriving a few minutes later at the ME's office. He strolled inside and swiped his card, glad to see his interns fully involved in the task he'd set them. "We have a double homicide in Stanton Forest. Dave and Jenna are on scene. It's cold, wet, and muddy—wear boots and wet weather gear."

Moments later they climbed inside the van and he punched in the coordinates for the murder scene. "Do you have classes this afternoon?"

"Yeah." Emily peeked out from the hood of a raincoat two sizes too big for her. "But we'll be through by three."

Wolfe turned onto Stanton Road and peered through the swirling mist. The few people braving the weather hustled along the sidewalk, bowed over into the wind, chins tucked in and holding tight to the brims of their hats. "We'll delay the Robinson autopsy until four. I'll see what we have here, but I'll leave the autopsies of the Stanton Forest victims until the morning. I'll want you in my office after breakfast as you don't have classes until after lunch."

"Oh, Dad, why so early?" Emily shivered. "It's freezing."

"Have you changed your mind about becoming an ME?" Wolfe kept his gaze on the murky road ahead.

"Don't be silly." Emily pulled an aghast expression. "I'm entitled to ask, right?"

Wolfe bit back a grin. She was so like her mother. It warmed his heart to see she'd inherited her mother's grit. In her chosen profession, she was going to need it. He glanced at her and shrugged. "Nothing we do in this job is particularly enjoyable, Em, you just gotta grin and bear it." He cleared his throat. "Any problems, Webber?"

"No, sir." Webber frowned. "Three homicides in twelve hours. I hope we're not having a Halloween killing spree."

Wolfe glanced at him. "Don't jump to conclusions before we've completed the autopsies. Many things are not what they seem."

"Dad." Emily looked at him. "Has Jenna determined how Mr. Robinson's killer entered the home?"

Wolfe shrugged. "I haven't read her report yet. I'd guess she was called out to this murder before she had time to file it." He frowned. "I've never seen weather like this before, so windy with sleet and yet the mist still hangs around."

"It's because we're at a higher altitude." Webber rubbed the condensation from the side window. "Or it's just because it's Halloween. They say strange things happen around this time, spirits and all coming through from the other side."

"So you'll be planning a visit to the Old Mitcham Ranch on Halloween to sleep over?" Wolfe chuckled. "Or are the college students too old to do that these days?"

"There's no way I'm going near that place." Webber gave a choked laugh. "I'm not afraid of ghosts, it's just way too cold to hole up there overnight."

"Right." Wolfe kept his eyes on the road.

Ahead the wig-wag lights on Kane's black truck loomed out of the mist. Wolfe slowed and, turning on his hazard lights, pulled up in front of it. He removed his warm leather gloves and exchanged them for surgical ones from a box on the dash. "Glove up, use the masks. Webber, get the metal detector from out the back. If the killer used a rifle, we might find casings."

"Do we need our coveralls?" Emily thought for a beat and then shook her head. "No, we don't, right? It's been raining for two days and any trace evidence will have been washed away?"

Wolfe noticed Jenna and Kane emerging from the forest, rain dripping from the brims of their hats. "Probably not. Wait here and I'll take a look." He slid from the van and walked up to Jenna and Kane. "What have we got?"

"Looks to me like the vehicle was chased, the driver lost control, crashed through the trees, and came to rest over there." Jenna pointed. "The doors are wide open, so they left in a hurry. I checked for footprints, from back here where the bushes are broken from the path of the truck."

"I found skid marks on the road, but with the sleet, it's hard to determine how long they've been there." Kane peered in the truck and then straightened. "I found nothing to point to the shooter following them into the forest. The pine needles are so thick, they're like a carpet. It looks like the shooter used a rifle. We haven't found any casings using the flashlight. It's so dark in the forest today, we could've missed them."

"Two gunshots per victim, from what we can determine." Jenna's mouth turned down. "We disturbed a bobcat, so one of the victims is torn up some. We've taken photographs of the scene. I'll forward them to you now."

Wolfe nodded. "Okay." He turned and waved to Emily and Webber to join them.

He took his forensics kit from Emily and turned to Webber. "Run the metal detector from the edge of the road to the bodies. Photograph the position of anything you find before bagging it."

"Yes, sir." Webber went to work.

Wolfe turned to Jenna. "Lead the way." He looked at Emily. "Follow behind Jenna and be aware there's a bobcat close by."

As he walked, Kane moved beside him. Wolfe turned to his friend. "Coincidence?"

"I'm not sure." Kane ducked to avoid a low branch. "Both crime scenes have the feeling of professionalism, although in this town, we have a number of marksmen." He slapped him on the back. "Just another string of mystery deaths for you to solve in Black Rock Falls."

Wolfe shook his head. "Me? Nah. It's usually no mystery discovering how a person died, but if these murders are connected and as professional as you say, I don't envy the investigation you and Jenna have to wade through."

"Me either." Kane frowned. "I thought I'd seen every side of human nature before I moved here." He sighed. "Man, I hadn't touched the surface."

CHAPTER THIRTEEN

Midday Wednesday

The waitress at Aunt Betty's Café brushed past his table, spilling his coffee all over the plate of cinnamon buns. He didn't have much time to spare after waiting in line for ages beside a man who smelled of wet dog, and the thought of the delay waiting for a replacement made his blood boil. Not wanting to make a scene and bring attention to himself in the crowded café, he waited for her to turn around and pointed at the ruined food. "You bumped into my table."

"Oh, I seem to be clumsy today. Can I get you anything else?" She wiped the table and refilled his coffee cup, and then waited expectantly.

"I'm not buying anything else. I'd like you to replace my food."

"I'm not sure I can do that." She glanced over one shoulder to the front counter. "It will come out of my pay."

He gave her a long look. Aunt Betty's Café was renowned for its great food and customer service; heck, it said as much on the sign out front. "Tell me something, if I wrecked your car, do you figure I should pay for the damages?"

"Sure, it would be your fault." The waitress rolled her eyes and let out a bored sigh. "That's the law."

He nodded as a familiar anger rose up inside him. The need to grab her by the throat and squeeze the life out of her was overwhelming. "Exactly."

It was as if he'd been speaking to a brick wall. She just picked up the plate of soggy buns, edged her way through the tables, and went back to the kitchen. Pushing down the rage, he scanned the room, making sure his conversation with the waitress had gone unnoticed. He gripped his hands together in a practiced move to regain control as the woman who'd taken his order glanced in his direction. He dropped his chin, allowing the shadow from his hat to cover his features, but in his peripheral vision, he noticed her slip from behind the counter and head his way. As she got closer, he made out a pin on her shirt that said, *Susie Hartwig, Manager.*

"I'm sorry, it's Ruby's first day." Susie smiled at him. "I'll replace those cinnamon buns and your meal is on the house."

He tipped his hat. "Thank you, ma'am."

Moments later, Susie returned with a plate of cinnamon buns and a wedge of apple pie, fresh from the oven.

He glanced up at her. "Is Ruby new in town?"

"Yeah, she's down from the city." Susie smiled. "She'll be fine once she gets to know our ways."

He sipped his coffee. "I bet she will."

Making plans as Susie walked away, he eyed Ruby from under the brim of his hat. Guys that tried to play chicken on the highway asked to die fast, but smart-mouthed women really ticked him off. A shiver of excitement ran through him as his gaze locked on her face. He'd plan something real special for her.

CHAPTER FOURTEEN

It was past lunchtime before Jenna dropped into her chair in her office. She'd stopped by the Sunnybrook Nursing Home to see Mrs. Grainger. The desperately ill woman was comfortable and grateful for Jenna's lenience toward her son. On Doc Brown's insistence, she'd asked Dirk to commit to a psych evaluation, which Doc Brown insisted would keep him in the hospital for a week. She'd also dropped by the plant and spoken to the owner. The man hadn't known about Dirk's mother and had fired him on the grounds of not returning to work after a vacation. He reinstated him at once and made sure his health insurance was in order. She sighed. It had been worth her valuable time to make things right for the Grainger family.

Trying to ignore the unrelenting battering of sleet on the window-panes, she placed the wallets of Parker Louis and Timothy Addams on her desk and then pulled up their names in the database. Like the first victim, Lucas Robinson, neither of them had a rap sheet. They carried no weapons in their vehicle; in fact, on paper they appeared to be ordinary people going about their lives. *Why would someone want to kill them?*

She stared at the driver's licenses of the two men and shook her head; both carried the gold star denoting them to be Montana Real ID licenses but they didn't prove the men's identity. The headshots had destroyed any chance of asking next of kin to identify the bodies. By now, Wolfe would be checking the victims for any distinguishing marks or tattoos. He'd take an impression of the teeth in hope the men had seen a local dentist at one time. Of course, she'd have the awful task of visiting the next of kin, and asking questions to establish identity and getting permission for the dentist to release his files.

The victims' truck had a bumper sticker promoting the new ski resort, and by the tools inside, it was possible both men had been heading to work at the time of the murder. Kane and Rowley had hotfooted it to the growing resort to speak to the site manager and see if he recognized either of the men. Jenna had turned her attention to searching social media for all three victims when someone knocked on her door. She lifted her head. "Yes, come in."

"Afternoon, Jenna." Atohi Blackhawk, a good friend and the Native American tracker who helped them with cases, waited in the doorway.

Jenna smiled, glad to see a friendly face. "Hey, what drags you out in this weather?"

"I come bearing gifts." Atohi placed a holder containing three to-go cups of coffee and a bag of takeout on her desk. "I ran into Dave outside Aunt Betty's. He was buying you lunch, but seeing as we were coming to see you, he asked me to bring it along." He flashed white teeth. "So, I grabbed some extra coffee." He turned and looked at the door. "There's someone here I'd like you to meet."

"Sure, get out of your wet coat and take a seat." Suddenly famished, she peeked into the takeout bags.

"Jenna, this is Brad Kelly, a cousin of mine from the res." Atohi waved in a tall man in his twenties. He had tiger's eyes, and when he removed his soaked Stetson, it revealed dark, straight hair to his collar. "Brad came to us after his mother went missing. He went away when he turned eighteen but is now back on a mission and we need your help."

Jenna took the to-go cup with her name printed on the side and nodded. "Sure, what do you need?"

"When I was a boy, I saw my pa kill my mom." Brad's tiger gaze never left her face. "He killed my brother as well."

Jenna frowned. "Have you spoken to the tribal police? In the first instance, it's really a matter for them."

"No, it occurred here in Black Rock Falls." Brad appeared agitated. "Atohi believes you might have records we can use to establish our case."

"Sure. How long ago did this happen?" Jenna took out her pen and made some notes on the pad on her desk.

"Twenty years." Brad frowned. "I'm kind of foggy on the exact date. I didn't tell anyone about my mom because I didn't remember. Atohi remembers it being late fall when I arrived at the res. I know now I blanked it out for a long time. It wasn't until the cops told me my pa had died, it came back in bits and pieces."

Not sure how factual his recollection could be after so long, Jenna met his gaze. "So, where have you been since you turned eighteen?"

"Alaska." Brad frowned. "I left the res because my pa was hunting me down."

"At eighteen you could've spoken to the law enforcement on the res or come here to speak to the sheriff and had him arrested. There's no statute of limitation on murder."

"I didn't remember how I'd gotten to the res at that time, and if I had recalled that morning, do you think the sheriff would've taken notice of me?" Brad clenched his fists on the table. "The only thing that would've happened is my pa would've killed me too. I had to get as far away from him as possible. The only thing I remembered at the time was my mom telling me to run."

"What he says is true. My mom took him in and told me the story of how he returned to the res." Atohi's dark eyes settled on her face. "He was in shock and not talking. The family was suspicious and my father went to speak to Joe Kelly on the pretext of inviting the family to my grandfather's birthday. He was told Luitl, Brad's mother, had left him and taken the boys." He shook his head and sorrow filled his eyes. "That is the edited version of what happened, but trust me when I tell you Joe Kelly was a wife-beating coward and too scared to set foot on the res. My family hoped one day Luitl would return."

"See, nothing was done. If I'd been able to remember, no one would have heard my voice." Brad's eyes bore into her. "I'm wasting my time. We'll let our people deal with this."

"I'm listening to you, Brad, but you'll have to help me. I need all the details, names, birthdates, addresses, anything you can remember." Jenna made more notes as he responded and then raised her head to meet his penetrating eyes. "I gather your father is not a Native American?"

"Nope, but my mom was a Blackhawk, Atohi's cousin." Brad shrugged. "After what happened, I ran through the forest. My mom had told us what to do if we had to run, to follow the river until we came to the rock like a bear and then follow the road to the res. It took me days but I found it, and they took me in and cared for me."

Jenna was finding his story strange. If his father had killed his mother and brother, someone would've found their bodies. They would have notified the authorities and they'd have hunted down his father and brought him to justice. "So why come forward now? Your father is dead, there is no charge to pursue."

"Maybe not, but if I can find my family's remains, I can ask the ME to put the case forward to the state coroner for an inquest. I want the truth to come out. Why weren't my mother and brother ever listed as missing? Someone was covering up for my pa and I want them charged."

Jenna nodded. "On the day your mother and brother died, do you remember anything? Do you remember what made your father angry enough to kill them?"

"He was always hitting her and us." A flash of anger so intense moved across Brad's face and startled Jenna. "Mom wanted to escape to the res. She could hide there and her family would protect her. They'd never allow him near her. I recall, creeping down the stairs and running for the truck. We'd gotten to the forest before he caught us. He came after us with a shovel and Mom told me to run and don't look back. I ran some ways but I stopped to see what had happened. They were both covered in blood and my pa was standing over them with a shovel. He yelled at me to stop but I ran like the wind. I heard him crashing through the forest after me and he hunted for me for a long time but I holed up in a hunter's blind. I fell asleep, and when I woke, all I remembered was I had to run away from my pa and get to the res."

Jenna tapped her pen on the table. "When did you remember the details?"

"Like I said, it started coming back to me the day the cops told me my pa had died." Brad pushed a hand through his thick black hair. "A little came back each day and then I remembered everything. I had to come back. My mom's ghost will be walking the forest unable to rest."

"Okay." Jenna turned to her computer. "Over the last couple of years, we've been uploading old hard copy case files into our system. I'm not sure if they go back that far but I can do a search." She smiled at him. "As luck would have it, not many things happened in Black Rock Falls twenty years ago—unlike now, we have three murder cases." She turned to the screen and placed the names into the search engine.

"Really?" Brad leaned back in his chair. "Maybe we can help. Atohi tells me you often ask for his assistance."

"Tracking, most times, but Jenna can always call on me if she needs help." Atohi glanced at him. "Don't underestimate our sheriff. She has hunted down many a serial killer."

"Yeah, I know." Brad reached for his coffee. "Her reputation isn't a secret."

Jenna stared at the computer screen in disbelief. "There's a report from his teacher expressing concern she hadn't seen you or your brother for a week. The sheriff says in his notes he spoke to your father and he told him your mother had taken his sons and returned to her people." She looked at Brad. He stared back with an expression carved in stone. "There was no follow-up." She frowned. "The procedure was different back then I guess. I'd have made sure your mother was safe on the res."

When Brad said nothing, Atohi cleared his throat as if to break the awkward silence. "We've been searching the places Brad can recall in the forest before the first snow. There's a group of us, and I've contacted the forest wardens so they know where we're working and will keep the hunters away from the area."

Jenna nodded. "That's a good idea. Keep me informed if you find any remains. Don't touch anything. Wolfe will check it out, and he knows a forensic anthropologist out of Helena who has assisted him with other cases." She looked directly at Brad. "Is there anything else you need?"

"I didn't realize we needed your permission to touch anything in our forest." Brad pushed to his feet. "But if it means justice for my mom and brother, I guess I can live with it this time." He turned, grabbed his coat and hat from the peg behind the door, and stormed out.

Jenna stood and walked to the door to stare after him. "Was it something I said?"

"Nope." Atohi sighed. "He came back with a chip on his shoulder. Don't take it personal."

The anger radiating from Brad had unnerved her to some extent. She shook her head. "I won't but he seems so angry. I feel as if I've let him down somehow." She leaned against her desk.

"You've been very helpful. Now we know why nobody searched for him." Atohi pushed to his feet and gave Jenna a hug. "Thanks for your help."

"Any time." Surprised by the gesture, she glanced away from Atohi and her gaze settled on Kane standing in the doorway. "I hope you find them. It will bring him some closure." She stepped away and reached for Atohi's hat and coat.

"Thanks." Atohi smiled at her and then bent down to greet Duke as the dog pushed past Kane, tail wagging. He took his coat and hat from Jenna and then raised his gaze to Kane. "I'll be on my way."

"Sure." Kane stepped to one side. "Get things sorted?"

"Jenna will bring you up to speed." Atohi pushed on his hat and then pulled on his coat. "Catch you later."

"Uh-huh." Kane shut the door and leaned against it.

"What?" Jenna raised one eyebrow.

"Should I be jealous?" He removed his coat and hung it on the peg, and then removed his black Stetson and shook off the raindrops before dropping it on her desk.

Stifling a smile, Jenna shrugged. "No, but he is a remarkably handsome man, don't you think?"

"I don't really take much notice of other men's looks." Kane folded his arms across his substantial chest. "What happened to make his friend bust out of here like his tail was on fire?"

Jenna shrugged. "Not sure, but he did add another murder to our growing caseload. A cold case, but from what he described, twenty years ago his father brutally murdered his mom and brother. He believes his mother's ghost is walking the forest unable to rest."

"Hmm, do you figure it's payback for what we did before coming here?" Kane sat down and peered up at her. "I mean, a case waiting twenty years for us to come along. You talk about strange things happening around Halloween, now that's darn right spooky."

CHAPTER FIFTEEN

Head bowed against the weather, Atohi increased his stride to catch up with Brad. The penetrating cold seeped through his already damp coat, and the wind blew icy rain into his face sending dribbles of cold water down his neck. He leaped to one side of the sidewalk to avoid two bulldogs dragging a huge woman behind them. With only her eyes showing from beneath the hood of her coat, she resembled a huge ball of red wool in rubber boots. He dashed on, and looking ahead, caught sight of Brad heading inside Aunt Betty's Café. He slipped inside the café's door and inhaled the food-infused warmth. He removed his hat and smiled at Susie Hartwig behind the counter. "Seems you can't keep us away today."

"I've just taken a batch of cherry pies from the oven." Susie chuckled. "Did the smell of them lure you back?"

"No." Brad gave Susie an agitated stare. "We're cold and wet and this seemed like a good place to dry out. I'll have the chili and apple pie."

"Sure, and what about you, Atohi?"

"The chili sounds good but I can't resist the cherry pies." Atohi grinned. "I'm surprised you have any left, with Dave Kane in town."

"We made extra." She called out the order and turned back to him. "Ruby will bring it out for you—and be nice, she's having a bad day. Poor girl has been spilling drinks all day."

Atohi nodded. "Okay." He waved Brad to a table and they removed their wet coats. "Do you have to be so rude? These are good people." Atohi hung his coat on the back of his seat before sitting.

"Are they?" Brad mimicked him and dropped into a chair. "We'll see." His mouth curled into a grin as Ruby, the waitress, headed toward them with a pot of coffee and two cups.

"Back again?" She smiled at Brad as she poured the coffee. "Your order will be right out."

"I hear you're having a bad day, spillin' drinks and all?" Brad leaned back in his chair and looked up at her. "Maybe I can make it better. Can we go out for a coffee sometime?"

"Oh…" Ruby looked at him and her cheeks pinked. "That would be nice. I don't know many people in town."

"Where do you live?" Brad gave her a slow smile. "I'm out on the res."

"Oh, I'm out on Elk Creek." She rolled her eyes. "It's my aunt's house. I'm staying with her until I can get a place of my own. It's a pain. I take the bus and it stops at the end of the road. I'll be wet through by the time I get home."

"I can come by Friday night; we could have that coffee and I'll drop you home." Brad flicked a glance at Atohi and his eyes danced with mischief.

"Yeah, sure." Ruby jumped when a bell sounded at the counter. "That will be your meal." She turned and hurried away.

Atohi stared at him. "Are you trying to prove a point or something?"

"I guess." Brad shrugged. "I was sure she'd refuse." He gave him a long look. "So, where do I take her for a coffee and maybe a meal around here?"

"There's a new pizza place, just opened up the other end of town." Atohi added cream and sugar to his coffee and stirred slowly. "I don't figure you for the Cattleman's Hotel."

"Nope, the pizza place sounds fine." Brad sighed. "I guess I have a few days to clean out my truck."

"You'd better take my ride." Atohi chuckled. "That's if you're planning on making a good impression. I'm surprised that old thing you're driving is running."

"It runs fine, and I'll fix up the body soon." Brad drummed his fingers on the table. "Finding my mom takes priority." He gave him a long look as if considering his offer. "I will take your ride. Thanks."

"What are your plans for after the melt?" Atohi leaned back as Ruby arrived with the plates of food. "With the influx of tourists, we have now, I make a good living from the tour guide business. People like to hear the old stories about the forest, and it makes them respect the land."

"I've never been a people person." Brad scooped up a spoonful of chili. "I'll find work. I've survived this long on my own."

Unease rolled over Atohi and he flicked his gaze over him. What had happened to Brad in Alaska to change the friend he'd known so well? His frequent and varied mood swings concerned him. The angry man before him had switched in an instant, in front of Ruby, into a laidback, nonchalant Romeo to convince her to go on a date with him. Moments later, the sarcastic Brad had returned, and Atohi wondered which of Brad's personas was the real deal.

CHAPTER SIXTEEN

Late Wednesday afternoon

Kane picked up the pen from the holder and turned to the whiteboard. Jenna had already sectioned the board into three, and added Lucas Robinson to the assumed names of the other two victims with the information she had to date. He turned to look at her and Rowley. "Okay, we've confirmed Parker Louis and Tim Addams worked at the ski resort. They were involved in the construction of the second phase of cabins." He waited for Jenna to stop chewing her sandwich.

"Who did you speak to?" Jenna sipped her coffee.

"Site manager." Rowley glanced at his notes. "Sid Glover."

"I ran the plates of the vehicle, and the truck belongs to Parker Louis." Jenna pulled the other half of her sandwich from the takeout bag. "With the vehicle and licenses match, we have enough information for Wolfe to speak to the next of kin. If both men are missing, he'll get permission for the dental records and we'll have a positive ID."

Kane wrote all the information on the whiteboard and noticed Jenna's raised brow. "Did I miss something?"

"Nope." She grinned. "Even your writing has military precision. How do you fit so much in such a small space and make it readable?"

"I'm not sure." Slightly embarrassed, Kane cleared his throat. "I have some information on Lucas Robinson. We dropped into the bank and spoke to a few of his associates. Rowley has a list of his friends—from what we gather, he was a player."

"As in gambling or women." Jenna looked interested.

Kane narrowed his gaze. "Women. From what we heard, he was having a not-so-secret affair with Ann Turner, a hair stylist working at the beauty parlor here in town."

"I know Ann." Jenna leaned back in her chair and looked at him. "She's young, maybe eighteen or nineteen. I wonder if his wife knows?"

"It would give us motive." Rowley smoothed down his curls and shrugged. "I mean, if Mrs. Robinson was aware of the affair, maybe she hired a hitman." He looked at Kane. "You did say the murder looked like a hit." He turned back to Jenna. "If so, where do we go from here?"

"As no hard evidence points to Mrs. Robinson being involved at this time, we'll need more than suspicion." Jenna made notes. "We'll attend the autopsy and wait for Wolfe's report. If he considers the possibility of a hit, we have probable cause and can ask the judge for a court order to view their bank and phone records. If Mrs. Robinson withdrew a large amount of cash, for instance, we'd have enough evidence to bring her in for questioning." She looked up at Kane. "We'll take the investigation in that direction for now."

Kane made notes on the whiteboard and then turned back to her. "What about Ian Clark, the guy we charged with break and enter last fall? He's just out of jail." He met Jenna's gaze. "He's living back at home, with his folks, on Maple. It would be unusual for him to go from B and E to murder, but we don't know what happened to him in jail."

"Sure, I have his address on file—we'll drop by after the autopsy and talk to him." Jenna chewed on her bottom lip. "Okay, let's move on to the Stanton Forest murders."

Kane added two names to the whiteboard. "We hunted down a possible suspect, maybe two. Cliff Young was in a fight with both victims outside the Triple Z Bar last Saturday night, according to the site manager of the ski resort. He was there having a few beers and the fight was a carryover from something that happened at work."

"Do you have his details?" Jenna was making notes.

"Yeah, Rowley has them." Kane added a second name to the board and waited for Rowley to finish speaking. "Then we have his close buddy Kyler Hall, and this is where things get interesting."

"How so?" Jenna lifted her gaze to him.

"Complicated more like." Rowley sighed. "These cases are more involved than you think."

Kane sat down in the chair in front of the desk. "Okay, we spoke to a number of the workers at the ski resort and discovered Young and Hall are close friends. Cliff Young was dating Ann before she hooked up with Lucas Robinson. Young wasn't too happy about seeing his girl with an older man."

"Okay." Jenna tapped her pen on the table. "And Hall? How does he fit into this mess?"

Kane rested one boot on his other knee and leaned back in his chair. "He went to Robinson for financial advice last year and ended up losing his shirt."

"So, both men could have a motive for killing Robinson." Jenna stared into space. "And if they're as close as you say, maybe they murdered the men in the forest as well. Do you know if Hall was involved in the fight at the Triple Z?"

Kane nodded. "We know he was there. We'll need to drop by the bar and hunt down witnesses to the fight."

"Good luck with that." Rowley grinned. "Those boys don't like talking to law enforcement."

"The reason for the fight might shed light on a motive for the murders in the forest. We have a lot of ground to cover." Jenna stared at the whiteboard for a beat and then over to Kane. "Take Rowley and head out to the Triple Z—see if you can hunt down any information on the brawl. I'll finish up here, and if you're not back by four, I'll go to the ME's office for the Robinson autopsy."

Kane stood. "Roger that." He pushed on his Stetson and then reached for his coat. "Coming, Duke?"

To his surprise the dog stood, shook himself from nose to tail, long ears and lips flapping, and then waited as he dressed him in his thick, waterproof coat. Kane straightened and looked at Rowley's amused expression. "He gets cold."

"He has a fur coat." Rowley pushed on his hat. "You spoil him."

Kane looked down into Duke's trusting brown eyes, remembering how he was when he'd found him in the mountains during a case. He'd been skin and bones. It was a wonder the dog was so gentle after surviving such horrific mistreatment. He rubbed Duke's ears. "He's worth it."

The sleet had pounded Kane's vehicle in an unforgiving blast all the way to the Triple Z. The limited visibility on the highway made it tough going, and even the eighteen-wheelers moved slower than usual. By the number of cars in the parking lot, the miserable conditions hadn't prevented the patrons from visiting the Triple Z. He parked as close to the entrance as possible and called Duke to follow him inside. The dog just opened his eyes for a beat and then closed them again. "Okay, stay here." He pulled a blanket over him and shut the door.

"My dog spends most of his time outside in all weathers, by choice." Rowley pulled his hat down to shield his face from the sleet. "He comes and goes as he pleases through the doggy door." He sighed. "There's only one problem: I can only give him access to the mudroom and usually have to clean him up when I get home."

Kane chuckled. "Maybe you should buy him a coat."

He pushed through the doors and winced at the stench of stale beer, sweat, and what could've been corn dogs. Weaving through the tables, he led the way to the bar, ignoring the dagger-like stares from the varied clientele, and waited for the barkeeper to serve a customer. Unless called out to sort out a ruckus, the sheriff's department usually let the Triple Z and its patrons be. This bar was like a beehive, better left alone than stirred up to cause trouble. When the barkeeper finished wiping down the bar and flicked the cloth over one shoulder, Kane beckoned him. "What can you tell me about the fight out in the parking lot on Saturday night?"

"Uh-huh." The barkeeper's mouth stretched into a grin. "There's a fight here most days, Deputy. It's kinda hard to keep track of them all."

Kane leaned across the bar and, dropping his voice to just above a whisper, glared at him. "You won't find it so funny when we don't respond the next time you call 911." He straightened and glanced around the bar. "I recall saving your hide the last time a brawl broke out in here, and the sheriff making sure you received damages. Our deputies went beyond the call of duty and suffered personal injury." He snorted. "I need answers. Two of the men involved in a fight here were found murdered in the forest." He leaned on the stained wooden counter and eyeballed him. "So, I'd suggest you wipe that grin off your face and start cooperating. Who was involved? If you don't know who caused the fight, I want the names of people who do."

"Murdered, you say?" The color drained from the barkeeper's face. "I'll tell you what I overheard but I won't stand up in no court to testify. A barkeeper is like a priest—people know they can talk to us and we don't blab all over town."

Kane took out his notebook and slid out the pen. "Why don't you start from the beginning? Who was here and what did you overhear?"

"Cliff Young and Kyler Hall were sitting at the bar when Parker Louis and Tim Addams walked in." The barkeeper stared into space for a beat and then narrowed his gaze at Kane. "They were arguing about an appliances delivery." He looked around nervously and started to polish the bar with vigor. "Cliff and Kyler are stealing from the ski resort site. They know when the deliveries of appliances arrive at the cabins and have been helping themselves to items. Apparently, it was one or two things at first. Parker and Tim found out and wanted in on the deal."

"So, what caused the fight?" Rowley moved closer.

"Parker threatened to spill his guts to the boss unless they included them on the next delivery." The barkeeper turned away, filled two glasses with soda, and slid them across the bar to Kane and Rowley. "Cliff went ballistic, saying he'd kill Parker before he let him blackmail him." He frowned. "Then they took it outside." He indicated with his chin to the emptying bar. "Is that all? You coming in here is bad for business."

Kane took down notes and then lifted his gaze to the barkeeper. "I don't have your name."

"Hank Dunaway. I live out back in one of the rooms."

Kane slid his pen back into the holder on his notepad and met the man's gaze. "Well, Mr. Dunaway, unfortunately, being a barkeeper doesn't entitle you to the Seal of the Confessional. This information makes you a material witness with important evidence about the case. If the prosecution calls on you to testify, you have no option."

"I'll refuse." Dunaway looked horrified. "You can't make me."

Kane noticed the sweat beading on the man's brow. "It's out of my hands. The prosecutor can issue a subpoena ordering you to appear in court. If you refuse, a warrant will be issued for your arrest. A judge could send you to jail for contempt of court if you refuse to testify." He dropped a few bills on the bar for the drinks and smiled at Dunaway. "Just in case someone in here figures you're bribing us." He turned and headed for the door.

"That was smooth." Rowley chuckled and followed him outside.

Kane smiled. "Just doing my job." He dashed back to his truck and slid inside, turning to look at Duke curled up asleep on the back seat. "I wonder why you insist on coming with me, Duke, when you won't get out in the rain."

"He's smarter than you think." Rowley climbed into the passenger seat and grinned at him. "Where to next?"

Kane started the engine and then glanced at his watch. "If we hurry, we'll be back in town before Jenna leaves for the ME's office."

His thoughts turned to the case and the possibility they had two killers stalking victims in Black Rock Falls. Or maybe one murderer and a follower, which was often the case. Alpha male psychopaths often led others to kill. He turned onto the highway, and as they reached town, he looked at Rowley, who seemed lost in thought. "How are things going with Sandy? You haven't mentioned her all day."

"Things are going fine… well, better than fine." Rowley chuckled. "I'm getting used to having her around. I'm thinking of asking her to marry me real soon."

Kane smiled at him. "Not planning on letting this one get away, huh?"

"No way." Rowley had a dreamy look in his eye. "She's the one, I just know it." He glanced at Kane. "Do you think Jenna will allow us to live in the house, after all it does belong to the department?"

"Yeah." Kane nodded. "I can't think of a reason she'd turn you out on the street just because you decided to get married. She likes Sandy, we all do. She's becoming part of our family."

"That's nice." Rowley cleared his throat. "But I'll make sure to ask Jenna about the house, before I tie the knot."

Kane parked on his spot outside the sheriff's department and opened the back door for Duke to jump down. The dog lowered his head and dashed up the steps nosing his way inside the glass doors. He stared after him. "You're welcome."

CHAPTER SEVENTEEN

After listening to Kane's report about the conversation between Kyler Hall, Cliff Young, and the two alleged victims from the forest, Parker Louis and Tim Addams, Jenna rolled her eyes to the ceiling. "This sounds too easy." She looked at her deputies. "And since when have any of our cases been open and shut?"

"Maybe we got lucky this time?" Kane sipped the hot coffee she'd given them on their return.

Something didn't feel right and Jenna frowned. "This is Black Rock Falls and luck has nothing to do with it. Sure, check out the suspects, but I believe we need to investigate this case some more. Rowley, head on over to the mortician's—Ian Clark, our other potential suspect, is working as a cleaner over there. I want you to find out his whereabouts at the time of the murders. I've read his sheet and I find it difficult to believe he'd break into a house, kill someone, and not take anything. Nor is he intimidating enough to hunt down two men and shoot them." She rubbed her temples. "But I guess he could've changed during his time in jail."

"Yes, ma'am." Rowley hesitated before leaving and looked at her. "Ah, can I ask you a personal question before I go?"

"Yes, what's the problem?"

"If I decided to get married, would I still be able to live in the house, seeing as it belongs to the department?"

Jenna couldn't stop smiling. "Yes, of course, you can stay there for as long as I'm sheriff, but I do hope someday you'll have a place of your own. The townsfolk might get tired of me one day."

"I hope to buy a ranch close by in a year or two." Rowley grinned. "Oh, and please don't mention it to Sandy, I haven't asked her yet. I was thinking of asking her at Christmas."

"I won't say a word." As Rowley went out the door, Jenna walked around the desk and grabbed her coat. "Come on, Kane, we'll be late for the autopsy." She glanced down at Duke. "You'd better stay with Maggie. Come on, boy." She patted her leg and Duke led the way out the door.

At the front desk, Jenna waited for Duke to climb into his basket behind the counter and looked at Maggie. "How's our handyman getting along?"

"He's a hard worker." Maggie met her gaze. "I don't know if he has any cash. He didn't take a break, so I sent him down to Aunt Betty's to get something to eat. Susie Hartwig made sure he was fed." She frowned. "He seems like a lost soul."

"A bear ate all his supplies and the plant laid him off." Jenna frowned. "Pay him two hundred this afternoon and if you get time, see if you can find him any work around town."

"I sure will." Maggie grinned. "I'll start with Rowley. He's been complaining his garage needs to be cleaned out before the snow arrives."

Jenna smiled. "Good idea." She gave her a wave and, following Kane out the door, pulled up the hood of her coat.

She didn't mind the snow—the cold had a refreshing, cleansing feel about it—but the sleet drove her nuts. Everything was damp, and the freezing rain seemed to seep through all her clothes. The constant fog closed in around the town, obscuring the views. It was oppressive. She ducked her head and made her way to Kane's truck through the slow-moving pedestrians, bundled up for winter and looking like drowned rats. Inside the truck, she fastened her seatbelt and turned to Kane. "I hope this weather blows through soon. It will ruin Halloween."

"Weather forecast said it would clear by this afternoon." Kane started the engine and backed out of the space. "The wind has picked up; maybe it will blow the clouds away. Then the temperature will drop like a stone, and with everything wet, the blacktop will be slick with ice. Dangerous times." He groaned. "Oh, I forgot to tell you. One of the investors in the ski resort heard about the Old Mitcham Ranch and has purchased it as a tourist attraction. They already have flyers out and advertisements all over the media for Halloween."

A shiver radiated through Jenna as the memory of the place slammed into her mind. It had started with a murder–suicide decades ago, and more recently the brutal murder of two young women had made the ramshackle building a legend. The locals insisted the ghosts of lost souls haunted the Old Mitcham Ranch and it carried a curse. After coming close to dying there, and witnessing the fate of the previous owners, she didn't need convincing the curse was real enough. "Who would want to go there for fun?"

"Not me but that sort of thing attracts people. They like to be scared." Kane sounded the horn as a stray dog dashed out from the curb.

As he hit the brakes, Jenna's seatbelt snapped so tight, she could hardly breathe. "Yikes."

"Dammit, that dog is going to cause an accident." Kane pulled in at the curb.

Jenna stared after the bedraggled mixed-breed. "Drive. We don't have time to chase after it now, Kane. I'll call the council and have the dog catcher keep an eye out for it." She made the call.

They arrived at the ME's office a few moments later and although the sleet had turned to light rain they dashed inside. Jenna swiped her card at the door and they dragged off their coats and then hung them on the pegs provided in the hallway. As they headed toward the morgue, Emily Wolfe poked her head out the door and waved to them. Jenna smiled at her. "Sorry we're late."

"We haven't started yet." Emily met them in the hallway and handed them masks and gloves. "I'll let Dad know you're here. It's an interesting case. I'm looking forward to discovering all the victim's secrets." She turned on her heel and marched back inside the room.

Jenna looked at Kane and noticed a flash of amusement in his eyes. Kane's macabre sense of humor seemed to spill out in the most inappropriate moments. She'd come to view it as his release from the stress of seeing so many dead, and sometimes mutilated, bodies. "Okay, Dave spit it out."

"Oh, nothing." Kane pulled on his mask but it didn't hide the smile. "I was just wondering how much information a practically headless man can tell us."

Unable to reply, Jenna lifted both arms into the air and then dropped them at her sides. She composed her expression and pushed through the door. The usual unmistakable smell of death and antiseptic greeted her. "Afternoon, everyone."

"Okay, it's getting late, but before we start, I've obtained positive IDs on the Stanton Forest victims. We'll conduct their autopsies tomorrow." Wolfe looked at Jenna over his face mask. "Let's get on with the Robinson case. I collected blood samples and conducted a blood-alcohol test at the scene last night before decomposition set in. I'd say from the reading, Mr. Robinson had a few drinks before retiring." He pulled back the sheet from the corpse. "I'm running a full tox screen on the samples as well."

"Do you have reason to believe someone drugged him?" Emily's pale gray eyes flicked toward Jenna.

Jenna shook her head. "No. From his wife's statement, she heard someone in the house and tried to wake him before the shooter entered the room."

"Exactly." Wolfe pulled down the recording device from above the examination table. "The amount of alcohol he consumed wouldn't have placed him in a stupor. So, we look for other reasons she couldn't wake him. Even though we found no gunshot residue on the wife's skin to indicate she shot him, we still need to rule out the possibility she was involved."

"I sleep like the dead." Webber cleared his throat. "Maybe he was the same."

"I'll take everything into consideration, but that question will have to be directed to his wife." Wolfe looked at Jenna. "Okay, no more questions. I'll record my findings as I go."

Jenna waited patiently as Wolfe described a healthy male, weight normal for his height. Nothing seemed out of place until Wolfe paused the recording and Webber turned the body over. Her gaze drifted over the torso, trying to ignore the shattered neck where part of the head had been, and centered on a mark. "Is that a bite?"

"Sure looks like one." Wolfe lowered a magnifying glass complete with light to the mark. "Webber, get a few shots of the area." He stood back. "Any suggestions?"

"How old would you say that is?" Kane moved closer and peered at the mark.

"It's not fresh—three or more days." Wolfe turned to look at him. "Although the teeth broke the skin, healing is well underway. Also, note the purple tinge to the bruising. You'll typically see a bruise change from red to blue to purple within the first few days after an injury. Maybe his wife bit him?"

The implications of the bite mark whirled through Jenna's mind. "If she didn't but noticed it, she'd be aware he was having an affair." She let out a long sigh. "Heck, how do you ask Mrs. Robinson if she was in the habit of biting her husband without opening a can of worms? For all we know, she's totally oblivious to her husband's lovers."

"Then we ask the girlfriend." Kane looked at Wolfe's astonished expression. "I'm sorry, we haven't had time to bring you up to speed. We only just found out Robinson was a player. He was seeing Ann Turner."

"The hair stylist?" Emily stared at them. "She was seeing him?"

Jenna nodded. "Seems so. I guess we'd better speak to Ann."

"I'd guess she doesn't know he's dead." Kane frowned. "Nothing worse than being the bearer of bad news."

CHAPTER EIGHTEEN

Wednesday evening

It surprised him that people never realized someone was following them until it was too late. The sleet had cleared and yet Ruby hadn't noticed his truck following her to the bus stop. He'd stayed well behind, waiting to discover her stop, crawling along the curb like someone out viewing the limp, rain-soaked Halloween decorations out front of most yards. The houses became scarce at this end of town, the perimeters of the properties turning from white picket fences to barbed wire. This close to the forest, many of the ranches had tree-lined driveways, and people used the alleyways as a shortcut to their homes rather than follow the road. His heart picked up as Ruby stepped down from the bus and it chugged away, leaving a puff of black smoke in its wake. He pulled to the curb, well away from a streetlight, as she walked a few feet along the sidewalk and then turned onto an alleyway.

Coldness dropped over him in an almost trance-like illusion. His body seemed to have a mind of its own as he slid from the truck. He walked hunched over and added a limp. Anyone glancing out a window and seeing him would see an old man battered by the wind heading home in the dark. He moved slowly to the entrance of the alleyway. Ahead he could hardly make out Ruby's slight figure as she kicked aside the thick coating of fall leaves on the well-trodden pathway.

Underfoot the gravel crunched beneath his boots and he sensed more than saw Ruby stop and look at him over one shoulder. He increased his speed and could taste her fear as he came within a few yards of her. Her breath puffed out in great clouds of steam as she increased her pace. It made her appear ethereal as if she might take flight and he'd lose her forever. He stamped his feet as he gained on her, amused by how she zigzagged like a scared rabbit. Ahead, he could see the yellow glow of a streetlight at the end of the dark alleyway, and with a sigh, he turned and walked back in the other direction. Ruby had whetted his appetite, and the next time they met, she wouldn't see death coming.

CHAPTER NINETEEN

Thursday morning

The sun had just peeked over the horizon as Kane leaned on the fence surrounding the corral. He smiled at the horses racing around snorting with their ears pricked. At last the sky was clear for miles and he could turn out the horses during the day to enjoy the lush green grass. He stared into the distance, feasting on the view. It was so darn good to see the mountains again. When Jenna walked up beside him with straw caught in her hair, he grinned at her and plucked it out. "Thanks for helping with the horses."

"They're my horses as well." She yawned. "Getting up to work out and then muck out the stables before we leave is a pain when we have murder cases as well." She turned and headed toward the house. "You've been carrying me far too long."

He chuckled and fell into stride beside her. "You help me tend them every night, and I did say I'd do the chores if we could have them in the first place."

"Hmm, but we'll be missing the autopsies on the Stanton Forest victims if we don't get a move on." Jenna glanced at her watch. "Can you shower and fix breakfast in time? I told Wolfe we'd be there before nine."

Kane whistled for Duke and turned toward his cottage. "Sure, and I'll drive real fast with lights and sirens if we're late." He smirked at her and jogged along the path.

Over breakfast, he allowed the case to filter into his mind. "As far as I'm aware, Wolfe will have started the autopsies already. With two to cover, he'll be using Webber as a law enforcement witness." He lifted a forkful of eggs to his mouth. "We could interview the hair stylist at the beauty parlor and then drop by the ME's office for Wolfe's findings."

"Yeah, we could cut a few corners, but then I'm not there to ask questions." Jenna frowned. "I know you take the majority of evidence from the crime scene but I believe the victims still have something to tell us."

"Sure." Kane stood, collected the plates, and scraped the uneaten eggs into Duke's bowl. The dog had cleaned them up before Kane had loaded the dishwasher. "Need more coffee?"

"No, thanks, I'm good." Jenna pushed to her feet, rounded the table, and added her cup to the dishwasher. "We'll speak to the hair stylist later. What was her name?"

"Ann Turner." Kane strapped on his duty belt and then pushed on his hat. "Ready?"

"Yep." Jenna slipped her phone into her pocket. "Is Duke coming?"

Kane headed to the door, snagging his jacket on the way, with Duke hot on his heels. "It's not raining so he'll stick to us like glue. I guess he'll be able to wait in Shane's office during the autopsies. I don't think we'll have time to drop by the sheriff's department."

"He'll be fine—Wolfe, I mean." Jenna headed toward Kane's truck. "It's not like it's a sterile area. Duke will probably sleep the whole time."

Kane opened the back door of his truck, lifted Duke inside and then went about attaching his harness. "Although, he might start to howl if he smells the corpses."

"Oh, that would make the news. I can see the headlines now." Jenna jumped into the passenger seat and turned to grin at him. "Ghostly howling heard at local morgue over Halloween."

"Can you imagine Shane's TV interview?" Kane started the engine and headed down the driveway. "Mr. Wolfe, have you been howling at the moon lately?" He chuckled. "Oh, don't mention any of this or he'll get his I-just-bit-into-a-lemon face." They turned onto the highway.

"I won't mention a word." Jenna's bright demeanor faded as her phone chimed. "It's Rowley, I'll put him on speaker. Morning, is there a problem?"

"No, ma'am. As you're heading straight to the ME's office, I thought you'd like me to bring you up to speed with the suspect I interviewed yesterday, Ian Clark." Rowley's enthusiastic voice came through the speaker. *"He has an alibi for the Robinson murder. I checked it out on the way in this morning and the mortician confirmed he was with him, preparing a body for burial for three hours that evening, and never left the parlor."*

"Okay, we can take him off our list. Thanks for letting me know." Jenna leaned back in her seat and looked at Kane. "One down. Hey, is that ice?" She pointed to glossy patches on the blacktop.

"It sure looks like it." Kane slowed to maneuver around them. He'd hoped the morning frost would've melted by now. "The temperature is dropping fast and the rain-soaked blacktop hasn't had time to dry."

The next moment a black cat dashed across the road, its coat spiky and damp. Kane slammed on the brakes, barely missing it. The back wheels of his truck hit an ice patch and they fishtailed so close to the ditch alongside the road, the front wheels crashed through the dried bushes before he regained control. He stopped inches from the edge of the ditch. "Where did that come from? There isn't another occupied ranch here for miles." He peered out the window but the cat had vanished into the undergrowth.

"Oh Lord, we didn't need any more bad luck." Jenna's attention had fixed on the clump of trees. "There was a cat sitting on the gatepost of the Old Mitcham Ranch last time I went by and it probably belongs to one of the contractors working there. It can't belong to the snowplow guy, he's in Florida, and he wouldn't leave a cat unattended."

When Duke barked and let out a howl, the hair on the back of Kane's neck stood to attention. He started back along the highway. "I didn't expect that reaction from Duke, but then I don't recall running into a cat with him lately." He glanced at Jenna. "You don't really believe black cats are bad luck, do you?"

"I guess not." Jenna cleared her throat. "I had a neighbor who owned a Bombay. Its coat was glossy black and it had amazing copper eyes. It was a lovely cat. I cared for it for a time after her house burned down." She sighed. "Poor woman lost everything but that cat."

Kane looked at her before pulling back onto the road. "So maybe not so lucky, huh?"

The moment they turned onto Main Street, Kane slowed to a crawl. The ice-covered blacktop glistened in the sunlight, and two rear-end accidents blocked the way. A crowd had gathered among the bedraggled Halloween bunting on the sidewalk, their faces obscured by the scarves and hats they wore to keep out the bitterly cold air. He pulled to the curb and stared into the distance. "They look like minor collisions."

"Dammit. More delays." Jenna slipped from the truck. "I'll call Rowley. He'll have to deal with them. Go check to make sure everyone is okay. We'll have to take the backroads or we'll miss the autopsies." She sighed. "I'll get someone out here to brine the roads as well."

The chill shuddered through Kane's head the moment he stepped from the truck. The temperature had dropped considerably in the short drive from Jenna's ranch and the metal plate in his head, the result of a car bombing, caused severe headaches in winter. He ducked back inside the cab, dragged his woolen cap from between the front seats and pulled it on, leaving his Stetson on the seat. He pulled up his hood and ground his teeth against the threatening pain. His boots crunched on the patches of ice as he made his way to the first collision. "Are you injured, ma'am?" He peered into the vehicle.

When the young woman shook her head, he nodded and moved on to the next vehicle. Underfoot the blacktop was treacherous and his feet slipped with each step. After checking each of the people involved, he slipped and slid his way back to Jenna. "No injuries this time. The sudden drop in temperature has covered this end of Main with black ice. The other end of Main should be clear, the sun is already on that part of town. Here the blacktop is in the shade."

"Brine spreaders are on their way." Jenna moved out into the middle of the road and directed traffic toward Ronan Road. "We'll need to keep the traffic flowing so the brine spreader can get through." She glanced at him. "You're as pale as a ghost. Headache?"

Kane winced. She could read him like a book. "Yeah, I'll take some pills, as soon as we get to the ME's office."

"No, you won't." She frowned at him. "You'll take them now. Rowley is picking up Deputy Walters and he can handle the traffic. Rowley will file the accident reports. You can wait in the truck." She turned away and walked down the center line, the yellow sheriff's logo splashed across the front and back of her winter uniform giving the oncoming traffic no doubt as to who was in charge.

CHAPTER TWENTY

"Feeling better?" Jenna turned to Kane as he pulled into the ME's parking lot.

"Yeah, thanks." Kane pulled his cap down over his ears and his hand went to the door handle.

Jenna rolled her eyes. She had a macho, ex-special forces deputy, who she believed resented her telling him how to care for his injury, but he often pushed himself way beyond the call of duty. As his superior and friend, it was her responsibility to make sure he took care of himself. "Wait up."

"We're late." Kane flicked her a glance, his hand hovering over the door release.

She gave him a direct stare. "I'm not going to apologize for insisting you take your meds." She took in his narrowed gaze and swallowed. "You should know better than to go out in this weather without a cap."

"I was in kind of a hurry this morning." Kane slid out the truck then reappeared at the rear door and unclipped Duke's harness. "You see, I have this demanding boss who has me working before sunup. I removed my hat when I dashed in for a shower before making her breakfast and forgot to replace it before I left home. It was my bad." He flashed her a smile and his eyes danced with amusement. "I *do* appreciate your concern, Jenna. It means a lot to me."

She jumped down from the truck and met him at the front door. "Demanding? *Moi?*" She pushed open the glass doors and went inside. "Never."

Jenna didn't wait for Kane to secure Duke in Wolfe's office and headed straight to the morgue. She removed her coat and hung it on one of the pegs in a row beside the door, grabbed a mask and gloves, flashed her card on the scanner, and moved inside. The smell of decayed flesh hit her as she glanced around the room. Monitors held X-rays and crime scene photographs in an array of horror. She stared at them, unable to recognize the location of a few of them. When Wolfe looked up and halted the recording device, she nodded to him. "Sorry we're late. We had to attend a couple of accidents on Main. There's a patch of black ice there. What have we got, and where is that crime scene? I don't recognize it."

"It's not one of ours, but the Stanton Forest murders have a similarity to a case in Butte. Emily did a search last night to see if we could find a pattern. I have a gut feeling these cases are linked." Wolfe glanced toward the door as Kane entered. "Two men gunned down and left to rot at the side of the road."

Intrigued, Jenna studied the unfamiliar crime scene photographs. "Both shot in the back and then head."

"You'd imagine the shooter dropped them and then came in to finish them at close range, but this isn't the case." Wolfe looked at Kane. "I believe this shooter has left his signature behind."

"Are you referring to the feathers we found at both scenes?" Kane moved closer to peer at the body on the examination table.

"Nope. There wasn't any mention of a feather. Maybe they missed it." Wolfe used a remote control to zoom in on an autopsy image of another victim. "The angle of the shots isn't consistent with that theory. These injuries are the same as Parker Louis and Tim Addams. What do you see, Kane?"

"From the trajectory of the bullet, I'd say shoulder shot, and as they fell a follow-up to the head, so he fired rapid shots at the same distance." Kane moved his gaze to Jenna. "One victim might be a coincidence, but two identical ones that tie up to victims in another town is a signature method of killing to me. He could've easily taken them down with a headshot. It would've been a clean kill, and if he is a hitman, one shot and get the hell out of dodge is usual. This indicates to me he wanted to inflict maximum pain." He pointed to the X-rays of the Stanton Forest victims. "To smash the clavicle like that takes precision. That injury is excruciatingly painful."

Fascinated, Jenna examined the X-rays. "With the headshots coming so fast, the pain wouldn't have lasted very long, seconds at best. It hardly seems satisfying enough for a psychopath." She turned to Kane. "We've seen many who torture their victims, and a slow death feeds the thrill. What kind of crazy are we dealing with this time?"

"I'd like to hunt down any other matches to this case and maybe speak to the profilers involved before I make a decision. You see, these crimes cover both ends of the spectrum." Kane rubbed the back of his neck. "We have what looks like a definite hit, likely paid. So, say we consider that's the reason the killer is in town. The Robinson murder was almost clinical, but then we have these two." He waved a hand toward the victims. "These aren't hits. I figure it was their unlucky day. They pissed off a psychopath."

"Hmm." Jenna turned to Emily. "How far did you extend the search?"

"Montana. I used the newspaper archives and followed up with a call to Butte to obtain the files." Emily shot a haughty look at Wolfe. "I don't have clearance to search the other databases."

Jenna smiled behind her mask. "Don't worry, it's our job to hunt down similar crimes." She turned back to Kane. "So how far would a hitman travel?"

"That would depend on several factors: is he a freelancer or does he work for a boss?" Kane raised both eyebrows. "He could be a cartel heavy, but unless Mr. Robinson was into drugs, gambling, or people-smuggling, which I doubt, or has been subpoenaed to testify against someone, I'd say he's a freelancer."

The enormity of the problem rested heavily on Jenna's shoulders. "If we find similar murders, we'll need to liaise with other law enforcement departments and speak to the officers on those cases."

She could think of nothing worse. Dealing with different filing systems was one thing, but people had their own way of investigating crimes; sure, they followed procedure, but only a few could match her team, and sometimes it was the small things that people missed in an investigation that could solve the case.

"Any other questions or shall I continue?" Wolfe's voice jolted her out of her thoughts.

Jenna shook her head. "No, what else did you discover?"

"I'll send you a full report once the toxicology results are available, but as far as I can determine, both Louis and Addams were healthy men for their age. Cause of death in both was a gunshot wound to the head. Again, by the small entry wound, the permanent cavity exit wound, and brain matter spatter at the scene, we can safely say hollow-points, and from the damage sustained, I'd say the weapon was a rifle."

Jenna peered at the body of Tim Addams. "Why do the shoulder exit wounds differ from the headshots? Would this indicate two shooters?"

"No." Wolfe cleared his throat as if to get Emily's and Webber's attention. "We're talking about kinetic energy, or the size of a bullet and how fast it travels before it hits the target. The damage inflicted depends on the type of tissue it hits. Soft tissue absorbs less energy from the projectile so allows it to pass through, causing less damage. Hard areas, like skulls or bones, often absorb most of the energy and result in the bullet causing massive damage."

"But all we found were fragments at the scene. Is there nothing we can use to do a ballistics test?" Jenna glanced at Kane, worried they'd missed vital evidence. "Surely if the bullets went through soft tissue, as you say, we'd have found at least one of the bullets inside the victim."

"I'm afraid not. The bullet hit bone before exiting. Soft tissue absorbs the kinetic energy and slows down the bullet, so they often remain inside the body. If a hollow point hits bone, it increases the kinetic energy, which mushrooms the bullet, spreading the damage and causing a permanent cavity exit wound. I have fragments from the Robinson case and what we found at the Stanton Forest crime scene. Wolfe looked at her. "I'll examine them to see if they're from the same weapon, but I doubt it. The shooter wouldn't have used a rifle for the Robinson murder, and from the damage to the two in the forest, he used a rifle to make the distance at that velocity. Find me the killer's weapons, and I'll conduct a test and see if we have a match."

Easier said than done. Jenna turned to Emily. "Can you send me the Butte casefiles? We'll head back to the office and see what else we can hunt down."

"I'll do it now." Emily moved to the computer and tapped away at the keyboard. "Done."

"Okay." Wolfe turned to Webber. "You can close up Mr. Louis for me. Emily, I'll leave Mr. Addams to you. When you're done, take the tissue samples to the lab." He pulled off his gloves and headed for the door. "I need to speak to Dave and Jenna in my office."

Jenna followed him into the hallway with Kane on her heels. "Is something wrong?"

"I have a very bad feeling about this killer." Wolfe waved a hand toward the morgue door. "I've seen this MO before and read about similar cases in other states." He led the way toward his office. "I have a contact in the FBI who worked on cases in Baltimore involving the killer leaving a black feather, and I think you should talk to her. With these last two and the ones I uncovered, there has to be more. We're talking about an extremely dangerous and active serial killer moving from state to state. If this is the same person, we'll need all the help we can get."

CHAPTER TWENTY-ONE

Snakeskin Gully, Montana

Exhausted, Jo Blake dropped into her office chair and pushed both hands through her hair. *What am I doing here?* The truth slapped her in the face and she pushed it to one side, unable to cope with any more stress. As if moving homes with her seven-year-old daughter and setting up an FBI field office in a remote, backwoods town in Montana wasn't enough to deal with, now her phone was ringing. "Special Agent Jo Blake."

"Jo, it's Shane Wolfe."

Jo brightened, stood, and walked into the main office. "Now there's a voice from the past. Last I heard, you'd given up the good life and gone into forensic science. Where are you living now?"

"I'm out of Black Rock Falls, Montana, aka Serial Killer Central. I'm the medical examiner for here and the neighboring counties." Wolfe cleared his throat. *"We have a fine profiler here, but if you have time, could I pick your brains on a case that's come our way?"*

"Montana? Small world that's where I am too. I'm out of Snakeskin Gully." Jo's voice echoed in the massive, almost empty room. "Yeah, I'll be glad to help as soon as I get settled. Give me a couple of days. I don't have any staff and haven't located the agent assigned to me. I'll put you on speaker but don't worry, this place is like Fort Knox. They used the old firehouse, so it's a huge building and has a helipad on the roof. I even have my own bird but no one to fly it."

"What? Why did you leave DC?"

The sinking feeling in Jo's stomach lurched again and she swallowed hard to prevent the anger and remorse from welling up inside her. "Long story, but after a messy divorce, the boss sent me to here to set up a field office. I'm here with Jaime, and you'll remember Clara, her nanny?" She sighed. "But enough about me. I was so sorry to hear about your wife's passing. Are the girls coping okay?"

"Thanks, and yes they're fine."

Jo's mind filled with memories of a happy family and amazing barbecues. "Okay, what do you need?"

"Do you recall the string of unsolved murders in and around Baltimore?" Wolfe paused a beat. *"The kills had similarities, in particular a black feather left on scene, and you thought they'd been committed by the same person?"*

Jo thought for a moment and nodded to herself. The brutal murders and their strange twists had her mind working overtime. "Yes, I remember. The Chameleon Killer. I found similarities in murder cases in other states as well. Some of the murders resembled hits and the others more personal. He's had me baffled a few times because we're either looking at three or more killers or a person with a variety of violent personality disorders. He may be suffering from dissociative identity disorder. He's still out there, we never caught him."

"I think he might be here."

A cold chill seeped through her as if warning her to stay away. Images too horrific for her mind to comprehend blindsided her for a moment before she pulled herself together. "Send me the file. I'll see if it matches anything I have on file. If this is the same killer, I'll need a team to assist your sheriff; right now, it's just me."

"There's no rush. We have an excellent team here. Jenna Alton has solved many murder cases, and she has an ex-military profiler for a deputy." Wolfe sounded proud of the people he worked alongside.

"I'll talk to her. If this is the same man, you know him better than we do. I'll send out to all agencies to contact me if any similar cases have happened in their state. This killer may be spreading himself wide."

Jo googled Black Rock Falls on her computer and peered at the map. "I'll get back to you as soon as I've gone over the files and unpacked." She blinked at the remote town, sitting snug in the mountain range. "I've found your location; it's almost as remote as here. It must be at least three hours' drive away. If it's the same man, I can give you a few days, but I can't be away from home too long. We've just arrived and Jaime starts at her new school in the morning. She's taken the divorce pretty hard." She stood and wandered to the window overlooking the local sheriff's department.

"I can imagine. Anna went into herself for weeks after her mom died. Look, I don't want to upset her. We can make a video call if necessary. The roads into Black Rock Falls aren't safe for someone traveling alone, and the weather out here has been unpredictable." Wolfe sounded exhausted. *"It's a beautiful town, lovely people, but for some reason a magnet for murder."*

Jo walked back into her office and sat down behind the desk. She turned the chipped mug on her desk with the words "World's Best Mom" on the side and selected a pen from the stack inside. She added notes to the list of to-do items. "I don't intend to drive there with the first snow forecast. It will depend on when I can get someone to pilot the chopper. I have an off-the-grid operative out in the woods, Carter. I have the task to go tell him he's now back on active duty."

"Don't tell me they've assigned Ty Carter to work with you?" Wolfe sounded astonished.

Jo dropped her head into her hands. "Oh Lord, please don't tell me he's a problem." She stared at her cellphone screen. "All his jacket tells me is he's thirty-six, an ex-Navy Seal turned FBI. He's a first responder and spent five years in the crime investigation division.

Top in his field. Helicopter pilot and arms expert. On leave for PTSD after three innocent kids died during a raid and does not intend to return to work any time soon."

"He's good—one of the best crime investigators around." Wolfe cleared his throat. *"Well, he was before he went off the grid. He had a few family problems around that time too. It must have been substantial because his trail kinda ran cold around two years ago."* He paused a beat. *"He was involved in cybercrime as well. Do you have an agent to cover that end of things?"*

"Allow me to explain." Jo rolled her eyes. "Do you remember Alexis Davenport, the head of my department?"

"Oh, yeah. She comes with a warning."

"John was having an affair with her and gave her some personal information on me that could ruin my career." Jo gripped her hands so tight her knuckles ached. "Alexis wanted my signature on the divorce papers and me as far away from Washington, DC as possible. She gave me an ultimatum and I had to comply or end up penniless on the street. She gave me the mission from hell. I'm in the backwoods of the Wild West with orders to scratch up a team and set about creating an FBI Crime Scene Investigation go-to for the remote sheriff's departments." She forced her voice not to tremble. "She gave me a list of possible staff members—let me see, she supplied me with three. An office administrator, a local who didn't show this morning, then we have Ty Carter. The third is our cyber superstar Black Hat Hacker from juvi turned White Hat with the tag 'The Undertaker,' who works at the local computer store." She snorted. "So, my friend, life here is just peachy."

"Oh, I see. You'll need an ME. You can call on me if you don't have anyone."

Jo straightened in her chair. "I might steal you. We have a state-of-the-art facility here. One thing I did insist on was a building outfitted with everything we need. I must admit, Alexis did supply me with the best equipment. I guess she believed my husband was worth it."

"And what do you think, Jo?" Wolfe's voice soothed her shattered nerves.

Forcing down the need to laugh hysterically at the way her life had disintegrated, she stared at the phone. "To be honest, I believe they deserve each other. Enough about me. I'll look over the files and call you back."

"Thanks, Jo." Wolfe disconnected.

Jo waited for the files to arrive and scanned them quickly. The familiarity of the crime scenes made her stare into space trying to make sense of it all. The Chameleon Killer had moved into Black Rock Falls. She shook her head in disbelief. "And so it begins."

CHAPTER TWENTY-TWO

Stanton Forest, Black Rock Falls

Atohi Blackhawk stared down at the unmistakable top of a skull poking out from beneath a white snowberry bush and swallowed hard. He took a few steps back and then took a roll of yellow tape from his pocket and marked the tall pine growing close by. He turned and walked back to Brad Kelly, stepping over the carefully constructed grid they'd searched tirelessly. "Brad, I've found something." He gripped Brad's arm. "Don't go over there, it's best we don't disturb the evidence."

"I need to see." Brad stared at him, eyes wild with distress, and pulled away.

Atohi held him in a bear hug. "No! There is nothing to see. Act like the son she knew—be strong and brave." Under his arms, Brad's muscles relaxed, and Atohi sighed with relief. "It's out of our hands now. Shane Wolfe is a good man. He will treat her with respect, you have my word."

"He knows nothing of our ways but I'll agree. We have no choice, do we?" Brad shook his head. "She's where I saw her in my dream." He turned and pointed through the trees. "I remember running toward that rock and hearing the sound of water."

Atohi nodded. "If it is her, she will rest easy now. We'll take her home."

"Is my brother with her?" Brad's head turned in the direction of the grave.

Atohi gave him a shake. "I don't know. There is only one bone. It may not even be her or your brother. We'll have to wait and see." He waved over one of his friends. "Take Brad back to camp and wait for me. I'll contact Shane and he'll be able to give us more information." He took out his phone and found Wolfe's number.

"Okay." Brad turned away, shoulders hunched.

"Shane, it's Atohi." Atohi walked back to the gravesite. "I've found a skull. I'll send you the coordinates. When can you get here?"

"Are you sure it's human?" Wolfe sounded busy, and Atohi could hear other voices in the background.

"Yeah, the top part of the cranium is visible and part of both eye sockets. I've marked the area but no one else has disturbed the scene." Atohi glanced at Brad sitting on a log, drinking something from a cup, and sighed. "Brad is concerned she won't be respected, but I've explained. He seems okay now."

"He led you right to the spot?" Wolfe sounded skeptical.

Atohi stared at the grave. "No, the general area. He recalled landmarks. We searched an area back from a stream he remembered from the night his father killed her. We did a grid search and split up. I pulled the lucky straw."

"I'll come take a look to confirm. Then all I can do is secure the remains. We'll need a forensic anthropology team to recover the body and any evidence left behind. I have a friend in Helena; I'll have her come down." Wolfe cleared his throat. *"It's likely the killer buried both victims together in a shallow grave. It would be better if your friend wasn't present."*

Atohi stared into the distance. "He won't agree. I figure, he'll camp out here until he's sure she's safe. He said he's been having dreams. I'm not sure how stable he is. I've known him for a long time and he's changed. It's as if remembering what happened has sent him a little crazy."

"I'm not surprised—it would have been a shock." Shane's voice was muffled as he spoke to someone else. *"Ah, sorry, I've just asked Emily to call Jenna and explain. I'll leave now and be there as soon as possible. How far are you from the highway?"*

"Not far at all. Only a few hundred yards. You'll see our trucks parked alongside the forest. I'll send Jenna the coordinates as well." Atohi turned to see Brad staring at him. He gave him a nod.

"I'm on my way." Wolfe disconnected.

CHAPTER TWENTY-THREE

The wind buffeted Jenna as she made her way along Main to the beauty salon. The ice had melted and the damp sidewalk glistened in the sunshine. The cold air blowing from the snow-capped mountains rising in the distance held the promise of snow and yet not a cloud marked the brilliant blue sky. She loved this about Black Rock Falls. No matter what happened in her town or how lousy she felt, the scenery made every day worth living. She nodded to the townsfolk as she passed by and all greeted her as a friend. Yes, life in this town was special.

The beauty parlor was busy as usual, and a girl came to the counter to greet her. Jenna wrinkled her nose at the confection of chemical smells accosting her and smiled. "I'd like to speak to Ann."

"She's just finishing up with a client." The girl waved to a row of chairs. "Take a seat, she won't be long."

Jenna glanced at her watch. The autopsies had taken longer than expected and she wanted to catch Cliff Young and Kyler Hall at the ski resort site this afternoon. To save time, Kane had gone by Aunt Betty's to grab lunch. They could eat on the way. Her phone chimed and she frowned at the caller ID. "Hi, Em, what's up?"

After Emily explained about Atohi Blackhawk's call, Jenna leaned back in her chair and her shoulders slumped. She'd need another team of deputies to handle the current caseload. "Okay, tell your dad we'll be there as soon as I've finished an interview." She glanced up as Ann walked toward her, ushering a client toward the counter. "Ah, Ann, is there a place we can talk?"

"Sure, come in here." She led the way into a small kitchenette. "Has there been a complaint? If so, you need to speak to the owner. I just work here."

Jenna shook her head. "No, I need to talk about Lucas Robinson." She waited for a reaction. It wasn't what she expected. The girl's expression was belligerent. "You do know him, don't you?"

"It's his wife causing trouble, isn't it, sending you around to my workplace to get me fired?" Ann's hands went to her hips. "He told me she wasn't too happy when he asked her for a divorce. He said we had to cool things for a while until he moved his assets into a place where she couldn't get to them. They haven't slept in the same room for over a year."

Interesting. Jenna took out her notebook and made notes. "When did you last see Mr. Robinson?"

"Sunday morning." Ann giggled. "He told his wife he was going to church."

Jenna raised one eyebrow. "And how long has your relationship been going on?"

"About three months." Ann met her gaze. "We're in love."

"You were seeing Cliff Young before him, is that correct?" Jenna glanced at her notes.

"Yeah." Ann twirled a strand of her hair. "He wasn't real happy when I broke it off with him."

"You better sit down." Jenna pulled out a chair and waited for her to sit. "Lucas Robinson is dead. Someone broke into his home and shot him."

"Oh my God!" Ann followed a horrified expression and rapid breathing by a wail that brought people running.

Jenna stopped the owner at the door and quickly explained. She returned to the kitchenette, poured Ann a glass of water, and then sat opposite her, so their knees were almost touching. "Ann, did

Lucas ever mention anyone who might want to harm him? Was he worried at all?"

"Nooooo." Ann lifted a tear-streaked face. "Only his wife. She didn't understand him."

Not able to keep the truth from this distraught young woman, she leaned forward and squeezed her shoulder. "Lucas was known to have several girlfriends." She took in the girl's astonished face. "Men who have affairs usually tell their girlfriends they're leaving their wife. His wife didn't have an argument with him, and he died in the bed beside her." She sighed. "Ask anyone he worked with; it was common knowledge. That's how I found you."

"He was just using me?" Ann's eyes rounded in surprise. "The pig."

"There's one very important thing I need to know." Jenna used her most comforting voice. "You're not in trouble but I have to eliminate something important. Did you happen to bite Mr. Robinson in the last few days?"

"Oh God." Ann looked horrified. "That's how his wife found out, isn't it? Yes, that was me—we were fooling around and it got out of hand is all."

"I don't know if his wife knew about his affairs." Jenna stood and closed her notepad. "That's all for now, Ann. I'm sorry for your loss." She handed the girl her card. "If you think of anything at all, anyone he mentioned who might have a grievance against him, call me." She headed for the door, leaving the stunned girl staring after her.

As she stepped onto the sidewalk, Kane pulled up to the curb and she jumped inside. "Great timing."

"Did she have any idea who might have killed Robinson?" Kane waited as a truck carrying pigs drove by, and then he turned toward Stanton Forest.

Jenna shook her head. "No, she had no idea he'd died. I had a call from Emily: Atohi found bones in the forest. Wolfe is on his way.

We'll help secure the scene and hope we get to the ski resort before Hall and Young leave for the day." She sighed. "That's assuming they went to work today and aren't halfway to Canada by now."

"Did Wolfe mention the name of the FBI agent he wanted to call about the murders?" Kane reached blindly into the bag of sandwiches on his lap.

"No, I haven't spoken to him since the autopsy." Jenna opened the takeout bag and peeked inside. "Are you worried it might be someone you know?"

"Not really." Kane shrugged. "When Agent Josh Martin dropped by a few months ago to assist with the missing girls case, he didn't recognize me, and I've worked alongside him, so I believe I'm safe." He frowned. "I'm wondering who it is, is all."

As they drove along Stanton, Jenna could see several trucks parked off-road at the edge of the forest, and Wolfe's white van with the Medical Examiner decal on the side. "We'll be able to ask him soon." As Kane pulled in behind the van, Jenna pushed the last of the sandwich into her mouth and grabbed her to-go cup of coffee. "Oh, good, he hasn't left yet." She hurried to the van.

"Jenna, Dave." Wolfe climbed from the van, gripping his GPS in one hand. "The grave is about two hundred yards in that direction." He pointed into the forest. "I guess we take this trail and see where it leads us." He adjusted his backpack and led the way through the trees.

Jenna followed behind him. "Did you speak to your FBI contact?"

"Yeah, Jo Blake." Wolfe ducked under a low-hanging branch. "She's willing to look at the files at least. She's opening a branch office in Snakeskin Gully. That's a small town tucked in the shadow of the same mountain range as Black Rock Falls, but it's at least a three-hour drive from here."

"When was her most recent case?" Kane crunched through the undergrowth, pushing low pine boughs away.

"The same year as I arrived here." Wolfe trudged on, checking his GPS. "She handled the profiling of a sadistic killer and found herself tied up in knots because of the variants in each kill."

Jenna frowned. She had Kane, why would she need another profiler? "What makes Jo Blake so special?"

"She was the behavioral analyst for the FBI's CSI out of DC and has a reputation for being one of the best profilers in the business." Wolfe glanced over one shoulder. "It's not her expertise we need, it's her knowledge of the killer. From the old case files, I studied, our current killer might be the same man. There is a similarity we can't ignore."

"And that is?" Kane moved beside Jenna as the trail widened.

"The switch from hit to personal." Wolfe stopped walking and turned to face them. "Jo had a theory. The killer she was hunting down in Baltimore was not only exhibiting criminal psychopathy but was perhaps suffering from dissociative identity disorder as well. He killed with almost clinical precision one day, like a hit, and the next he'd mess up the victim; with some he'd be horrendously cruel. He didn't have a preference for type or gender, and Jo couldn't pin him down."

It was obvious to Jenna that both men understood the conversation. She held up a hand. "Just a minute, you lost me at 'exhibiting.' What is dissociative identity disorder?" She sighed. "In plain English."

"Oh, sorry, Jenna." Kane frowned. "You'd know it by the term 'split personality.' Over the last few years, new and less demeaning terms have been used for patients." He met her gaze. "I find it hard keeping up myself."

Jenna snorted. "As if, your nose is always stuck in a book." She glanced ahead. "How much further?"

"From the trampled undergrowth, I'd say they went off the trail just ahead." Wolfe took the lead again.

"Now you know that information, do we really need an FBI agent on the team?" Jenna looked at Kane, wondering what was going through his mind. "Wouldn't you be stepping on each other's toes?"

"I don't think so. I'm a sniper who studied profiling; she is a behavioral analyst. She is way above me." Kane shrugged. "I'd be able to learn from her, much like Wolfe learns from his forensic anthropologist friend."

"What's she like?" Jenna wrinkled her nose at the smell of bear scat. "Some of these professional types can be unbearable."

"Not Jo." Wolfe turned to look at her. "She speaks her mind and jumps in boots and all. Her job and her daughter are her life."

Jenna winced. "I hope not in that order. So, she's unattached?"

"Divorced. Think on it, Jenna, and I'll contact her again if you're interested in bringing her in on the case." Wolfe moved on through the trees. "Ah, I see Atohi. He has a group of people with him."

After exchanging pleasantries, Jenna followed as Atohi moved away from the small clearing to an area marked off in grids with yellow tape. Ahead, Wolfe held up a hand and they all stopped, forming a half-circle. "What can you see?"

"Human skull." Wolfe took a brush from his pocket and crouched down. With gentle care he brushed soil from the rounded skull. "It's been exposed for some time. It has moss growing over it. I'm surprised no one has discovered it before now." He flicked Jenna a concerned glance. "Substantial head trauma. I'll have to call in a forensic anthropologist—you'll remember Dr. Jill Bates from Helena?"

Jenna nodded. "Okay, we'll secure the scene and inform the forest wardens. They've already posted notices saying there is an archaeology dig taking place in this area, so with luck we might be able to keep people away."

"No need." Atohi touched her arm. "There will be two of us camping close by. She is family and we don't fear her spirit."

"Secure a wide boundary." Wolfe pulled out his cellphone and walked some distance away, disappearing behind bushes.

Jenna, Kane, and Atohi soon had the area enclosed with crime scene tape. Checking her watch again, she waited impatiently for Wolfe to return. "We need to leave now if we're planning on speaking to Young and Hall."

"We'll make it." Kane checked his own watch. "Here's Wolfe now."

"Jill will be here in the morning by chopper with her team. She'll need accommodation and transport for six. Can you get Maggie to arrange that for me, please?" Wolfe raised both brows as he looked at Jenna. "I'll leave everything to Jill. She'll be able to use one of my labs for the remains and then give us a report." He sighed. "I'll have to get back to the lab. I haven't finished my investigations into the cases we have already."

Jenna nodded and turned to Atohi. "How is Brad handling all this?"

"Disturbed but I think relieved." Atohi smiled at her. "Don't worry, go on your way, I'll make sure no one disturbs anything."

"Thanks." Jenna turned to the others. "Let's go."

"Disturbed, huh?" Kane glanced at her as they followed the path back to their vehicles. "Maybe we need to look a little closer at Brad Kelly."

CHAPTER TWENTY-FOUR

Kane accelerated along the highway, lights flashing and sirens blaring. It was good to be able to drive his truck fast on the open road, and the way his engine roared made him smile. The drive alongside Stanton Forest and high into the mountains was one of his favorites. It was almost like flying as they gained altitude at speed. All good things must come to an end, and he slowed, turned off the lights and sirens, and then took the new off-ramp leading to the ski resort.

The mayor's vision for a winter tourist boom was working well. Wide roads snaked their way to the top of Black Rock Mountain and gave spectacular panoramic views of the forest as far as the eye could see. The snow-covered mountain offered a natural array of ski runs without destroying the beauty of the area. So well concealed, even the ski lifts didn't spoil the views. Surprised by the interest and investments coming in by the dozen, the mayor had commissioned another ten cabins. He'd set them in a little picturesque village within walking distance of the main lodge. It seemed since the popularity of the White Water Rapids Park, everyone wanted a share in the prosperity of the town.

Trucks littered the road alongside dumpsters filled with discarded building materials, and radios blared from the small cabins like a badly tuned orchestra. He turned into the village and parked out front of the site manager's trailer. "I guess we should start here."

"Okay." Jenna pulled out her notebook and gave him a stern look. "It's freezing out there. Are you wearing the thick cap I got for you?"

Kane smiled at her. "I never leave home without it." He pulled the cap down over his ears and climbed out.

The cold blast of wind made his eyes water as he hurried into the trailer with Jenna hot on his heels. They stepped inside a temporary construction, desks with computers and papers everywhere. From the array of equipment on-site, the building work employed many different trades. He'd met the large man sitting at the main desk behind a sign saying "manager" on his last visit. Wearing a hunting cap lined with sheepskin and glasses resting on the end of his nose, he looked up curiously as they entered. Kane nodded to him. "Sid Glover, this is Sheriff Alton. We're looking for Kyler Hall and Cliff Young. Are they working today?"

"Just a moment." Glover hammered on his keyboard and ran his finger down the screen. "Yeah, they're working on number six." He narrowed his gaze. "Not in any trouble, are they? I don't want any criminals on my site."

"Not that we're aware." Jenna stepped forward. "Have they been working here long?"

The man used the keyboard and nodded. "Yeah, according to the payroll, since the project started, over a year now."

"And yet you acted as if you didn't know them when my deputy asked you." Jenna pressed one hand flat on his desk and glared at him with an intimidating stare. "Why is that?"

"Oh, I know them." The manager waved a hand as if to include all around him. "I just don't know where each individual man is at a given time. We have two hundred men working here in a variety of crews. I can't keep track of all of them in my head."

"Okay, what are their usual hours?" Jenna made notes.

"Ah, any time between daylight and dusk." The manager smiled. "It's contract work here for the most part, and crews work longer hours. The faster they work, the more they get paid."

"Is that usual for this type of work?" Jenna straightened.

"It's usual practice for most building work these days. We have a project manager who arranges for trades to come and do the work; it's not like a plant where people are employed by the firm."

"Point us in the direction of number six." Jenna headed for the door.

"First right, halfway down on the left. The numbers are outside." The manager leaned back in his seat. "You can't miss it."

Kane followed her out. "Thanks."

"We'll drive, the wind is cruel up here." Jenna climbed into the truck. "I had the weirdest feeling the manager was hiding something; he seemed distracted somehow. Did you notice the way his eyes kept flicking to the door?"

Kane nodded and drove the short way to number six. "I didn't see anyone hanging around. He gave you the information you asked for, I figured he was cooperating." He pulled up beside a truck loaded with a variety of waste. "Whoever owns the truck doesn't take too much pride in keeping it nice."

"Maybe they don't have time, working all hours." Jenna slid from the seat and headed to the door, swinging her small forensics kit over one shoulder before Kane had time to unclip Duke and let him down.

Kane started after her, and Duke bounded off, tail wagging and ears pushed back flat against his head by the wind. The dog wasn't letting Jenna out of his sight. Kane scratched his chin. *What's wrong with him? Is there someone here we should know about?*

He made it to the front door of the cabin in long strides, scanning the area in all directions, but nothing seemed suspicious. Men moved in and out of unfinished cabins, and the cacophony of different tunes surrounded him. Inside the cabin, Jenna waited for a man using a nail gun to stop what he was doing. Kane moved to her side, and the man raised his head and started at the sight of them. The nail gun rose in his hand and Kane instinctively drew his weapon. A gas-driven nail gun could be lethal. As Jenna stepped closer, Duke's hackles rose and he gave an uncharacteristic growl and showed his teeth.

"Aim that someplace else." Jenna's voice sounded loud in the empty room. "In fact, lay it down on the counter over there. What's your name?"

"Cliff Young, ma'am." He turned away and placed the tool on the counter. "Is there a problem, Sheriff?"

"Where's your friend?" Kane holstered his weapon, noticing the concern in Young's eyes.

"I'm here." A man in his late twenties, tall and muscular, walked out from another room. "I'm Kyler Hall. What do you want with me?"

"I hear you were in a fight with Parker Louis and Tim Addams at the Triple Z Bar on Saturday night." Jenna lifted her chin and stood her ground. It was obvious this man's show of hostility hadn't fazed her. "We have reason to believe you were all involved in a racket to steal appliances from the site." She narrowed her gaze at his arrogant bark of laughter.

"Nah, it wasn't about anything of the sort." Hall gave her an insolent grin. "It was over a woman. We'd all had too much to drink." He looked at Kane and winked. "You know how it is? Things got nasty. I had to put those boys down to teach them a lesson."

Kane met his gaze. "Are you admitting to shooting Louis and Addams?"

"What?" Hall gave Young an astonished look and swallowed hard. "No! I don't know nothing about no murders."

"Can you account for your movements on Wednesday morning between daybreak and eleven?" Jenna opened her notepad.

"Just a minute." Young's Adam's apple bobbed as he swallowed. "Do we need a lawyer?"

"I'm not arresting you." Jenna passed a meaningful look at Kane. "I'm here to hunt down suspects in a shooting incident, and if you pulled the trigger, I'd say 'yes.' As you have some concerns, we'll make it official." She glanced at Kane. "Read them their rights."

"We didn't kill anyone." Hall straightened as if regaining control. "We share a house. We had breakfast together on Wednesday morning and then headed here before seven. We left here around four."

Kane frowned at their responses. They'd not informed them either man had died and yet Hall and Young had mentioned murder and killing. He read them their rights, and when they refused legal representation, he moved on with the questioning. "Do you live in town?"

"Yeah, on Lake." Hall leaned against the counter, his tool belt scraping against the granite top.

There was only one way out of town to the highway, and that put both men in the area at the time of death. "Then what time did you hit Stanton Road, and do you recall any other vehicles passing by?"

"Lake runs into Stanton so around seven, I guess." Hall glanced at Jenna. "I had trouble seeing a few feet in front of me. A thick mist was coming in from the forest. Some vehicles passed us but I don't remember anything about them at all."

"Okay." Jenna nodded. "What do you carry in your truck for protection? I mean, working up here, you can't be too careful, can you?"

"There's a shotgun on a rack in the cab." Hall shrugged. "Most guys carry one up here."

"And when was the last time either of you fired a weapon?" Jenna slipped her small forensics kit from one shoulder.

"Not for about three months—we went to the practice range." Young moved around restlessly. "We didn't shoot no one."

"Then you'll agree to a gunshot residue swab?" Jenna opened the kit and looked at them expectantly.

"No way." Hall gripped his friend by the shoulder. "They're looking to blame someone. We need to have this done legal. We're not answering any more questions, we want a lawyer. You have to provide one free of charge, we don't have any money."

Dammit. Kane sighed. They needed information about their involvement with Robinson. Both men had an ax to grind, and now they'd have to pull them in in for questioning. He rolled his eyes at Jenna and she sprang into action.

"Fine, then get your gear together. I want you back at the sheriff's department for questioning." Jenna looked from one to the other. "I'm giving you a break by allowing you to drive back to town, but if you take off or do anything stupid, trust me you won't like the consequences." She glared at them. "I'll call you a lawyer and have him meet us. We'll wait for you outside." She headed through the door and leaned against Kane's truck. A huge puff of steam came from her mouth as she sighed. "I sure misjudged them. I thought they'd welcome a gunshot residue test to clear their names."

Kane whistled Duke to his side and lifted him inside the truck. Once he had the dog secured in his harness, he looked at her. "They've tipped their hand. We never mentioned anyone was dead; it's a pretty big assumption. Duke didn't like them either. I've never seen him become aggressive before today."

"Maybe we should give him the scent of the victims and see how he reacts to Hall and Young then?" Jenna threw her arms up in the air. "That's not conclusive either; we know they were in a fight."

Kane watched the men pack their truck and climb inside. "This is going to be interesting. Why didn't you just cuff them and take them in?"

"Well, they'll have Cross for their lawyer, and at this stage of the investigation I don't want to give him any excuse to undermine me." She climbed into the truck. "This way, it appears they agreed to come in for an interview." She turned to look at him. "Between you and me, I think they're as guilty as hell."

CHAPTER TWENTY-FIVE

Rattled didn't come close to the way Samuel J. Cross, the local lawyer, made Jenna feel. The man dressed like a cowboy, straight from the rodeo circuit, but the casual look was deceiving. Sam Cross was as smart as a whip and she needed to be on her toes with him. She peeled off her coat and hung it on the peg in her office, and noticed Duke had stuck to her like glue since the encounter at the ski resort. The dog usually went to visit Maggie at the front counter, looking for snacks, and would lie under her desk in a basket or at Kane's feet most of the time. It was unusual for him to be so protective, and the growling and teeth-showing was out of character. Jenna patted him on the head. "Can you feel my resentment toward the lawyer? Don't worry, he won't hurt me. While he's talking to his clients, why don't we go see how the handyman is doing in the basement?"

She walked through the office and took the steps down to the basement. One door led to the evidence locker, a secured area, and a second, currently open, led to the furnace and a storage area. She moved to the door and Duke barked, making her jump. The dog rushed forward and Jenna raised her voice. "Down boy."

Inside, Tom Dickson dropped the stack of old papers he'd been carrying and staggered back. Jenna grabbed Duke's collar and instructed him to sit. She looked at Dickson's face. He was an old, wrinkled mountain man with no hint of compassion in his hard gaze. "I'm sorry, I'm not sure what's gotten into him today."

"Dogs are nothing but trouble." Dickson raised his gaze to her and bent to pick up the papers.

Jenna ignored his comment. So, he wasn't a dog-lover; it made no difference to her. She considered him for a moment. He looked so down on his luck, she wanted to help him in any way she could.

"Is there something else you wanted me to do, ma'am?" Dickson dropped the papers into a carton and straightened. He pressed a gloved fist to his back and groaned. "Sorry, my arthritis plays up something fierce in the winter."

Jenna shook her head. "No, I was just checking on how you were going down here."

Rowley had offered him a day's work over the weekend, but he really needed something else now. She searched her brain for a job for him to do. "If you can come by my ranch first thing in the morning, it would be a great help if you could make some room in my barn. I have the winter feed delivery due soon. I'd planned to help Kane over the weekend, but we're snowed under right now and I need to be here."

"You won't be there?" Dickson frowned.

"No, but the house and cottage are under CCTV surveillance." Jenna shrugged. "If you enter the perimeter of the house or cottage, you'll risk setting off the alarm system. So long as you avoid those areas, you'll be fine."

"I'll be there by seven." Dickson bent to pick up more papers. "As long as that mutt isn't running loose."

Jenna headed for the door. "No, he'll be leaving with me. Just remember, bring everything you need with you because once you leave the perimeter of the ranch, you won't be able to get back inside without tripping the alarm. I'll be happy to leave you some lunch." She ran up the steps with Duke on her heels. *Time to face Sam Cross.*

She made her way to the interview rooms and found Kane sitting outside, sipping a cup of coffee. "This seems like a waste of your time—shouldn't you be chasing down a court order for Mrs. Robinson's bank account details?"

"Cross said his clients would be ready to talk at any time now, so as you'd gone missing, I thought I'd wait here." Kane lifted a second to-go cup from beside his chair and handed it to her. "Rowley has taken the paperwork over to the courthouse and although the probable cause is vague, we might be lucky."

Jenna sat down beside him in the cramped alcove and sipped the coffee. "Hmm, seems to me it was common knowledge Lucas Robinson was having affairs for some time. I find it hard to believe the wife was that naïve. We'll go and speak to her again as soon as the doctors have finished their evaluation of her state of mind. I'm still convinced there's a link to her that we've missed, and she is left-handed like the killer." She smiled at him. "I've asked Tom Dickson, the handyman working in the basement, to drop by in the morning. That's where I vanished to. He's going to reorganize the barn before the winter supplies are delivered."

"You planning on leaving him there while we're out?" Kane frowned at her and shook his head. "You don't know him from Adam."

"No, but what could that old man possibly do?" Jenna sighed in frustration. She had to believe people were inherently good. "We have a security field around the houses. If he so much as moves inside the perimeter, we'll know. He can't access the saferoom, and the rest of the barn holds feed and stables. Nothing to steal. He's worked here without a problem, kept to himself and not wandered around. He's going to be there by seven, so we'll set him to work and leave." She could see he was unconvinced. "I'll put his lunch in the old refrigerator so he doesn't have to leave during the day; he'll be fine."

"Okay. You're making him lunch as well?" Kane gave an agitated roll of his shoulders. "You planning on inviting him to dinner too?" He indicated to Duke, who was leaning against her leg. "Duke is agitated, has been since we started working this case. He won't let you out of his sight."

Jenna laughed at his sour expression. "He's getting like you, overprotective. If you recall, Duke became aggressive when we spoke to Hall and Young. They posed a threat to me and he sensed it is all." She patted Duke on the head. "Although he did frighten Dickson enough to make him drop the papers he was carrying."

"He did what?" Kane chuckled. "Really?"

Before Jenna could explain, the light flashed outside the interview room, indicating Sam Cross had concluded his interview. She glanced at Kane. "That's one down."

"Nope, two." Kane threw his to-go cup into a nearby trash can and stood. "He didn't spend more than a few minutes with Young. Most of his time has been with Hall."

Jenna swallowed her coffee and tossed the cup beside Kane's. "Okay, I'll take the lead and you observe unless you have any of your own questions."

"Okay." Kane stretched and his long fingers touched the ceiling. He bent to pat Duke on the head. "Stay here, good boy." He swiped his card and they entered the interview room.

Jenna nodded at Sam Cross. "Afternoon, Sam. Is your client willing to answer a few questions?"

"Yeah, within reason, but I'm stating for the record neither he nor Mr. Young were involved in the shooting in Stanton Forest." Cross nodded at Kane. "Deputy Kane."

"Cross." Kane nodded and sat down. "I'll start the recording." He gave the date and time, and everyone in the room stated their names.

Jenna laid her notebook on the table and sat opposite Cross and a very belligerent-looking Hall. She glanced down at her case notes on Robinson; she already had what she needed from them about their involvement with the Stanton Forest murder victims. Both Hall and Young were in the vicinity at the time of the crime, and both men had history with the victims and had refused a gunshot residue swab. Now she needed information on Hall's interaction with Lucas Robinson. "Mr. Hall, can you account for your whereabouts on Monday night after eleven and Tuesday morning before three?"

"Yeah." Hall leaned forward on the desk and rested his head in one hand. "I was home with Cliff. We have to get up early for work so we don't go out weekdays."

"Did anyone else see you?" Jenna glanced up at him. "A neighbor perhaps? Did anyone call you, or did you interact with anyone online during that time?"

"No, I'd say I was sound asleep." Hall smiled. "Alone in my bed, unfortunately, so I can't prove it. Why?"

Jenna pushed on. "I believe you had a grievance with Lucas Robinson. Can you elaborate?"

"A grievance?" Hall snorted and his eyes flashed with anger. "Is that what you call swindling a man out of his inheritance?"

"How so?"

"He told me to invest in a crazy scheme and it went bankrupt two weeks after I invested my money." Spittle flew from Hall's mouth. "I'm sure he knew it was going to go bust. I shouldn't have trusted him to invest my money… if he invested it at all. Seeing the house he built at Majestic Rapids, I'd say he's been swindling everyone in town for years."

Jenna made a few notes and felt Kane touch her arm. She nodded at him.

"Did you make a complaint to the bank manager?" Kane leaned back in his chair, making it creak. "If you believed someone was running a scam, you could have reported it to us or the FBI."

"What's the point?" Hall choked back a laugh of disgust. "Who'd listen to me? And I don't have the cash to pay for lawsuits, I'm living hand to mouth since that guy ripped me off."

Jenna nodded. "I can see you're upset, Mr. Hall, and why. Did you enter Mr. Robinson's home on Monday night and kill him?"

"Don't answer that question." Cross sent daggers across the table at Jenna. "You said you wanted to interview my clients about a shooting incident; now you're bringing murder one to the table." He shook his head. "Lay it out for me, Sheriff. What are you accusing my clients of doing?"

Jenna bristled. She had wanted Kane to watch Hall's reaction, and rather than denying any wrongdoing, the man was glaring at her with malice. "Okay." She took a beat to shake off the hate radiating from Hall and lifted her gaze to Cross. "Both your clients were in the vicinity of the Stanton Forest murders at the TOD. Both were involved in arguments at their place of work and later at the Triple Z, where there was an altercation witnessed by a number of people. Both your clients have grievances against Lucas Robinson, and they can't verify their whereabouts during the time he was gunned down in his home." She gave him a direct stare. "I believe your clients are involved in three murders."

"Where's your evidence?" Cross stabbed a finger into the table. "Do you have anything to prove my clients were at either crime scene?"

Jenna shook her head. "Not at this time."

"Not at this time." Cross barked out a laugh. "Circumstantial evidence will not amuse the DA. Nor will it convince him to charge my clients. No jury will convict them without evidence."

"I asked for a gunshot residue test and they refused." Jenna glared at him. He was right, of course, but she had to interview suspects to get answers. He was going way over the top. "If they are innocent of the crimes, why not comply?"

"Because a gunshot residue test from two known shooters would likely show positive, as both my clients have current hunting licenses." Cross pushed to his feet. "That alone is reasonable doubt. Now, if you'll open the doors, I'm taking my clients out of here."

Jenna stood her ground. "Not yet. I want to speak to Cliff Young. His girlfriend broke up with him over Lucas Robinson. I need to know if he met with Robinson."

"I wouldn't allow you to ask that question, Sheriff." Cross flicked a glance at Kane and then back to her. "This may be a backwoods town but we don't allow intimidation from law enforcement."

In her periphery, she noticed Kane stiffen just slightly and get slowly to his feet. He had her back as always, and from his cold expression, he wouldn't allow too many more judgmental remarks from Sam Cross.

"Why don't you take a seat, Mr. Cross?"

"So you can try to intimidate me as well?" Cross glared at Kane.

Infuriated, Jenna shot up from the table. "I resent that. It's unprofessional, and I thought you were better than that, Sam. We always treat people with respect. I asked you here because I need to ask questions to eliminate your clients from my inquiries. You're impeding my investigation. This time you can remove your clients, but rest assured the moment we find evidence against them, the talking is over. I'm taking it straight to the DA for an arrest warrant." She swiped her card on the scanner and walked into the hallway without a backward glance.

CHAPTER TWENTY-SIX

It had been a long day and Ruby Evans rubbed her sore feet on the bus trip home. Glad the sleet had stopped at last and the evening was clear and crisp, she slipped her shoes on and stood to make her way to the front of the bus. The vehicle slowed with a squeak of brakes and she moved down the steps. The doors banged shut behind her, and as the bus disappeared into the distance, she had the awful sense of being totally alone if someone attacked her.

It seemed darker than usual, and although the sky was clear, a heavy mist swirled across the blacktop from the forest. Halloween was a few days away, and the mist resembled ghostly forms drifting along the sidewalk as if searching for souls to steal. To make things worse, the streetlights were out between the bus stop and the pathway she took on her way home, through the woods. After the upsetting meeting with the strange man the previous evening, her nerves were on edge. Ruby couldn't push the thought from her mind that someone was following her again, and she had to force one foot in front of the other along the shadowy sidewalk. As she walked, she searched her purse for her phone; the screen would offer her a modicum of light but the battery was low.

Ruby walked the fifty yards to the alleyway and stopped, listening for any sound. An owl hooted in the forest and a breeze rustled the leaves, but nothing seemed to move in the darkness. She took a few hesitant steps and then paused, looking ahead at the patch of inviting light from the streetlight, one hundred or so yards away. She *could* take the long way home. It would take maybe another half an hour, but her feet ached and she had an early shift in the morning. She peered into the darkness. The picturesque walkway she'd taken earlier had turned into a musty-smelling tunnel leading into an unknown void of uncertainty. Should she take the shortcut home and maybe risk running into the strange man again?

Fear churned her stomach. It was so dark in there, and the canopy of trees hid any hint of light. Anyone could be hiding in the gloom, waiting for an unsuspecting victim to walk by. How easy it would be to pluck her from the pathway and drag her into the bushes. Biting her bottom lip, she sucked in a deep breath as indecision made her falter. Home was on the other side of the alleyway; a meal and a hot bath called to her. She ignored the little voice in her head telling her to avoid dangerous situations, gathered her courage, and entered the pitch-black tunnel. The light from her screen was of little comfort but better than nothing. As she quickened her pace, the blue glow faded and blinked out. Surrounded by a suffocating wall of black, she stuffed the phone inside her bag and, using one hand to guide her, she hurried along the wall of leafless bushes, stretching her eyes wide to see in the dark.

The musty smell of rotting vegetation filled her nostrils, and underfoot wet leaves covered this part of the gravel path, muffling the sound of her shoes and the footsteps of anyone following her. Rising panic made it hard to breathe. She had to get out of the claustrophobic tunnel and increased her pace, stumbling over the uneven pathway. Petrified of every creak of the surrounding tree branches, she moved forward and then her hand touched fabric. A hint of cologne drifted on the air. She froze, too terrified to speak. Under her palm, the fabric moved and a low chuckle came on a breath, so close she could feel the warmth of it on her cheek.

"Hello, Ruby."

CHAPTER TWENTY-SEVEN

Friday morning

Jenna ducked and then spun on one foot, aiming a kick at Kane's head. The next moment his large hand gripped her foot and flipped her face down. The mat made a whooshing sound as Kane's two-hundred and fifty pounds landed beside her, pinning her with ease. "Dammit, Kane, let's try that again. I'm getting slow."

"It's to be expected." Kane rolled to his feet and offered her his hand. "You can't expect to be in top shape when you work on cases half the night."

She took his hand and he pulled her to her feet. "You do."

"True but I'm used to surviving on no sleep." Kane pushed a hand through his damp hair. "I just need food and I'm good." He grabbed a towel from the back of the chair and smiled at her. "I'll hit the showers. The horses are squared away and it's your turn to cook breakfast." He glanced at his watch. "Then I guess it's a meet-and-greet with the handyman."

Jenna watched him walk away and then headed to her bathroom. Although he hadn't said another word about allowing Tom Dickson to work at the ranch, he'd spent a great deal of time checking the security on her house and his cottage. They both had installed a home security alert on their phones. If Dickson decided to wander near either home, they'd know, and he'd be under CCTV surveillance. She wasn't in the least worried, but she'd seen the concern in Kane's eyes. The thing with Kane, he was always on the job. It would've come from his time protecting POTUS, no doubt, but she wished sometimes he'd just loosen up. She'd seen his gentle side and he had a vulnerability. He'd place his body in front of a bullet to protect the innocent and she feared, one day, someone would use it against him.

As Jenna closed the dishwasher door and set it working, she glanced at the clock. "Dickson will be here in about thirty minutes." She turned to speak to Kane but he held a finger to his lips and pointed at Duke.

She stared at the dog. It was as if he'd frozen in time, and from his raised hackles and the low rumbling growl, something was wrong. She pulled her weapon, slid to the back door, and checked the locks. When she returned to the kitchen Kane indicated with hand signals to move along the hallway and into her home office. Keeping her back to the wall, she eased inside. She studied the array of CCTV cameras, showing all the external areas. Only the horses moved around in the corral; she couldn't see anyone near the house. "All areas clear."

"He's indicating toward the front door." Kane moved to her side. "I can't see anyone out there either, but I trust Duke—he senses more than people."

A shiver of a memory caught Jenna unawares. She'd once hit a tripwire and set off an explosive device, sending them sky-high. "A bomb?"

"No one could get in here undetected unless they dropped something using a drone." Kane frowned. "I'm pretty sure that's the only way in unless someone used a chopper, and then they'd have tripped the motion sensors."

When Duke barked and ran at the door, Jenna exchanged a puzzled look with Kane. "Do you figure he's ill or something? Do dogs go crazy?"

"Only with rabies and he's had his shots." Kane walked to the door, peered through the window, and then turned and raised both eyebrows at her. "I've found the problem. It's that black cat. It just peeked its head out from under the porch."

Jenna frowned. "Poor thing is probably starving."

"Not likely—they are superb hunters and there are plenty of mice and rats in the barn." Kane looked again and then frowned. "It might be hurt. It's covered in blood."

"Blood? Hold onto Duke." Jenna hurried to the door and opened it. "Puss, come here, puss." She bent and held out one hand.

Instead of coming to her, the cat bounded away and she could see its tail waving above the long grass in the direction of the Old Mitcham Ranch. Jenna straightened and stared at Kane. "It's not acting as if its hurt. I hope nothing has happened to its owner."

"It wouldn't hurt to check." Kane stared in the direction the cat had gone.

"Okay, we'll drop by the Old Mitcham Ranch on the way to the office. We haven't met the new owner yet." She trunked back to him. "I wonder if they've gotten a pile of black cats for Halloween and left them there?"

"Maybe." Kane glanced at his watch. "I doubt the owner would stay there. There's a crew working out of trailers turning it into a Halloween attraction." He grinned at her. "Woo woo. Let's hope the curse hasn't taken them yet."

Jenna shook her head. "That's not funny."

The buzzer sounded at the gate and Jenna went to the small screen set beside the front door. She peered at the man staring at her from the window of his truck. "It's Dickson." She pressed the button to unlock the gates. "I'm glad he's early. I want to get over to the Old Mitcham Ranch just in case something has happened. The cat was upset about something."

"Hmm. It was making enough noise." Kane frowned at her. "Unfortunately, I don't speak cat."

Jenna grabbed his coat from the peg in the mudroom and tossed it to him before getting her own. "Neither do I." She set the alarm and opened the front door. "Cats are more intelligent than you think."

"Yeah, but if it's witnessed a bloody murder, getting it to testify in court is gonna be a problem." Kane chuckled and followed her down the steps.

They greeted Tom Dickson and Jenna explained what they needed him to do. She pointed out the sandwiches and drinks she'd left in the refrigerator. "See how you go. Get as much done as you are able but I don't expect you to work all day. We'll finish up this weekend. I'll leave cash with Maggie at the front desk, same deal as before."

"Thanks, Sheriff." Dickson touched his hat and talked slow. "I'll be working alongside Deputy Rowley on Saturday, and next week Maggie has found me a few days' work out at the livery stable." He peered at her over his glasses. "You've all been mighty kind to me, ma'am."

Jenna looked at the old man and smiled. "That's great. We'll leave you to it." She walked away and heard low voices behind her but didn't turn around and headed for Kane's truck.

"Hmm." Kane slid behind the wheel.

Jenna turned to look at him. It was obvious from his grim expression he was annoyed. "What?"

"Nothing for you to worry about." Kane started the engine and drove down the driveway, staring straight ahead.

"Uh-huh, so I'm going to get combat-face Kane all day, am I?" Jenna sighed. "Loosen up, Dave. It's me, Jenna. He said something to you, didn't he?"

"Oh yeah, he said something." Kane glanced at her and then looked back at the road. "Nothing for you to worry about, he's just an old man is all. Probably going senile and lost his filter."

Jenna sat back in the seat and stared out the window. It was a short drive to the next ranch and Jenna's mind was running at maximum speed. "If he said something about me, I need to know. I'm recommending him for employment. My reputation is on the line."

The truck stopped with a jolt and Kane turned in his seat and looked at her. Annoyed by his stubbornness, she met his gaze. "Don't go all macho on me, Dave, it doesn't work. I can order you to tell me."

"Yeah, I guess you can. Fine. He asked me how I kept my cool with you ordering me around all the time." Kane's gaze didn't leave her face. "And how I felt being kept in my own little house like your prize stallion."

Shocked, Jenna stared at him. "After all we've done for him, he said that? He's a strange one. He probably never had a filter. He was likely raised to believe women should be chained to the kitchen sink." She frowned. "Do you want me to ask him to leave?"

"Nope." Kane turned the truck back on the highway. "He's just an old man, and I'm sure he was just teasing me." He snorted. "I'm not easily provoked but he got under my skin is all."

Mind reeling, Jenna looked at him. "You don't think that, do you?"

To her surprise, Kane laughed.

She turned in her seat. "What's so funny?"

"I'm the luckiest man on Earth." Kane flicked her a glance. "I came here broken and you gave me a place to live. You nursed me back to health when I'd lost my memory. I'm not perfect but you don't care. Most women would've given up on me after six months but you understand me." He turned into the Old Mitcham Ranch. "You don't care you're living with a killer, albeit, a government assassin. There are no secrets between us—well, apart from my real name—and we're happy. So, who cares what people think?"

Jenna sighed. "Well, I sure don't give a damn and I don't believe the townsfolk do either." As they drove past the line of trailers, she looked at him. "I thought this place would be a hive of activity. Where is everyone?"

"Not sure." Kane moved the truck closer to the dilapidated ranch house. "Maybe it's finished or they're working inside."

Jenna's attention moved over the elaborate Halloween decorations on the front porch of the Old Mitcham Ranch. A skeleton hung inside the window, and the ghoulish mannequins sitting upright in chairs looked so real among the grinning jack-o'-lanterns. She stared as they got closer and her stomach did flip-flops at the sight of a blood trail on the front steps. It looked too real somehow, and the next moment the smell of death seeped into the cab. "Err, Dave, I don't think the dead bodies are Halloween decorations."

CHAPTER TWENTY-EIGHT

Shots rang out and a tree beside the truck shattered into a million pieces. Wood splinters rained down on the truck in a strange brown dust.

"Dammit!" Jenna scanned the area, looking for the shooter. "Get us out of here."

More shots peppered the ground, sending up plumes of dust. "Move it, Kane. With the sun in my eyes, I can't see if it's coming from the ridge. We're sitting ducks here. Go, go, go."

"Hold tight. This is gonna be rough." Kane spun the wheel and hit the gas.

As the truck reversed at speed, Jenna ducked down and gripped the seat. The engine roared as they flew backward, bumping over the uneven driveway. "Did you make out the shooter?"

"No." Kane had turned to look out the back window. "Rifle, from the west I figure."

Jenna looked up at his grim face. "Get us out of range. Head back to the ranch. We'll suit up and get backup."

The truck rotated and rocked for a second and then, wheels spinning in the dirt, careered down the driveway. Trees rushed by in a blur and the truck bounced like a bucking bronco as Kane maneuvered over the deep grooves. Thrown forward, Jenna hit her head on the console but held on for dear life as the world turned again. The truck seemed to rise at the front as Kane pushed it to full speed. They slid onto the highway, drifting around the corner and fishtailing in a scream of tires as he accelerated away from the carnage. A wave of nausea hit her and she looked up at Kane's combat face. "We good?"

"If he's on the ridge, we will be once we make our driveway." Kane didn't take his eyes off the road.

"I'll call the cavalry." Jenna eased her cellphone out of her pocket and called Rowley. "Shots fired. We need backup, my ranch. No sirens. Call Wolfe. Tell him to bring Webber and pack for bear. Wear full gear including com packs. We have a mass murder at the Old Mitcham Ranch."

"Holy cow. Are you okay?"

"Yeah. Move it." Jenna disconnected.

"Okay, we're coming up to our gate now." Kane slowed to make the ninety-degree turn and then hit the brakes, waiting for the gate to swing open.

Jenna pushed up and rubbed her forehead. "Okay, what is your take on the scene? It sure looked like a mass murder to me."

"From what I could see, the men on the porch are all headshots. I'd say the killer allowed the woman to bleed out. The blood is fresh."

Jenna stared at him open-mouthed. "Your eyesight is obviously better than mine. Could she still be alive?"

"Nope." Kane pulled up outside her ranch and rubbed his thumb over the bruise on her forehead. "Sorry about that, it's just a bruise."

Jenna batted his hand away and glared at him. "You had a few seconds to take in the scene, how could you possibly know she was dead?" She touched the throbbing egg on her forehead with trembling fingers. "I only figured out they were people and not store mannequins from the smell."

"I've seen a lot of death, Jenna, and I recognized the woman. Her throat was cut." Kane's expression was grim. "She was the new girl at Aunt Betty's. I think her name is Ruby."

Horrified, Jenna swallowed hard. "*Jesus.* What kind of lunatic are we dealing with now?"

"If he's the same man who murdered the others, unpredictable and escalating fast." Kane gave her a concerned look. "We'll probably need an army to take this one down."

Jenna had never seen Kane this on edge, and a wave of anxiety slid over her. "It's never easy." She cleared her throat. "Get your gear, backup is on the way."

Although she'd handled many murders in her time in Black Rock Falls, it didn't get any easier. She hadn't become hardened to seeing mutilated bodies, and under the bravado of leadership, she still had to conquer her fear and force her legs to move. "I'll suit up and then tell Mr. Dickson to go home. From the smell, he's already fired up the incinerator." She slid from the vehicle and then went around the back to collect her new liquid Kevlar vest and helmet.

"Why? We need that work done." Kane joined her.

Jenna pulled on the vest and then shrugged. "Dickson doesn't like dogs and Duke doesn't like him, so you can't leave them together."

"Okay, Duke can stay in the truck." Kane assembled a rifle in seconds and laid it in the back. "I'm ready."

Wolfe's ringtone chimed on Jenna's phone. "We're safe, Shane. What's your ETA?"

"I was on the way to my office. I'll be there in ten." Wolfe disconnected.

Jenna looked at Kane. "Ten minutes. We'll do an equipment check."

They spent the next few minutes stuffing useful items into their pockets. Jenna went inside the house to exchange her buff-colored Stetson for a black woolen hat. As she went down the steps and headed for Kane's truck, she caught sight of movement near the barn. She heaved a sigh of relief when she spotted Dickson coming from around the back.

"Is there a problem?" Dickson limped toward them. "Anything I can do to help?"

Jenna turned to look at him. "Nothing to concern you, Mr. Dickson. We're just picking up a few things." When he nodded and headed back to the barn, she took one of the rifles out of the gun locker in the back of Kane's truck and checked it. "Hand me some spare clips." She shoved them in her pockets. "Let's go, we'll wait at the gate for the others."

She climbed back into the truck and waited for Kane. He was staring at his phone and passed it to her as he climbed behind the wheel. She glanced at the screen. It was the CCTV feed from the front gate. "Ah, good thinking."

"Did anyone follow us?" Kane headed down the driveway.

Jenna took the recording back to when Dickson arrived at the gate. She could see them leave and return but no one else had used the road since they'd arrived home. "No, and I wouldn't expect to see many people. The guy that owns the snowplow and brine spreaders is the only other person who uses this road, and he's in Florida. There is access overland, even from here. There are tracks all over, left from when the Old Mitcham Ranch was split up. Most of the ranches use them to move livestock."

"What about the crew working on the Old Mitcham Ranch?" Kane waited for the gate to creak open and then drove through and pulled out onto the road. "They'd be back and forth collecting supplies."

The sight of the dead bodies set up on the porch shuddered into Jenna's memory. She rewound the feed a full twenty-four hours, and apart from her and Kane, no one had passed. "The shooter must be one of the men working on-site."

"Unless they know about the dirt roads. You can get to town via the other ranches if I recall?" Kane took his phone from her and slid it inside his pocket.

"Yeah, apart from mine there are three ranches over the hill. They all have dirt roads that lead to the highway. I would imagine I'm the only owner who has a perimeter alarm system, and they didn't set off any of our alarms, so they came from a different direction. Since the last owners sold the land, I have no idea if anyone uses the old tracks anymore." Jenna turned in her seat. "Here comes the cavalry."

"How do you want to play this?" Kane looked at her.

Jenna thought for a moment; she had a tactical professional in Kane and yet he asked her opinion. "We should split into two teams. We take the front with Rowley, head up beside the trailers, and Wolfe and Webber go around back of the ranch house and come in from there. Any suggestions?"

"I'm not sure we'd have enough cover for a frontal approach. The shooter could be holed up in one of the trailers, or the barn." Kane turned and looked at her. "Or maybe he was using a hunting rifle from up on the ridge. We've been shot at from there before."

Jenna nodded. "Okay, I've got a better idea." She slid from the seat as Rowley pulled up behind them and Wolfe stopped his van in the middle of the road. Webber jumped out, rifle in hand. She waited for the men to gather. "Okay, we have four men with gunshot wounds to the head, one woman with her throat cut. No one has left or visited the ranch in the last twenty-four hours so we have to assume the shooter is on scene or has escaped overland." She turned to Wolfe. "Webber is with you. Head up the road with caution, don't slow down, go past the ranch. There's a trail just on the bend; you can park there and come in on foot around the back of the house. Use your coms to keep in touch." She turned to Rowley. "You're with us. Leave your truck here. There's a dirt road just before the Old

Mitcham Ranch's driveway which leads to the paddock at the back of the barn. We'll go in from there and use the barn for cover." She looked at Kane and noticed a slight nod of approval. "This way, if the shooter is there, he won't know we're coming."

"If there's one shooter." Kane frowned. "From the carnage it could be two. I made out single headshots but that was from a distance."

Jenna nodded. "Okay, move out and stay safe." She looked at them one by one. "We could be facing a psychopath responsible for homicides across the country. No heroics, he won't give you a second chance. Shoot to kill."

CHAPTER TWENTY-NINE

A strange excitement descended on Jenna, but deep down she understood the danger, and becoming a victim was a sobering reality. The adrenalin pumping a mixture of dread and uncertainty triggered her flee response each time she chased down a felon. Her heart pounded, and relying on her years of training to bolster her, she headed into danger with her head screaming at her to run away. Her mind filled with the ghastly scene on the front porch of the old home, the blood spatter on the steps and empty sightless eyes. She slowed for just a second before pushing the images away and increasing her stride. Having Kane and Rowley to watch her back gave her courage as she bolted along the trail toward the barn overlooking the house. The thick covering of leaves dampened their footfalls as they moved swiftly without making a sound. As they came to the tree line, her com crackled.

"Jenna, we're coming up on the ranch house now." Wolfe's voice came in her ear. *"It's almost too quiet and I can smell death. Moving in now. There are swarms of flies crawling over the side of the house beside the back door. We may have more victims inside."*

Cold fingers of unease slid down Jenna's back. She ignored the warning screaming in her head not to move forward and glanced at Kane beside her. He'd heard Wolfe through his com and winced. Jenna pressed her mic. "Stay in position. We're coming up alongside the barn and will have eyes on the front porch in five."

"Roger that."

Jenna looked over at Kane to give him an order, but he was already scanning the area with his binoculars. "All clear?"

"We're good to go but the undergrowth is at least waist-high." Kane glanced at her then his attention went back to the barn. "Do you want me to go first and open up a path?"

"Okay." Jenna nodded. "Single file once we leave the cover of the trees. You and Rowley go first, I'll watch your backs."

They scurried through the trees and she waited as Kane made a dash to the side of the barn. He peeked around the corner and waved Rowley over, and Jenna followed close behind. She moved up behind Kane. "What do you see?"

"Nothing moving." Kane leaned his back against the wall and looked at her. "I can't see inside the trailers. We could have a shooter waiting to pick us off one by one."

Jenna nodded and dropped into her combat zone. "We'll clear the barn first—we can gain access by the side door." She pressed her com. "Wolfe. Hold your position. We'll clear the barn. Wait for my signal. When we have eyes on the front of the house and the trailers, you can go inside and clear the house. Be aware of IEDs; we don't know who we're dealing with right now."

"Roger that. No sound from inside, and the back door is open. No explosive devices or tripwires in sight."

"We're entering the side door of the barn now." Jenna nodded at Kane. "Go."

"Wait!" Kane handed her his rifle and bent to examine the ground. "No soil disturbance." He checked all around the doorframe before standing to one side to ease the door open and turkey-peek inside. He pulled back and then looked again, using his binoculars. "Damn Halloween."

Jenna stared at his annoyed expression. "What is it?"

"They've recreated the Mitcham hanging scene inside." Kane shook his head. "It's going to be a nightmare sorting out what's real." He pulled his weapon and moved inside. "Clear."

Jenna followed and waved Rowley into the barn. She scanned the area. The new owners had made changes for Halloween by adding false cobwebs with huge fat black spiders and eerie lighting. A mannequin of a man swung back and forth from the rafters, making a creaking sound that would set anyone's nerves on edge if they'd heard the ghost stories surrounding the place. Many years ago, Mitcham had murdered his wife and committed suicide. Later, people claimed to have heard him swinging back and forth in his death throes.

"This place is every kid's nightmare." Rowley paled. "It seems wrong to commercialize the murders committed here."

Jenna shook her head. "I can't believe the mayor allowed this." She handed Kane the rifle.

"It happens all over." Kane shrugged and pressed his mic. "Wolfe. We've found re-enactments of crimes here. You may be facing the same inside the house."

"Copy."

Jenna pulled her weapon and moved to the barn door, trying to ignore the entrance to the root cellar. She could see the bolt secured over the hatch and wondered if the new owners had recreated the brutal murder of a young woman who'd died there. She swallowed hard, trying unsuccessfully to push the murder, that had even stunned Kane, from her mind. With Kane and Rowley in position, she turned to them. "Kane, keep your rifle on the first two trailers, Rowley take the third, I'll watch the house." She pressed her mic. "Wolfe, we have you covered. Move in."

"Roger that."

The smell blowing in from the house had intensified, and the congealing blood appeared black in the sunlight. The killer had staged the macabre scene on the porch to gain maximum effect. Jenna shuddered and froze on the spot as something brushed against her leg. She'd seen prairie rattle-snakes on her ranch and dare not move. She lowered her voice to just above a whisper. "Kane, something touched me. Is it a snake?"

Her eyes moved to meet his and she bit her lip as he looked down. When he grunted and aimed his rifle out the door, she glared at him. Panic rose in her throat as the sensation came again. "There's something here. I can feel it."

"It's that darn cat again." Kane was using his rifle to scope the trailers. "It's rubbing around your legs."

She glanced down and a pair of big copper eyes looked up at her. The cat let out a contented purr. "Not now, pussycat."

A loud bang broke the silence. Startled, Jenna swung her weapon up and down and side to side, searching. "Where did that come from?" She hit her mic. "Wolfe. Come in."

Nothing.

Another bang and Kane moved forward through the barn door and took a position behind a tree. Jenna tried again. "Wolfe."

Nothing.

CHAPTER THIRTY

Wolfe flattened against the wall of the kitchen. He'd heard the bang from outside and Jenna's voice through his earpiece, but with both hands firmly on his weapon, he wasn't removing a hand to reply. He'd heard something moving in the house and wasn't taking any chances. He glanced at Webber's face, eyes wide at the three fly-infested hands on the kitchen table, next to a bloody ax. Webber was a trained police officer, and to Wolfe's relief, he shook his head and snapped back into action.

"Wolfe, come in." Jenna was getting insistent.

Wolfe dared not make a sound but turned on his mic and tapped it twice. It was code to let her know he'd heard her but couldn't talk. He nodded to Webber and they eased their way down the hallway. Heart thumping in his chest, he took a quick glance into the first bedroom and ducked back. A mannequin of a woman wearing old-style clothes lay on the floor in a pool of blood. He looked again, slower this time, at a grisly scene, designed for Halloween. Moving to the next room, he vividly recalled the murder scene of a young girl he'd attended. Whoever had purchased this ranch had used crime scene photographs to depict the murders. Although, the last one wasn't how he remembered it. The noise came again, and he glanced back at Webber. "Did you hear that?"

"Sounds like rats in the walls." Webber moved ahead and peered into the family room. "This room has skeletons playing cards. The rats are a bonus." He hit his mic. "House is clear, Sheriff. We're heading onto the porch next."

"Roger that, Webber." Jenna sounded relieved. *"Wolfe, the banging was the wind catching the trailer doors and shutting them. The occupants must have left in a hurry to leave them open. All clear so far. No sign of the killer at all. No shell casings either. This is a strange one."*

"Copy." Wolfe holstered his weapon as he followed Webber into the family room and, batting away flies, peered out the window. "The porch is a crime scene. Stand down until it's secured. It's going to take time to process, but if you want to get up close, wear gloves and booties. There are footprints on the porch floor. My kit is outside the back door—grab what you need from there and come around the front. The inside is set up for Halloween but the killer has added his own touch by littering the kitchen table with the victims' hands. It looks like he used an ax. We're going to need help to catch this lunatic, Jenna."

"Copy that. I'll leave you to handle the scene and we'll continue to search the grounds. There's a bunkhouse out back I want to check. I'll leave Rowley here on surveillance." Jenna cleared her throat. *"Oh, did you check the cellar? It's in the pantry."*

"No, we're on our way."

Wolfe waved Webber from the room and they soon found the pantry. With Webber's assistance, he pulled open the door and peered at steps vanishing into darkness. He fumbled for a switch, but of course, the bulb was missing. Standing in the light at the top of the stairs, they might as well have had targets pinned on their shirts. He ducked back and listened with his back against the wall, Webber beside him. After what he'd witnessed, he had no intention of becoming the killer's next victim. Risking his life when he had daughters to care for at home was not an option. He sucked in the putrid air, aimed his flashlight along his Glock, and peered around the door to search the small room. The old furniture stacked all over could be hiding anyone, and in one corner a huge chest freezer hummed. He pulled back and looked at Webber. "I don't see anyone but they could be hiding behind furniture. There's an old freezer in the cellar and it's running. Where do you figure the power is coming from?"

"I noticed solar panels on the trailers, and they'd need power to set up here." Webber scratched his chin. "Maybe there's panels on the roof as well."

Wolfe nodded but his gut was telling him not to venture down the steps. "If so, why didn't they replace the light in the cellar? Unless someone removed it to hide down there."

"Maybe it's all part of the Halloween experience?" Webber was staring at the body parts on the kitchen table. "Do you want me to go down?"

Wolfe shook his head. "Nope, I'll go. I believe it's clear down there but this house is giving me the creeps, and trust me that doesn't happen often." He raised his weapon. "Keep your back to the wall and watch the door. I don't like the idea of the door shutting and locking me down there."

"No worries." Webber gave him a curt nod.

Glad of his liquid Kevlar vest and the new helmet he'd obtained for the sheriff's department, Wolfe headed down the creaky steps. "Is anyone down here? This is the medical examiner. I'm armed and the sheriff has the house surrounded. Call out."

His flashlight moved across spiderwebs heavy with dust and picked up reflections of red eyes in dark corners. Underfoot his boots crunched on rat droppings covering the step treads. The scurrying sounds from below made the hairs on the back of his neck prickle. He wished he'd worn a face mask. The stench of vermin turned his stomach but he'd smelled worse things in his career. The stairs creaked and moved unnervingly with each step, and the handrail looked as if it would crumble away at the first touch. He moved the flashlight around, up and down, but no one lurked in the corners.

The beam of his flashlight moved to the chest freezer, and Wolfe moved closer to examine the dark stains on one side. It was as if something had spilled over the edge and run down the sides, leaving a sticky mess on the floor. He moved closer and examined the deep cherry pool. *More fake blood?* He pressed his mic. "Webber. I've found something. I'm opening the freezer."

"Roger that." Webber's voice came through his earpiece and seemed to echo from his position at the top of the steps.

Wolfe holstered his weapon and attempted to lift the freezer lid without success. He placed the flashlight between his teeth and, steeling himself for what may be inside, dragged open the lid a few inches. As he bent to peer inside the crack, the lid sprang open and a figure sat bolt upright.

Surprised, the flashlight slipped from Wolfe's mouth, bounced across the floor, and went out. In complete darkness, he hit the floor and rolled away, drawing his weapon. "Shit!"

CHAPTER THIRTY-ONE

He peered over a boulder on the top of the small ridge overlooking the Old Mitcham Ranch and smiled. The old backroads had cut the distance from the highway in half and made for a fast getaway. Even so, the view through his scope had been worth the risk of running into the sheriff and her posse. He'd watched her move her men around like chess pieces across the board he'd created. He'd waited patiently to see their reactions to his art—and it was art. He wondered if they would've enjoyed watching the shocked faces of the men he'd mutilated as much as he had. The way they'd run around in panic as the girl bled out made him chuckle. They'd tried to save her and hadn't seen him coming. The moment they laid eyes on him they'd sealed their fate. They'd acted tough, throwing out threats as if they could manipulate him. He laughed at the memory. They couldn't escape—no one ever escaped—and after a few well-placed shots, they'd have strangled their own mothers to get away from him.

He didn't hear pleas, promises, or prayers; in fact, the more they tried to reason with him, the more pain he needed to inflict. Seeing people die made his memories go away. It was as if each one ticked a box on an imaginary list of things to do. If the cops ever caught him, he'd have difficulty remembering all his kills. At the time, it was like watching himself from afar, as if he hadn't cut the girl's throat or used an ax to remove body parts. By tomorrow, he'd forget them, only remembering them like a person would recall a slice of excellent pie or a strong cup of their favorite coffee.

He'd enjoyed this kill. It made up for Robinson. He took no immediate pleasure from a quick kill, and the exhilaration seemed delayed, coming later in a rush of technicolor images as he rode on an adrenalin high. He'd once thought everyone was like him but discovered being able to walk right up to a person and kill them was a gift. He'd gotten close to his targets with ease. No one ever questioned what he was doing, or why he was there. Why? Because he walked into every store, business, restaurant, or home as if he belonged there.

He cast one last look over the porch, seeing everything as he'd left it. It was his donation to the curse of the Old Mitcham Ranch, and it would outshine all the others. He could see the headlines now: Mass Murderer Commits Halloween Mayhem. *Yeah, I'd like that.*

CHAPTER THIRTY-TWO

Kane had his own ideas about the killer. He may not be a hotshot behavioral analyst, but he'd profiled murderers with success for some time. The current random killings, with no rhyme or reason to them, sent chills down his back. The unpredictability made the case difficult, and the pace the killer was escalating had exceeded all his expectations. He'd studied the behavior of many psychopaths and rarely did their condition fit into a neat little box. They all had different types of mental health conditions mixed into their psyche, which meant they were always dealing with an unknown quantity.

He followed close behind Jenna, constantly scanning the area. The old bunkhouse had been empty, with no recent sign of habitation. They reached the back door of the ramshackle house and Wolfe's voice came through his earpiece.

"We need backup. In the cellar."

"On our way." Jenna pressed her mic and, weapon drawn, ran up the back steps.

Kane followed and near gagged on the stench. He batted away swarms of flies and took in the scene. In the small pantry, Webber was against the wall weapon drawn. Before Jenna could speak, Kane hit his mic. "Wolfe. What's happening?"

"Not sure. I've lost my flashlight. Someone was hiding in the freezer. The light's out. I can't see a darn thing down here."

"Did you take a look?" Jenna glared at Webber.

"No, ma'am." Webber's cheeks flushed. "Shane told me to keep back and guard the door."

"Kane, get down there." Jenna met his gaze. "I'll have your back." She looked at Webber. "Watch the back door. I don't want any surprises."

Kane turned on his Maglite and found Wolfe leaning up against a wall, weapon drawn. He moved the beam around and found the freezer. He lifted the light up, taking in the spilled blood, and winced. Inside the freezer sat a grotesque mannequin, white-faced with black eye sockets. Seeing a dummy coming out of the freezer in the dark would've startled him after seeing the carnage on the porch. "Clear. Hold tight, Shane." He turned to Jenna. "It's all part of the show." He indicated behind her. "There's a box of lightbulbs on the shelf behind you. Hand me one and we'll get some light down there."

After fixing the light, Kane headed down the rickety steps. Wolfe was shaking his head over the Halloween display. Kane walked up to him and slapped him on the back. "Now that's just plain nasty."

"I must've stepped on the pressure pad." Wolfe shut the lid of the freezer. "Watch this."

The lid moved and a white, blood-soaked hand slipped out the crack. The next moment the freezer opened and the mannequin sat up, making a hissing sound. Kane pushed the lid down and shook his head. "Whoever set this up has collected crimes from all over Black Rock Falls. These aren't memories I want to revisit." He turned to see Jenna standing behind him.

"When you two have stopped playing with the exhibits, we have victims to attend to." Jenna turned and headed back up the stairs. "Get suited up. I'll meet you out front." She used her com. "Rowley, it's all clear here. We're moving outside now. Hold your position."

"Jenna." Wolfe followed her up the steps. "Wait, we'll use the front door. I'll take a quick look at the murder scene then I'll be starting in the kitchen. I'll be taking shots of the hands on the table and bagging them. There's a blood-spattered, balled-up jacket under the kitchen table—it may have some ID inside. I'd say the killer used it to carry the hands from the porch." He tossed Webber his keys. "I'll need my van."

"Yes, sir." Webber headed down the back stairs at a run.

They suited up, gloves, masks, and booties. Kane eased open the front door and pushed all his emotions to the darkest reaches of his mind. The porch resembled a typical Halloween scene until he took in masses of insects crawling over the corpses. As he moved outside, the smell of death was as thick as fog. The killer had secured the four male bodies to chairs with wide black tape. Some of the men had hands missing but their clothes were intact. Each had gunshot wounds to the head. The young woman, who he recognized as Ruby, sat in the middle surrounded by a pool of blood. In the crimson puddle floated a black feather disturbed only by a trail of bloody cat footprints leading away to the edge of the porch. He turned to Jenna and pointed. "The cat *was* here."

"So, I see." Jenna lifted one shoulder. "Go figure."

Kane went back to examining the scene. One man, with gray hair, sat in his shirtsleeves; beside him on the floor was a Glock 22 with the clip removed. He searched around and spotted the clip in the grass below the porch railing. He stood to one side to allow Wolfe to conduct a preliminary examination and moved to Jenna's side. "I'm finding it hard to believe this is the work of one man. If so, he is out of control."

"Or just enjoying himself." She peered at him over the top of her mask and then turned to Wolfe. "What have we got, Shane?"

"The woman is the central figure. The killer brought her here and secured her to the chair. I'd say when the men were asleep, so sometime last night." Wolfe glanced over at the trailers and then back to the crime scene. "The incision to the neck is post-mortem, and from the angle I'd have to assume the killer used his left hand. This ties him to the Robinson case." He looked at Kane. "Assuming you're correct about the shooting."

"It makes sense—a killer wouldn't juggle his weapon to turn on a light." Kane frowned. "He's either left-handed or ambidextrous."

Wolfe nodded. "The laceration to the throat is all the proof I need." He turned back to Ruby's body. "The female victim has a puncture wound to the thigh. The killer nicked the femoral artery and then hid close by. He knew where to put his wound, which also indicates he has some knowledge of anatomy or was trained to kill." He looked at them. "If he used her for bait, he'd have brought her around and she would've screamed for help. The men came running. From the first aid kit on the floor, someone tried to stop the bleeding. They wouldn't have been too anxious to call 911 because the wound is so small." He glanced at Jenna. "Maybe they believed it would be quicker to drive her to the ER once they'd stopped the bleeding."

Kane stared at the scene. "Yeah, I agree."

"How did he get the jump on four men, with one of them armed?" Jenna stared around her and then looked back at Kane. "There are two flashlights on the ground, they would have seen the killer."

Kane surveyed the immediate area. "There are tons of places here to lie in wait at night. The killer waited for them to concentrate on the girl, came out of hiding, and pointed his rifle at them; he'd have had the drop on them." He moved onto the porch, stepping carefully around the blood spatter. "He takes out a knee on the guy with the gun to show them he means business and then orders them to tie each other up."

"Then he has his fun." Jenna frowned. "All the while, Ruby is bleeding out." She looked at Kane. "It could be any number of killers. One man doing this much damage in one night seems a bit far-fetched."

"No, it's not." Wolfe straightened from examining the gaping gash on Ruby's neck. "It's possible. We don't know how much time he had, do we? Once I establish the time of death, we'll have a better timeframe to work with."

Kane bent and peered at the feather. "Three crime scenes and black feathers at each one. This is a signature. It means something to the killer."

"I've established the feathers come from crows." Wolfe frowned. "It's also the name of a local tribe of Native Americans. It might be significant, a message perhaps."

"I'll speak to Atohi." Jenna's lips flattened into a thin line. "Although he's kind of tied up with the cold case murder. I hear the excavation is going well but there's no sign of another skeleton."

"The boy's father could've buried them apart or wildlife could've scattered the remains. It will be some time before Dr. Bates finishes up there." Wolfe pulled out his phone and took shots of the crime scene. "I'd like to send these to Jo to compare with the crimes in Baltimore. You don't have to ask for her help, Jenna, but with this type of killer, we're gonna need all the help we can get."

Kane frowned. "Jo Blake is a behavioral analyst, a fancy name for a profiler. What can she bring to the table?"

"I'm not questioning your skills, Dave." Wolfe looked perturbed. "Not at all. It's that she had similar cases in Baltimore and there's been others. The FBI's codename for the Baltimore killings was the Chameleon Killer and he left black feathers at the scene. It's too much of a coincidence. From what I'm seeing, it could be the same killer or killers."

"Okay, so you want her here in an advisory position and not to take over and stamp all over our investigation." Kane shrugged. "What do you say, Jenna?"

"Will she be coming with her team?" Jenna balled her hands on her hips. "How many?"

"I'm not sure… only two of them, I believe, if she has located her detective. She was trying to locate Ty Carter but he's off the grid. She needs him to fly the chopper."

The name ignited a memory in Kane's head. "He's a loose cannon. Headstrong, works alone. I can't see him agreeing to work in a team or taking much notice of a behavioral analyst. He's a seat-of-your-pants type of guy."

"Do you know him?" Jenna looked concerned.

Kane shook his head. "Only by reputation."

"I know both of them." Wolfe smiled at Jenna. "You'll find Jo easy to get along with but she's as tough as nails, so don't underestimate her. Trust me, Kane, you'll be able to keep Ty Carter in line."

"I guess if it's the same killer, and she's been hands-on with his previous cases, she'll be able to help." Jenna glanced at Kane and shrugged, then looked back at Wolfe and nodded. "Okay, give her another call and bring her in on the case. So long as you're sure they won't pull the FBI card and use it to railroad us."

"You have my word." Wolfe pulled out his phone. "I'll call her now."

CHAPTER THIRTY-THREE

Snakeskin Gully, Montana

Annoyed by the lack of response to her messages and calls to Ty Carter, Jo Blake had called into the Snakeskin Gully Sheriff's Department to ask for assistance to locate him. It seemed when an off-the-grid ex-Navy Seal didn't want anyone to find him, he became invisible. The sheriff had insisted he take her to Carter's last known location and they'd left at once. The sheriff's cruiser, a massive SUV, bumped over a rocky path. Along the way, she'd kept vigilant and scanned the area, trying to memorize the turns they had taken, but the highway had soon become dirt roads leading into a dense forest. After reading the serial killer reports coming out of Black Rock Falls, being with a complete stranger in the middle of nowhere pushed her fear factor to maximum. "How much further?"

"Well, Last Chance Falls is at the end of this road. From there I guess we go on foot and look around for a cabin." Sheriff Cage Walker's mouth turned up at the corners. "You sure you're cut out for small-town life?"

"I don't really have a choice." Jo looked at his honest face and soft brown eyes. "I go where I'm needed."

"I haven't had more than a dispute over a fence since I became sheriff, and that's near two years now." Cage shrugged. "I'm not sure why the FBI decided we need a field office here."

The images Wolfe had sent through earlier spilled across her mind. "I guess they picked somewhere central, with a spare building for us to set up shop in."

"Maybe." Cage pulled the cruiser to a halt. "There's the falls— his place can't be too far away."

Jo frowned. "He owns a mess of land up here but I couldn't find a cabin on Google Earth."

"It's unlikely you would." Cage chuckled. "Not many come this way to map the forest." He gave her a long look. "You do know about the wildlife around these parts? You wouldn't want to find yourself in a showdown with a grizzly."

Annoyed, Jo stared at him. "Yeah, I'm aware. I wouldn't have asked you to come with me if it hadn't been so urgent."

"I'm happy to help out at any time." Cage slid from behind the wheel and pulled up his collar. "Looks like there's a trail into the forest. Watch your step; it's been snowing and underfoot is icy."

Jo swallowed her first reply and nodded. "Yeah, we have snow where I come from too. Can't we drive? The trail looks wide enough."

"I don't make a habit of driving onto people's property without permission." Cage frowned at her. "Walking up nice and slow, so they can see who you are, and yelling out will keep you safer."

"Hmm." Jo touched the Glock snug inside her shoulder holster under her jacket. She shivered. It was so cold and she wasn't handling the mountain temperatures at all. "So they shoot first and ask questions later around here?"

"If they've posted a notice, yeah." Cage grinned at her. "A might different than the big city, huh?"

Jo shook her head. "Not at all but in the big city they don't post notices, they just shoot you. Sometimes because you've looked at them the wrong way or they want your shoes." She slipped on the uneven surface and he grabbed her arm to steady her.

"You might want to buy a pair of hiking boots." Cage eyed her footwear. "The produce store carries a good range and you'll need snow gear too. You won't survive here unless you bundle up." He took out a pair of binoculars and scanned the area. "I see smoke. The cabin must be straight ahead."

Jo stumbled after him, realizing designer boots might look great but didn't stop the bitter cold. After three strides she couldn't feel her toes. They'd walked for ten minutes before the cabin came into view. Tucked into the side of the mountain, it was barely visible, but the signposts along the way warning the owner would shoot trespassers on sight had gotten her attention. She paused at the stairs to the porch and raised her voice. "Hello, inside. I'm Agent Blake, FBI. I'm looking for Ty Carter."

"You found him." A deep, masculine voice came from inside.

Relieved, Jo moved to the bottom step. "It's Jo Blake from the field office at Snakeskin Gully. We need to talk."

The front door opened a crack and she made out a tall figure inside. "I thought you were a man."

Jo held her ground. "Well, you were obviously mistaken."

"Mornin', Cage." Carter stepped to the door.

Jo swung around and gaped at Cage in surprise. "You know him? Why didn't you say?"

"You didn't ask if I knew him, you asked if I knew where he lived." Cage leaned against a tall pine. "I've never visited him before now."

Jo turned as Ty Carter walked out onto the porch and rested a rifle against the wall. He was not what she'd expected. Tall and strong with a square jaw and buzz cut was the image she remembered from his file. The man standing before her was a cowboy right down to his snakeskin boots. Piercing green eyes bore into her, and his shaggy blond hair poked out from under a well-worn Stetson. She straightened and walked up the steps to greet him. Grab your gear, we have an urgent case." She noticed a slight smirk and it made her blood boil. "Why didn't you answer my calls?"

"No bars up here." Ty shrugged and moved a toothpick across his lips. "I received my orders last week by mail. They informed me to wait for you to contact me and here you are." He stood to one side. "I guess you'd better come in and bring me up to speed."

Jo stood her ground. "We don't have time." She pulled her phone from her pocket, opened the image files Wolfe had sent her, and handed the phone to him. "Mass murder out of Black Rock Falls. The medical examiner is waiting for us before he removes the bodies. You'll need to pack for a few days."

"My duffle is always packed." Ty frowned at the images. "Give me five to put out my fire and get my weapons." He looked at the sheriff. "Cage, can you grab a bag of food for Zorro from my pantry and put it in my truck?"

"Sure." Cage walked in the door and stopped dead. "Ah… is he okay?"

Jo's attention moved to a Doberman, sitting ears tall, quivering lips pulled back displaying very white teeth. "Do you have someone to care for him?"

With one small gesture from Ty's hand, the dog dropped and watched them closely. Jo marveled at the condition of the animal. He was a fine-looking dog and held his head up with pride, looking like a Sphinx.

"Zorro goes where I go." Ty walked through the small, spotless cabin and into a room at the back. "He's the bomb squad."

She waited a few minutes for Ty to emerge from the other room. He'd changed into clean clothes and had a duffle over one shoulder, a gun case in one hand, and a pair of hiking boots in the other. He still resembled a cowboy.

"We'll go in my truck." Ty ushered her out the door.

Once they'd dropped Cage at his cruiser, Jo brought Ty up to speed with the murders in Black Rock Falls. He hadn't said a word to her for the past ten minutes. He had no conclusions or opinions on the case, which she thought strange. "Have you handled many serial killer cases?"

"Yeah, a few." Ty turned onto the highway and accelerated. "So, what is your part in all this? You're my boss—my orders made that perfectly clear." He tossed the toothpick out the window, letting in a blast of freezing air.

It was obvious to Jo that he didn't like the idea of her seniority. From his file, he'd been at the top of his field two years ago. He'd been much of a lone wolf before a slip-up by a team he was working a case with had resulted in the deaths of two young children. From what she'd read, Ty had suffered PTSD to such an extent he'd gone off the grid to recover. Although his psych tests had come back clean, he was still an unknown quantity. She turned to look at him. "The idea is we work together but I'll be taking the lead. I'm a behavioral analyst. I profile killers and attempt to anticipate their next move."

"I use my gut instinct and I've not been wrong yet." He shrugged. "Do you work on the fly?"

"If you mean will I stay in the office and send you out on cases, no. I prefer to be right in the action. I need to see the crime scene to determine the profile of the killer." Jo looked at the rigid set of his jaw. It was obvious he wasn't impressed to be working with her in the field. She cleared her throat. "I'm not a detective but my insights have solved many crimes."

"Can you handle yourself in the field in extreme conditions?" Ty flicked her a swift glance, taking in her attire. "It's going to be tough working the backwoods towns. Days of hiking through forests, hand-to-hand combat, and ducking bullets."

Jo set her jaw. Her boss and ex-husband's lover had given her a hardnosed, damaged partner with the intention of making her life a misery. She'd dealt with a bossy, demanding man during her marriage and was well versed in how to deal with egos. She didn't need to impress Ty Carter with qualifications. She'd earn his respect but he was correct, they would sure need to be tough. She lifted her chin. First, she'd need to convince him she wasn't a helpless woman. "I can handle myself just fine."

"Uh-huh." Ty stared straight ahead. "So, how many do we have on our team?"

Jo swallowed hard. "Right now, it's just you and me."

"Oh, boy."

CHAPTER THIRTY-FOUR

Black Rock Falls

It was after two by the time Jenna spotted the incoming chopper. She hurried into the barn, thanked Tom Dickson, and asked him to finish up. She gave him a full day's pay but didn't explain why an FBI chopper was landing on her ranch. Kane had dashed to his cottage with Duke and then hurried inside the barn to calm the horses as the noisy machine landed. Shielding her eyes from the whirlwind of dust from the spinning blades, Jenna waited on the front porch for the agents to emerge. She took in the two strangers and shook her head. Jo Blake, an attractive woman she imagined to be around thirty, had dressed in a tailored suit with fashionable boots and with her dark hair swept up; she reminded Jenna of her time working in DC. Agents had a dress code unless undercover, but when Ty Carter emerged from the pilot's seat, she did a double take. Bundled up in a sheepskin coat and wearing blue jeans, a battered Stetson, and one-way sunglasses, he looked as if he'd just walked off a ranch. *He's a DC agent?*

Carter obviously owned the sleek Doberman that jumped down from the chopper wearing a harness. It moved to his side and looked up at him as if awaiting instruction. She wondered what Duke would think of another dog in his yard. She turned as Kane strode out from the barn, and after the introductions, she looked at Carter. "I didn't know you'd be bringing a dog. Our Duke is pretty territorial."

"You won't have a problem. Zorro will just ignore him, and it takes two to tango." Carter smiled. "What breed is Duke? His name sounds like a hunting dog to me."

"Yeah." Kane moved to Jenna's side. "He's a bloodhound and a fine tracker."

"Zorro is our bomb squad." Carter patted Zorro on the head. "I haven't trained him to disarm one yet, but if there's one out there, he'll find it."

Jenna nodded. "Good to know. Bring him along. The ME is waiting for us at the crime scene." They climbed into Kane's truck and headed to the Old Mitcham Ranch.

"I hear you're the profiler of the team, Kane." Jo sounded interested. "Would you consider this a serial killer's work or are we looking at a terrorist?"

"Serial killer." Kane looked at her in his mirror. "We're here, so you can take a look for yourself."

"I hear you're an expert in catching serial killers." Carter instructed Zorro to remain inside. He removed his sunglasses and moved to Jenna's side as they stepped down from the truck.

Jenna looked at him to see if he was joking but she only saw genuine interest in his unusual green eyes. "Well, I have a great team." She waved toward the murder scene. "This is our first mass murder, and I believe Jo was involved in something similar in Baltimore."

"So she said." Carter took a toothpick from his pocket, pushed it into the side of his mouth, and moved it from side to side. "I only met her a couple of hours ago. She didn't say too much on the way here about her old cases; she was on the phone making arrangements for her daughter. She has a seven-year-old at home." He took the gloves and booties Wolfe handed him and put them on. "Let's see what we have here."

As Carter walked up the steps and nodded to Rowley, who was standing guard just inside the front door, shotgun in hand, Jenna pulled on her gloves and booties. She'd already listened to Wolfe's take on the crime scene but was interested to hear the discussion between Kane and Jo. They were speaking in hushed tones and doing a great deal of pointing and gesturing.

"Oh, I agree. Severe trauma-induced psychosis would push an already unstable psyche into this pattern." Jo looked up at Kane. "Using the girl as bait is the same MO as the Baltimore case but this is more violent, more advanced. It shows a power-induced frenzy. He loved the audience, and when they passed out from lack of blood, they lost their use to him, so he shot them in the head."

"What puzzles me is the first victim, Robinson." Kane turned to look at Jo. "His murder was too clean, unhurried, a walk in and walk out. It doesn't fit into this type of extreme behavior."

"This is what fazed me too. I've had several the same." Jo glanced at Jenna as if seeing her for the first time. "If this killer is working across the states, this investigation will become an FBI matter. Although, there's only the two of us available at the moment." She sighed. "I only arrived in Snakeskin Gully last weekend, and so far, I've only located Ty. The computer guy and receptionist are AWOL."

"Do you have access to the case files? We'll need them to compare the cases." Kane walked off the porch with her and they chatted on the way back to his truck.

"Sheriff Alton." Carter walked up beside her. "There's a few things I'd like to discuss with you."

Jenna turned to look at him. "Yes, of course."

"Wolfe said he's matched all the bloody footprints with the victims, yet the killer must have been covered in blood. How did he move around without leaving footprints? All the victims are secured, so it's not a murder–suicide." Carter waved flies away from the pool of congealed blood beneath Ruby's lifeless body. "I can usually sum up a scene in seconds but I'd be interested to know what you see here."

Is he testing me? Jenna scanned the array of footprints. "This isn't my first dance, Carter. I don't need a lesson in crime scene investigation."

"Then why the rush to get us here?" Carter gave her a long look. "You're clearly out of your depth. I've noticed an anomaly on Wolfe's preliminary examination—have you?" The toothpick moved across his lips and he grinned at her. "No?"

Kane had mentioned Carter was arrogant, and he was sure showing it now. She straightened and eyeballed him. "Wolfe doesn't make mistakes."

"I didn't say he did. I asked you what you see here." Carter stared at her, green eyes flashing with amusement.

Okay, I'll play your game. "I see everything perfectly clear, Carter. One set, the one with the swirls, appears to be more dominant than the others." She pulled out her phone and scanned the footprint comparison files Wolfe had made previously from the victims' footwear. "The first victim from the left owned these shoes, so I'd imagine he was the last to die. The killer ordered him to secure the others and then carry the severed hands into the kitchen, as the same footprints are throughout the house."

"Uh-huh." Carter scanned the scene again. "So, Wolfe figures the killer stood back here and ordered the big guy, we'll call him number one, to tie everyone up and then collect body parts in his jacket. The killer told him to carry them to the kitchen and display them on the table like a good boy. He expected him to come back here so he could tie him up and kill him?" He walked over to corpse number one and looked at him closely. He turned back to Jenna and rested the toothpick in the corner of his mouth. "That doesn't work for me. Not at all. I'd say he died first, he was the guy with the weapon, maybe the boss here." He frowned down at the victim. "How could he have carried the body parts with a hand missing, and why didn't he escape? According to the footprints he was alone in the kitchen. Any fool would have hightailed it out the back door." He snorted. "There's something else significant. Take another look."

Wolfe had backed his conclusions with physical evidence and Jenna had no cause to doubt his findings. Bemused, she stared at Carter and then back at the crime scene. He'd spotted something she'd overlooked. She went to each man, looked at their footwear, and checked the soles against Wolfe's record. When she got to victim number one, she did a double take. Large leather boots stuck out from the end of his jeans. She looked up at Carter. "His shoes are on the wrong feet."

"Yeah, I noticed that, and his jacket is missing and it's freezing out here. His must be the jacket Wolfe found in the kitchen." Carter stepped around the blood spatter and went to her side. "Wolfe had no reason to remove his boots. I believe the killer wore them to move around and put them back on the corpse when he'd finished. We know he used a jacket to collect the body parts. I would say he took the jacket from victim number one before he began his killing spree. The rest is much like Wolfe surmised. He held them at gunpoint and had one tie up the other. The last one he secured himself. He is smart—look here." He pointed to victim number two. "The murderer severed the right hand of the second victim but placed a tourniquet above the amputation to prevent blood loss. It's the same with the others. He wanted them alive and in pain."

Intrigued by Carter's insight, Jenna nodded. "Going by the damage to the arm of the chair, he used the ax Wolfe found on the kitchen table."

"Yeah, I would think so." Carter picked his way back to Ruby and stared at the pool of blood. "The feather. Jo said this is three for three, so we must assume the same man murdered all the current victims. I believe the feather is significant to him: it means something, and by leaving it, he's sending a message."

Jenna nodded. "I thought Jo was the behavioral analyst."

"She is but it doesn't take a degree to understand human nature in our business, does it?" He pushed back his Stetson and looked at her. "Anything else I need to know?"

"Wolfe believes the killer is left-handed from the laceration on Ruby's neck." Jenna waved a hand toward Kane. "Kane has the same theory with the Robinson murder. When the killer walked into the bedroom, he turned on the light, shot Robinson, and turned off the light, all in seconds. The switch is on the right going into the room, so Kane figures the shooter was left-handed or ambidextrous."

"More like left-handed; one hand is always weaker." Carter ambled off the porch. "I think we're done here and the stink is getting bad. Where's a good place to stay around here? And we'll need a vehicle."

Jenna frowned. "I guess you can use my cruiser. I ride with Kane most times." She waved a hand toward the house. "I'll speak to Wolfe about the victim's boots and then we'll drive you into town."

She picked her way back inside and noticed Carter sticking to her like glue. In the kitchen, Wolfe was bagging and labeling the body parts. She explained Carter's theory to him. "You didn't mention victim number one's boots, so is it a possibility the killer used them to disguise his identity?"

"Yeah, but I'll need to prove it. I've made a note of the boots being on the wrong feet in my crime scene report." Wolfe wrote on an evidence bag and then looked up at her. "I have to consider both scenarios, Jenna. The killer using another man's boots is a possibility, but he'd have to have the victims secured first." He sighed. "Then you have to consider the situation the men faced. It was the middle of the night, a girl is screaming, and they would've dressed quickly to rush outside to see what the noise was about. Victim number one could've easily put his boots on the wrong feet. If the killer did use his boots, I'll find evidence. For instance, I'll look for blood spatter from the other victims on his socks." He gave Carter a long look. "I can't figure out why the first victim didn't fire his weapon. He must have had it in his hand when he came out the trailer."

"Maybe the killer had the drop on them." Carter chewed on his toothpick. "Or he put down his gun to help the girl." He looked at Jenna. "Did you search the trailers for weapons?"

Jenna nodded. "Yeah, we didn't find any, which out here is more than a little strange, but there's a rifle in the truck."

"What I think is stranger." Kane walked in the back door with Jo on his heels. "Where are the other workers' vehicles? We have one truck parked behind the first trailer owned by Trevor Wilson; from the driver's license on record he's the shirtless victim. He's sixty-two years old, has been in the service, and we have his prints—it's a positive ID."

Jenna waved the flies away from her face. "What type of crazy boss drops their workers out here without transport or weapons to protect themselves?"

"Illegal aliens, maybe." Kane shrugged. "Cheap labor and ones who don't know the local legends or don't care."

"Or maybe they flew in from another state, and as the boss is living on-site, he'd be giving them a ride into town when necessary." Carter leaned against the doorframe. "There's time to discuss this later. Can we get away from this stink?"

Jenna looked at Wolfe. "Do you need our help? I'll leave Rowley here to watch your back."

"Nah, we'll work our way through and get them on ice, although I'd appreciate Rowley as backup just in case the killer is hanging around." Wolfe's eyes met hers over the mask and she noticed one raised eyebrow. "You'd better get the agents settled. We'll be just fine." He turned to Jo. "What're the chances of the killer returning to the scene of the crime?"

"It's possible, don't take any chances." Jo moved her attention to the body parts. "Although, this much carnage might satisfy him for a while."

Jenna headed for the back door. "I hope so, we're running out of space in the morgue."

CHAPTER THIRTY-FIVE

Deep in her own thoughts, Jenna allowed the light conversation drifting around her to go by and let Kane answer the agents' questions. The truck pulled up outside her front door and the passengers climbed out to retrieve their bags from the chopper. She heard Kane clear his throat and looked at him. "Did you say something?"

"Nope." Kane scanned her face. "Don't you think it would be a good idea to have them stay with us? We usually work into the night and it would be more convenient."

Unsettled by his suggestion, Jenna stared at him. "If you want Jo to stay with you, that's your call, but as sure as hell, I'm not sharing my house with Carter." She shook her head. "I've offered him my cruiser but I don't make a habit of inviting strange men to share my house."

"You did me." Kane smiled at her. "It must have been my irresistible charm."

Jenna glared at him. "I did not! Giving you the cottage was a kindness. I didn't ask you to move in with me."

"Uh-huh, I guess. Anyway, I was thinking of offering Carter my spare room and wondered if you might do the same for Jo. It's a temporary solution and would save time." Kane shrugged. "But if sharing with Jo is a problem, we'll find them rooms in town."

Seeing the sense in his idea, she nodded. "Sure, why not? But I'm surprised you'd risk having an FBI agent snooping around your house, and what about his dog? Duke will go crazy."

"Don't worry about Duke, I'll tell him to be nice." Kane cleared his throat. "Security isn't an issue either—he won't find anything, and since Rowley's stay, I've installed another safe in my bedroom. Trust me, it's like Fort Knox."

Jenna smiled at him. "Good to know." She slid out the door and went to greet Jo. "To save time hunting down a place to stay, would you like to bunk with me? I have all the equipment we'll need, and you're welcome to use my cruiser."

"That would be great." Jo smiled at her.

Jenna turned to Carter. "What about you?"

"Yeah, thanks." Carter nodded. "We'll dump our bags and then head into town for a meal. We'll meet you at the sheriff's office in an hour and review the cases. I'll think on how we can split the caseload, so make sure all your deputies are at the meeting."

His attitude took Jenna by surprise. She walked closer and eyeballed him. "Agent Carter, I'm the lead officer on this case. When I'm ready to hand it over to the FBI, I'll let you know."

"Yes, ma'am." Carter didn't disguise an eye roll. "I'm used to working alone but that's no excuse. I apologize, ma'am."

Unconvinced, Jenna nodded. "Okay."

"You'll be staying with me." Kane's stony expression hadn't changed as he looked at Carter. "I'll show you your room." He led the way to his cottage.

Jenna turned to Jo. "I'll have to make up your bed tonight. I don't have many visitors." She smiled at her. "Do you have a pair of jeans and some more substantial boots to wear? Most of the crime scenes are out of town and the forecast is for snow any day now."

"No, I don't." Jo pulled her suitcase wheels over the uneven ground. "I had no idea what to expect. The FBI moved me to Snakeskin Gully without notice." She smiled at Jenna. "The local sheriff there informed me I can buy everything I need at the produce store in town."

Jenna opened the front door, shut down the alarm, and waved her inside. "There are two places here in town that sell basic winter wear, but the jeans will need washing before you wear them. I have a pair that will fit you in the meantime, but a pair of hiking boots is a priority around here." She looked at Jo's suit jacket. "Do you have a winter coat with you?"

"Yeah, my FBI jacket is thick and I have my Kevlar vest with me." Jo stood in the family room and looked around. "You have a lovely home."

Jenna showed her to her room. "Thanks. I'll grab those jeans."

She hurried to her closet. Jo was smaller than her but she'd been thinner when she'd arrived in Black Rock falls and had three pairs of good jeans she no longer used. She took them into the spare bedroom and noticed Jo's drawn expression. "Is there something wrong?"

"I'm worried about my daughter, Jaime." She stared down at her phone.

Jenna's stomach gave a twist. "How so?"

"She took my divorce and moving away from her friends really hard. It was a messy divorce and it's been difficult explaining to her why her daddy prefers mommy's boss." Jo gave her a direct look. "That's why I'm working in the backwoods of Montana with a team of misfits."

Astonished, Jenna shook her head. "Hmm, I see. She wanted you out of the way."

"Exactly. We haven't unpacked yet and I'm off on a case." Jo shook her head. "Jaime has her nanny but I feel as if I'm letting her down."

Jenna sat on the bed beside her, surprised a virtual stranger had decided to confide in her. Perhaps she had no one else to talk to. "Divorce is hard on kids, but she is seven, isn't she? Halloween is coming up and she'll be involved in all sorts of fun things at school. Does she mix easily with other kids?"

D.K. Hood

"Yeah, and she's used to me going away for days on end on cases. I'm lucky, she's pretty easygoing." Jo indicated with her chin toward the door. "Like Deputy Kane. You're lucky to have him, he's a real gentleman. He's been calling me 'ma'am' all day." She chuckled. "I'm stuck with Mr. Grumpy. I'm told Ty is one of the best in his field, but it's going to be like working with a robot. He's old-school and this assignment must be his worst nightmare."

Jenna laughed. "Oh, Kane was pretty macho when he arrived too. It took him some time to understand that I could look after myself, but I'd trust him with my life. He's a good man." She stood. "I'll leave you to get changed. We haven't eaten yet either, so if you'd like to follow us to Aunt Betty's Café in town, we can discuss the cases over lunch and then I'll take you to the stores. It will be faster. Kane can take Carter back to the office. He'll have all the info you need by the time we get back."

Later, in Kane's truck, Jenna glanced at him. "What do you think about Carter?"

"Arrogant but being off the grid for a year, you tend to lose your people skills." Kane's mouth quirked at the corners. "You sure shut him down."

Jenna cringed. "Too much?"

"Nah, saved me the trouble of taking him out back of the wood-shed and teaching him some manners." Kane flashed a wide smile. "And to think I used to worry over you."

Jenna shrugged. "I'm a big girl and there's no way he was going to walk over me. He did try, but I must admit, after I took control of the scene, he came over as knowledgeable and allowed me to see the action through his eyes. You may be right. He's been alone too long." She turned in her seat to look at him. "And Jo. First impressions?"

"Smart, and she analyzes on the fly with incredible accuracy." Kane frowned and glanced at her. "I picked up a vulnerability but she's toughing it out. It's hard to hide insecurity from me. It makes me wonder why she was sent to a small town in the middle of nowhere with an arrogant SOB like Ty Carter." His gaze remained fixed on the road. "Wolfe gave me the impression she was super confident and used to running the show."

Remembering the devastation on Jo's face, Jenna wondered if telling Kane was breaking a confidence, but they had no secrets between them. "From what I gather, she's concerned about leaving her daughter. Jo is recently divorced."

"Oh, I see." Kane pulled up in front of Aunt Betty's Café. "That makes a lot of sense." He nodded toward the café. "Will you inform Susie Hartwig about Ruby's murder?"

"Not until I've notified her next of kin but I will ask her for Ruby's details." She frowned. "I'm surprised nobody has reported her missing."

"Maybe they have." Kane reached for his phone. "Do you want me to call Maggie and ask?"

Jenna slid from the truck. "We'll ask her when we get into the office. I'm famished." She waited on the sidewalk for Carter to pull up behind them in her cruiser.

They ordered their meals and sat at the sheriff's table. It was quiet, with only a few customers lingering after the lunchtime rush. Jenna looked at Carter. "We'll need to exchange case files; it will make life easier. What are your cell numbers?"

She took them down and the message ringtones chimed as the files flashed through cyberspace. After scanning the Baltimore case files, she glanced up at Kane. "What's your take on this?"

"From the crime scene images and the autopsy reports, plus Jo's profile, I figure we're dealing with the same man." Kane nodded to Jo. "Have you come to the same conclusion?"

"Yeah, unless it's a copycat, but the link we considered between the Baltimore murders wasn't released to the press. Although, nothing indicated our killer was left-handed." Jo refilled her cup from a pot on the table. "Did you get a read from any of your suspects?"

"We interviewed Kyler Hall and Cliff Young but they lawyered up. We don't know if either of them are left-handed." Kane spread cream over the top of his cherry pie. "To save time, I'll give you a rundown of the case against them. They were involved in a fight with the Stanton Forest victims, Louis and Addams. Young broke up with his girlfriend, Ann, over her affair with Lucas Robinson, our first victim. Robinson apparently swindled Hall out of his inheritance, so they all tie in. They have no alibis for TOD in the Robinson case and were in the vicinity of the Stanton Forest murders at the TOD as well." He glanced at Jo. "Are they capable of murder is the question. Volatile and angry can escalate into this type of behavior, as you know."

"Yeah, any of those scenarios could trigger a psychotic episode, but this anger seems more pronounced. It's ongoing, a deep hatred." Jo sipped her coffee. "Likely from a traumatic event in childhood."

Jenna looked from one to the other. "Okay, say they're the killers. What is the significance of the black feather? Why would it be significant to both men? They come from different family situations and it's unlikely they'd have both suffered the same trauma as kids."

"They could be a leader and a follower." Jo smiled at her. "A psychopath has charm in spades, and this is attractive to a weaker man; he may look up to him. In this case they usually go along with them and get dragged into their world without really understanding the reason." She placed her cup on the saucer and patted her mouth on a paper napkin. "Seems to me Hall and Young have common enemies."

"That's all very neat." Carter let out a long sigh and scrolled through the images of the crime scenes. "So how do they tie in with the mass murder? I'm no medical examiner but I know enough forensics to see that the first three killings are clean. The killer or killers didn't linger to enjoy their kills like the last one. Trust me, that amount of damage takes time." He shot a direct glance at Jenna. "Can *you* make out any possible link between the cases because I sure as hell can't."

Jenna dropped some bills on the table and pushed to her feet. "At least we have suspects. Looking at the FBI's past efforts, they've struck out on every murder."

CHAPTER THIRTY-SIX

Kane headed to the office, taking in the constant changes to Main Street. Few weeks went by between a celebration of one thing or another. After suffering weeks of sleet, the townsfolk had replaced most of the hail-ruined decorations for Halloween. He'd noticed how Black Rock Falls embraced the celebration for well over two weeks prior to the day, although the jack-o'-lanterns didn't come out until the last minute, when they lit up Main with eerie golden smiles during the trick-or-treat procession of kids collecting candy. He'd enjoyed patrolling with Jenna and seeing the happy faces and outrageous costumes. He hoped the current murders wouldn't prevent the kids' fun.

As they arrived at the sheriff's department, he turned to Jenna. She hadn't said too much to him since leaving Aunt Betty's. "I believe you're right about Carter. He has a good reputation of getting the job done; we can use his input same as Jo's."

"He sees things differently to the way we do." Jenna rubbed her temples. "I admit, I prefer the team approach to solving crimes. Sure, I lead the case, but I rely on your profiling skills and Wolfe's determination on the crime scene. Together, we consider all possibilities and go from there." She puffed out a breath that lifted her bangs. "Carter looks at the whole picture at once and makes a snap determination. He came up with a different scenario than we did in about fifteen seconds."

Kane rubbed his chin. "That doesn't make him right. Considering all aspects before jumping to conclusions is a sound strategy. Using all your resources is a mark of a good leader. You shouldn't doubt yourself. He's a lone wolf. I think Jo is going to have her hands full with him."

"The problem is, this time, everything he said made perfect sense." Jenna met his gaze. "Wolfe didn't mention he'd noticed the victim had his shoes on the wrong feet." She explained her conversation with Wolfe, and Carter's take on the murder at the Old Mitcham Ranch. "What Carter says is more than possible—he's probably right."

"Wolfe noticed the boots and will add it to his conclusions because he takes into account all the evidence." Kane shrugged. "If he said it could've happened because the men rushed to dress, then he's offering you reasonable doubt. Knowing him as I do, he'll be testing those boots for any foreign DNA and search for proof the killer removed the man's footwear. He doesn't jump to conclusions. He wants his evidence to be rock solid in court."

"Okay." Jenna gave him a direct stare. "We have to live and work with them for a few days, and from what Jo said, she will be our go-to local FBI branch, so getting on good terms with them now will be to our advantage." She smiled. "I kind of like Jo, and it's nice to have someone close my own age to talk to."

Bemused, Kane frowned. "I'm close to your age, Jenna."

"Oh, Dave, you are so funny." Jenna chuckled. "I mean girl talk. I've missed it, and Emily Wolfe is a great companion, but it was refreshing talking to Jo." She reached for the door handle. "I'm taking the cruiser for half an hour. Jo needs to pick up a few things. If you could collate all the info we have to date, we'll all meet up in my office when we get back."

Kane stared at her in disbelief. "Can't Carter take her?"

"No, I'm going with her. We'll need to show them the murder scenes and Jo doesn't have a decent coat or hiking boots. I know where to go, Carter doesn't. It will take no time at all." She slid out the truck and poked her head back inside and grinned at him. "Promise."

Kane scratched his head. "Uh-huh."

He waited for Carter and Zorro on the sidewalk and they walked into the sheriff's department. After introducing him to Maggie and Walters, he went straight to Jenna's office and pulled down the whiteboard. He stared for a few moments at the faces of the victims depicted in life beside the gruesome images of their deaths. It was as if they pleaded with him to find and stop their killer. "I'll print the images from the crime scene and get them up." He used his phone to access the file and sent them to the printer.

As the printer hummed and churned out the images, Ty Carter instructed Zorro to lie down on the mat and then walked up and down, staring at the whiteboard, stopping to examine photographs before moving on.

Kane rested one hip on the edge of the desk and looked at the dog. "There's not much for Zorro to do in this case. If he gets on okay with Duke, you're welcome to leave him at my cottage. I have an enclosed area out back they can access from the mudroom."

"Yeah, I might take you up on that offer. He doesn't like being cooped up inside."

Kane nodded. "Jenna mentioned your theory about the footprints."

"Not a theory, an observation." Carter chewed on his toothpick. "Wolfe will find blood on the victim's socks. From the blood spatter pattern around his feet, he wasn't wearing his boots when the killer severed his hand. "Did you find shell casings at any of the scenes?"

Kane shook his head. "No."

"Hmm that sure ties in with what Jo told me about the Baltimore murders." Carter turned and looked at him. "What do you think we have here?"

Kane collected up the photographs and then went to the whiteboard and attached them. "I figure we have to look into the victims' backgrounds to catch this killer." He stood back to admire his work. "The feather links them but apart from that, I'd say Robinson was a paid hit. The Stanton Forest murders don't resemble a random shooting. They're clean, like the Robinson case. It's as if something these two men did, triggered the killer to run them off the road and kill them." He moved along to the Old Mitcham Ranch killings. "This is completely different. It's messy and dangerous. I mean, how did a waitress from Aunt Betty's end up dead here? If the killer abducted her and brought her here with the intent of using her as bait, to kill the men, he's changed his MO again. Jo believes this indicates a particularly nasty personality disorder."

"Holy cow, are you suggesting he has a split personality and both sides are serial killers?" Carter dropped into a chair and scrubbed both hands down his face. "I'm going to need coffee intravenously to wrap my head around this one."

Kane waved a hand to the two coffee machines on the counter at the back of Jenna's office. "Well, make yourself useful and put on a couple of pots."

"Sure." Carter removed his coat and hung it on one of the pegs behind Jenna's door. "This is the first time I've worked in an office that smelled of honeysuckle." He chuckled and went about refilling the coffee machines. "Most times it's bad breath and body odor." He glanced at Kane. "I take it you're close to Jenna. I had her all wrong and wasn't expecting her to break my balls."

Kane didn't bite. "She has the respect of everyone under her command. The sheriff is professional all the way. I suggest you don't underestimate her."

"Hmm, I was warned the same about Jo, but at the time I'd assumed she was a guy." Carter moved the toothpick across his lips and sighed. "I haven't worked with many women."

"Not even in the service?" Kane narrowed his gaze. "Or in DC?"

"Nope." Carter shrugged. "I led my team and kept my head down." He gave Kane a long look. "You're wasting your talent here. Ever thought about applying to the FBI?"

Biting back a grin, Kane stood, turned away, and made notes on the whiteboard. "Nah, here I have one boss and I live on her ranch rent-free. I have wide-open spaces, fishing, and hunting on my doorstep. I'm a happy man."

"I have that too." Carter hit the switches on the coffee pots. "Well, I do now. Unless they call me back to DC. If they do, I might vanish again."

"I bet Jo would put up a fight if they do. There's no way she'll be able to run the Snakeskin Gully office alone. She needs a chopper pilot and a detective, so I figure you're safe." Kane turned at a knock on the door to find Rowley. "Oh, good, you're back. Is there anything to report?"

"No, all quiet at the Old Mitcham Ranch. I covered the entrance with crime scene tape, and the trailers and ranch house." Rowley dropped a takeout bag on the desk and pulled an evidence bag from under his arm and handed it to Kane. "The wallets from the victims. It seems they're all out of Wyoming. Wolfe checked the male victims against their driver's licenses and they all fit. He's taken prints as well and added the information to our case files. The girl we've identified as Ruby Evans, who worked at Aunt Betty's Café. You recognized her and so did I, so that's two for two, but Wolfe requires a positive ID. I spoke to Susie Hartwig and got Ruby's details. She lived with her aunt out on Elk Creek." He stared longingly at the coffee dripping into the pots. "It's been a long day."

Kane nodded. "I guess from the bag of takeout you haven't eaten yet? Grab a coffee and take a seat. Jenna will be back soon and we'll discuss the case."

"Thanks." Rowley pulled off his jacket and hung it on the back of the chair. "This is the worst so far, isn't it?"

Kane's attention drifted to the images on the whiteboard. "Yeah, this is a twisted, unpredictable mind and he's charging down victims like a mad bull."

CHAPTER THIRTY-SEVEN

A cool breeze scented with the promise of snow blasted Jenna as she hurried to the cruiser with Jo at her side, carrying bags filled with her purchases. She had to admire a woman who could select an entire wardrobe in twenty minutes flat. There had been no deliberation; she'd cast her gaze across the available range and had the goods at the checkout in record time. She'd pulled on her new hiking boots, jacket, hat, and gloves before dashing out the store. "My head's spinning. I've never seen anyone shop so fast."

"The time to go shopping is a luxury I haven't been able to afford since I joined the FBI." Jo waited as Jenna popped the trunk and dropped her bags inside. "Not if I wanted to be a wife and mother as well."

Before Jenna had the chance to start the cruiser's engine, she heard Atohi Blackhawk calling her name. She opened her window to speak to him. "Are you chasing after me?"

"Yeah." Atohi squatted by her door and his friend, Brad, placed one hand on the roof and stared down at her. "Jill, the forensic pathologist, has removed the bones and wants to take them to Helena to study them."

"You can't allow that." Brad's tiger eyes flashed in anger. "We won't allow it. She must remain here."

Unsettled by Brad's aggression, Jenna lowered her voice. "I'll speak to Wolfe. He'll know what to do." She looked back at Atohi. "Any sightings of Brad's brother?"

"He has a name." Brad stared at her. "It's Scott." He touched an angry-looking scratch along his jaw as he stared into the distance. "He's out there somewhere. I feel a connection to him."

Oh boy, we have another crazy. "Okay. Has Jill mentioned continuing the grid search?"

"Yeah, she's asked for volunteer archeology students from the college to assist." Atohi's gaze searched her face. "She'll be leaving a couple members of her team to oversee the excavation but we'd appreciate it if you could intervene on our behalf."

Wondering why Atohi hadn't expressed his concerns to Wolfe in person, Jenna nodded and started the engine. "I'll call him the moment I get back to the office."

As if reading her mind, Atohi stood.

"I've been calling him all day and keep getting his voicemail." Atohi frowned. "And he's not at the morgue."

Jenna sighed, unable to elaborate on why Wolfe was busy. "He's working a case. As soon as I speak to him, I'll get back to you. I've gotta go, I have a meeting."

"Sure." Atohi slapped the top of the cruiser and the two men walked away.

"Problem?" Jo stared after the men. "His friend sure has a ton of pent-up aggression."

"Cold case." Jenna turned into the flow of traffic and headed to the office. "They're talking about his mother's remains. They found them in the forest but his brother is still missing. Brad witnessed the murders when he was a kid."

"Well then anger is a better response than being charming." Jo raised one eyebrow. "With that traumatic event, he could easily have turned out a psychopath."

Five minutes later, Jenna was shucking her coat and hanging it on a peg in her office. She rubbed her hands together and went around her desk to her seat. A cup of coffee appeared beside her like magic and she smiled up at Kane. "Okay, the gang's all here. I see you've added the information to the whiteboard. We have a ton of ground to cover and can get the cases moving while Wolfe is busy with the forensic investigations. Just one moment." She picked up her landline and dialed the morgue. "Emily, I guess your dad is busy, but I need a favor." She explained Atohi's request. "Call me when you have time and let me know what he said." She disconnected. "Okay, back to the case. I'm going with Jo to interview Mrs. Robinson at the hospital. Kane and Carter, I want you to hunt down details about the victims, you know the drill. You'll need to contact the closest sheriff's office and ask them to notify the next of kin. Tell them we need someone to come by and identify the victims."

"Okay. We'll need space and a bank of computers, so we'll be working in the CCTV control room." Kane stood and Carter followed him out the door with Zorro at his heels.

Jenna looked down at her notes. "Rowley, head out to Ruby's address and speak to her aunt. She'll need to formally identify Ruby's body." She sighed. "Take her to the morgue and wait until Wolfe has prepared the body for viewing. I'm guessing he'll be doing her first as she lived locally." She tapped the pen against her bottom lip. "Wolfe is very busy but ask him if he's made headway on getting positive IDs for Parker Louis and Tim Addams, the Stanton Forest victims."

"Yes, ma'am." Rowley stood, picked up his empty takeout bag, and tossed it in the trash. "I'll call if he has any info. It's going to take time for Wolfe to make Ruby presentable." He pushed his Stetson on his head, grabbed his coat, and walked out the door.

Mentally exhausted, Jenna drained her coffee cup and pushed to her feet. "Okay, Jo, we're off to see the wife of the first victim, Lucas Robinson. She told us she was lying beside her husband when he was shot." As they walked back out in the rapidly dropping temperature, Jenna brought Jo up to speed.

"Do you think she pulled the trigger?" Jo slid into the passenger seat of the cruiser. "The spouse is usually the first suspect."

Jenna nodded, climbed behind the wheel, and started the engine. "My gut told me she's involved but we don't have enough to get a warrant to search her bank statements. I haven't followed up yet as we had the other murders in quick succession. It's not her on a killing spree— she's locked up in the psych ward at the hospital." She glanced at her. "That's why I want you to interview her. My gut is rarely wrong." She backed the cruiser out onto the road and headed for the hospital.

"How was she when you arrived on scene?"

"Rowley was the first responder. Mrs. Robinson called 911, and she seemed lucid, but by the time he arrived she wasn't saying anything. He cuffed her, thinking she could be responsible." Jenna sighed. "When we arrived, she'd spoken to Wolfe and I was able to question her; she seemed distant."

"Did she say anything unusual?" Jo turned to look at her.

Jenna allowed the memory of that night to percolate into her mind. "She'd hidden under the bed after the shooting, didn't check on her husband, just ran downstairs and hid in a broom closet. She was asking me if she could've saved him."

"Hmm." Jo went silent for some minutes. "Of course, we all react differently in a crisis. It's typical to experience a variety of emotions following a traumatic event. The incident triggered her flee response and she ran away. Running from the room and down the stairs knowing the shooter could be in the house is unusual."

Jenna turned into the hospital parking lot. "My feelings exactly. She'd waited for a time under the bed—she must have known the shooter had gone. Why didn't she check on her husband before hiding?"

"It's a question we need to ask her." Jo gathered her briefcase and looked at Jenna. "Usual feelings include fear, shock, numbness, grief, disillusionment, and anger. Some even say it's like an out-of-body experience."

Jenna got out of the cruiser and they walked into the hospital. "I've suffered from PTSD, so I do have some idea, and I've been trained to handle stressful situations. I thought I was unbreakable until I had a knife to my throat and then a man's head exploded next to my face. So, I can relate to what she went through."

"That must have been tough." Jo gave her a concerned look. "Did you have trouble sleeping and concentrating?"

"Yeah." Jenna pushed the memories away, into their safe place, and smiled. "I was indecisive forgot to eat, and acted stupid, but Kane hauled me back into shape."

"How so?"

Jenna pushed the button for the elevator and waited for it to arrive. "The incident happened because I'd let my guard down. Kane insisted on daily workouts, as in hand-to-hand combat, and he gives no mercy." Jenna flicked her a glance and stepped into the car. "He's got a metal plate in his head, so with the constant headaches it must have been difficult for him, but he drilled me until my confidence returned. He also instilled in me that he'd always have my back."

"He understands the condition." Jo smiled at her. "Support is very important, and making you feel safe would've been his first priority." She led the way out the elevator.

As the pieces fell into place, Jenna fell into step beside her. "I thought he was being overprotective and macho. I told him to back off."

"Really?" Jo chuckled. "But you felt safe, right?"

Jenna nodded slowly. "I still do." She walked toward the secure ward and swiped her card. The door slid open and she led the way inside. "Carol Robinson will be in here. As she's here for voluntary psychiatric assessment, we'll have to speak to the attending physician before questioning her."

The hospital smell surrounded Jenna as they walked to the nurses' station. She requested Mrs. Robinson's room number and asked the nurse to call the attending doctor. As luck would have it, the doctor was on the ward. The doctor, a man barely thirty, came to greet them, not in the white coat she'd expected but in jeans and a sweater.

"Dr. Bligh? Sheriff Alton and this is Agent Jo Blake." She held out her hand. "Do you have a report on Carol Robinson? We would like to interview her if possible."

"I don't see a problem. She is in surprisingly good spirits." Bligh's hand was warm and his grasp firm. "She is asking if she can go home. I'm surprised she wants to return to the house. For most people it's the last place they'd want to go. This is the reason I've kept her here. I'm still evaluating her condition."

"She can't return home. It's still a crime scene. For now, I'd prefer her to remain here. She doesn't have any relatives to go to and we may need to question her further."

"That would have to be voluntary at this stage." Bligh frowned. "In truth, she can walk out when she wants."

Jenna rolled her eyes. "I'll see if I can convince her to stay. Please contact me if she ups and leaves, won't you?"

"Of course." Bligh walked them to a room and went inside. "Carol, you'll remember Sheriff Alton. She wants a word with you."

The woman sitting in an easy chair reading a book didn't resemble the blood-spattered woman she'd met on the night of the shooting. Jenna introduced Jo and then turned to the doctor. "Thank you, Dr. Bligh, we can take it from here."

"Afternoon, Sheriff." Carol Robinson placed her book face down on the coffee table and looked at them. "Is it time for me to go home?"

Jenna pulled up a chair and Jo followed so they both sat opposite her. "I'm worried about your safety, so I'd prefer you to remain here for the time being, and your house is still a crime scene. I'm sure you don't want to return to it like it is?"

"No, I guess not." Carol stared into space. "I'll have to redecorate, and get new carpets as well."

Jenna nodded. "I think so." She indicated toward Jo. "Agent Blake has a few questions for you. Is that okay?"

"Yeah, sure." Carol turned her attention to Jo.

"What do you remember about the time before the intruder shot Lucas?" Jo casually took out her iPad from her briefcase and then looked at Carol. "Tell me about the days before it happened."

"It was the same as always." Carol blew out a sigh. "He went to work and came home late. Some nights he didn't come home at all. He had business meetings and refused to drink and drive, so stayed over in town."

"Did you ever worry about him having an affair?" Jo's face hadn't changed expression as if she'd just asked what she'd had for lunch. "I sure would."

"It entered my mind." Carol picked at her fingernails. "A woman called, asking after him, one night. Lucas said it was his secretary reminding him about an appointment is all."

"How did that make you feel?" Jo glanced down at her notes.

"I'd heard the rumors; you know, about him having an affair with one of the girls from the beauty parlor." Carol gave her a slow smile. "She didn't get him, did she?"

"No, I'd guess she didn't, if the rumors were true." Jo gave Jenna a meaningful look and then moved her attention back to Carol. "Did you shoot Lucas?"

"No, and the medical examiner swabbed my arms for gunshot residue." Carol looked straight at Jenna. "You know darn well I was in the bed beside him when it happened. I had his brains all over me." She looked back at Jo. "Why would you ask me a question like that?"

"We have to ask—it's a normal part of the questioning." Jo patted her arm. "So, in your own words, what happened that night?"

Jenna went through the notes she'd taken on the night as Carol recalled the shooting. The story remained the same, maybe a little embellished. "How long did you remain under the bed?"

"I don't remember. Five minutes maybe." Carol moved around in her seat, clearly agitated.

"How did you feel then?" Jo looked at her. "Angry, scared?"

"Scared." Carol dug her fingernails into her arm. "Lucas' arm was hanging over the edge of the bed and it was moving. I could see it with the light from my phone."

"So why didn't you help him?" Jo made some notes.

"I couldn't look at him. I had his blood all over me." Carol looked Jo straight in the eye. "I just ran."

Jenna checked her notes. "So how long after the shooting did you call 911?"

"I'm not sure... Time seemed to stand still." Carol looked out the window. "Is that all? I'm tired."

Jenna glanced at Jo and she nodded. "Yes, thanks for the chat." She stood and they walked from the room. "What do you think?"

"I think you need to look a little closer at her. She's involved. She didn't pull the trigger but maybe she has a boyfriend who did." Jo smiled at her. "I think your gut was right this time."

CHAPTER THIRTY-EIGHT

He noticed the sheriff's cruiser coming his way in the reflection in a storefront window. As it went by, he turned to get a better look. Sheriff Alton was at the wheel, and the woman wearing the FBI jacket, who he'd seen her with earlier, was riding shotgun again. He wondered if his time at the Old Mitcham Ranch had made an impression on them. He ran the exquisite pantomime through his mind, his payback to the big boss man who'd parked across the alleyway, blocking his truck. It had taken one question in Aunt Betty's Café to discover where the crew worked. The girl who'd spilled his coffee had been the perfect bait, and getting her had only taken a small amount of his time. The moment he'd stepped out of the bushes, he'd strangled her just enough to keep her unconscious until he'd decided her time to die.

He'd headed out to the Old Mitcham Ranch. Late at night, the boss man and his smart-mouthed workers would be slow from drink and drunk from sleep. He'd driven right in with Ruby out cold in the back seat. The chairs, he'd found stacked up on the front porch and set them out just before reviving Ruby and puncturing her thigh. He licked his lips, almost tasting the memory of the kill. Ruby had screamed like a banshee and the men had come running, falling over each other to get to her. They'd argued over how to stop the bleeding and not one of them had called 911. He'd walked right up to them unnoticed, a weapon in each hand, and the big boss man had wet himself. Once he'd made them secure each other to the chairs, he'd had all night. The smell of blood had been like perfume filling the air in a heavy fog. His vivid recollections of the terror in the helpless men's eyes, their screams of pain. The way they'd begged for mercy and twitched after he'd shot them had fed his hunger, but their faces he'd forgotten the moment he'd walked away.

He'd been so careful never to leave more than a single feather as a clue and laughed aloud when the sheriff and FBI agent dashed straight past him into a clothing store, cackling like teenagers. He slipped inside behind them and made his way around the store, so close he could smell the sheriff's honeysuckle scent. He walked around like he owned the place, and went about choosing a woolen hat, a new pair of leather gloves, and a hoodie. His heart pounded with excitement, being so close to them, and at one point he brushed against the FBI agent as he reached for a coat on a rack. He listened to snatches of their conversation and heard enough to know the FBI agent was staying with the sheriff. *How convenient.*

The hustle around the sheriff's department made him smile. He'd seen vehicles coming and going like buses at a terminal; better still the sheriff had called in the FBI. It seemed the law enforcement in town would be working long hours with eight murders to solve. Keeping them busy was a ploy he enjoyed. The dogged persistence and tunnel vision of law officers on a case meant that he had free rein to move around. He wasn't concerned when the cravings came; he could act without the worry of the law disturbing him. They'd never suspected him and never would. The problem was the *eight* victims. He preferred to do things in threes, and eight… well, the number eight didn't sit well with him. It had to be nine, or maybe twelve, before he satisfied the craving. He smiled and pulled on his new leather gloves, flexing his fingers. At this moment, the choice of who lived or died was in his hands. *I own this town.*

CHAPTER THIRTY-NINE

Saturday morning

Jenna was thinking seriously about asking Mayor Petersham to extend her office. In fact, a few additional rooms would be necessary with the caseload of late. She often needed to have everyone in her office, including deputies from other counties and Wolfe and his team, and things were getting more than a little cramped. She eased her way from the whiteboard and back to her seat. She had Kane on one side of her and Jo on the other; Carter, Wolfe, Emily, Webber, Rowley, and Walters stared at her expectantly. "Okay, I've been issuing press releases but we've had no call-ins from any witnesses. No one has been near the Old Mitcham Ranch or seen anything the morning of the Stanton Forest murders. So, let's start with Ruby Evans. Rowley, what do you have for me?"

"I notified her aunt and took her to the morgue. She gave me a positive ID." Rowley placed the paperwork on the desk. "I asked some questions about Ruby's movements. She had told her aunt she'd be working late. Her aunt slept late yesterday morning, and assumed Ruby had already left for work. No boyfriends and no friends, the aunt is aware of at all." He glanced down at his notes. "I followed up at Aunt Betty's. Susie was upset at the news. She said Ruby left at nine to catch the bus home. I called the bus company and have gotten hold of the driver. He remembers dropping her some ways from the cut through to Elk Creek around nine-twenty."

Jenna made notes as he spoke and then thinking ahead looked up at him. "Did you ask Susie if Ruby had any problems with any of the customers?"

"Yeah." Rowley nodded. "She did mention Ruby thought someone had been following her the night before. I asked her if she'd had any problems at work. The only person Ruby had spoken at length with was Atohi Blackhawk's friend and she didn't know his name. She was planning to meet him for a coffee on Friday night after work."

Jenna looked up from her notes. The image of the tall, muscular man with unusual eyes came into her mind. "His name is Brad Kelly."

"The angry young man." Jo leaned forward in her chair. "He didn't seem to have the time to chase women."

Jenna looked at Wolfe. "Did you sort out the problem with his mother's remains with Jill?"

"Yeah, if it's his mother's remains." Wolfe gave her a skeptical look. "It's female, and Jill is going to work out of the mortician's as the morgue is packed to the rafters. She's chasing down dental records; as Kelly is next of kin, we have his consent to obtain his mother's files and see if they're a match." He glanced down at his notes. "From the initial examination I did at the scene, the head trauma appears consistent with his story, but we're taking the word of a child's memories here."

"Traumatic memories as a child are usually more accurate than you realize." Jo glanced at Kane. "You'd agree?"

"Yeah, it's as if the incident or the face of the perpetrator is imprinted on their memory." Kane looked at Wolfe. "Although, head trauma in female murder victims is very common."

Jenna made a few notes. "Okay, then we need to speak to Brad Kelly as he interacted with her."

"He seems angry." Jo looked concerned. "Did you do a background check on him?"

Jenna shook her head. "We had no reason to. He came to us seeking help to find his mother's and brother's remains. His father was abusive and he witnessed their murder; he made his way to the res, left there when he turned eighteen, and didn't return until he found out his father had died."

"Well, I say he fits the typical description of a serial killer." Carter stretched out his long legs and crossed his cowboy boots at the ankles. "He had a seriously messed up childhood. How do you know he didn't murder his pa? Have you even considered him? Think about it: he's just arrived in town and the killings start. The killer leaves a black feather. Seems to me it would mean something to a Native American—the Crow Nation live in this state, don't they?"

"Is he a member of the Crow Nation?" Jo turned to Jenna. "If so, a black feather could be significant."

It all sounded feasible but Jenna wasn't convinced. "Okay, we'll chase down Brad Kelly's background and whereabouts at the time of the crimes, but you'll likely find twenty or so people will vouch for him. As far as I'm aware, he's been camping at the burial site since they found the remains." She looked at Kane. "Can you tactfully ask Atohi if the Blackhawks are members of the Crow Nation and ask about the black feather and its significance?"

"I could." Kane gave her a long look. "But I know he's a member of the Blackfeet Nation, so I doubt it. If I recall, he mentioned Brad saying his mother sent him to the reservation to be safe among her people. If he's Atohi's cousin, then he'd be the same." Kane raised one eyebrow. "Still want me to hunt down info on Brad Kelly?"

Jenna nodded. "Yes, but later. We'd better cover all the bases and find out how his father died as well." She glanced around. "Okay, where were we?"

"Ruby Evans." Wolfe met her gaze. "I've completed the autopsy, and my report is in the files. I'll give you a rundown of the main points.

The killer strangled her but that wasn't the cause of death. I would imagine by the bruises, her killer used strangulation to subdue her for a time before he stabbed her in the thigh. She died from blood loss, and the laceration to the throat was post-mortem and consistent to the killer being left-handed. I found DNA under her fingernails which could have resulted from her scratching herself as she tried to free her hands or during the strangulation. I'm waiting on the results of a DNA comparison and will call you if the trace evidence belongs to her killer."

"That would sure be a breakthrough." Carter smiled. "If it matches any of our suspects."

"I guess we'll wait and see." Wolfe shut him down with a look. "Kane and Carter hunted down the families of the victims at the Old Mitcham Ranch. We have all of them coming by sometime today to identify the bodies. I'll start on the autopsies as soon as we've finished up here." He looked back at Jenna. "From my initial examinations on scene and back at the morgue, I doubt I'll find more than is obvious. They were all tortured and finished with a gunshot to the head. The killer spaced the deaths over at least one hour as the rate of rigor is slightly different in each victim. The four men all appear fit and normal for their ages."

Jenna leaned back in her chair. "Have you had time to examine the boots of Trevor Wilson, the site boss? The man with his boots on the wrong feet?"

"Yeah, and I found traces of blood spatter that matched the spots on his socks. I can say, without doubt, his boots were removed and then replaced later."

"Ha!" Carter slapped his leg. "I was right!"

Jenna ignore Carter's grinning face and turned to Kane. "Okay, Kane, you've discussed the scenario with Jo—what have you come up with as a profile for our killer? Is it the same killer, or are we dealing with someone else?"

"The same killer."

Jenna nodded. She'd heard so many theories about what happened at the Old Mitcham Ranch but she needed Kane's. "How did you and Jo read the scene?"

"I believe the killer snuck up on the men and threatened them. He would feel powerful and in control." Kane shrugged. "Then I think he took the boots and jacket from victim number one and wore them. He planned the murders so had on coveralls and gloves. He's aware of trace evidence and made sure not to leave any, not one footprint or even a shell casing. Same as in the Robinsons' house and the Stanton Forest murders." He looked at Jenna. "I know he has a different MO but we're convinced it's the same killer."

"If I can take you back to the first murder." Jo leaned forward in her seat and cupped her hands on the table. "At first, we see a cold calculated killer. He killed fast and clean. He gained no pleasure out of killing Lucas Robinson, which we all believe was a paid hit."

"Then you move on to the Stanton Forest Murders." Kane folded his arms across his chest. "This was the same, disposal of a problem, a fast kill, clean."

"Then we have the mass murder." Jo looked at Jenna. "This is a killer prolonging the enjoyment, making it last. Maybe he felt he deserved it after the two fast killings. He needed a fix and took his time to set it up. He used Ruby as bait—why her, we don't know, unless it was opportunistic."

"I don't think so." Kane looked at Jo. "It's not easy to just grab a girl off the street at around nine at night. He likely discovered she took the bus and followed her. She mentioned to Susie that someone was following her, so it was probably him. He'd planned the kill and knew the men would be alone. Maybe he had a reason to go there, maybe he went there looking for work or something?"

He shrugged. "It's been all over the media there's a team up there creating a Halloween attraction."

Jenna nodded. "Okay. If this is the case, and he made the victims tie each other up, like we thought, they would have left trace evidence on the gaffer tape. Wolfe, that's a theory you'll have to prove or disprove."

"I've taken prints and swabs from everyone at the scene. I'll check the gaffer tape for prints and see if I get a match." Wolfe rubbed his chin, making a scraping sound on the bristles. "I can verify he mutilated the victims while they were seated. All of them have various blood spatter evidence on the front of their bodies. Apart from the blood spatter around their necks from the head wounds, their backs, from the shoulders down, clearly show the outline of the chairs. The victims would have suffered."

"He sounds like a monster." Emily had paled. "The way he laid out the hands, like trophies on the kitchen table and yet so far he doesn't seem to be taking trophies. That's unusual isn't it?"

Glad that Wolfe's daughter, Emily was involved in the case, Jenna made a note of her comment. "That's a good point. He doesn't take trophies."

"Either that or he's smarter than we think." Carter reached for a bottle of water on the desk cracked it open, and took a sip. "Taking trophies is a killer's downfall and usually leads to their arrest. We know he is cold and calculating, but the way he flips his MO makes him different to any killer I've known before."

"We have." Jenna shot Kane a glance. "Trust me, Black Rock Falls has seen just about every type of killer known to man."

CHAPTER FORTY

Mind reeling from all the information, theories, and ideas from her team, Jenna closed her eyes for a few seconds to think before taking a moment to look at the whiteboard. "Let's just take a minute to consider the suspects in this case. Kyler Hall and Cliff Young are persons of interest because they tie in with Lucas Robinson and the Stanton Forest murders. We've interviewed both men and they lawyered up. The evidence we have on them is circumstantial at best. I'll need more to tie them into the mass murder." She looked at Rowley. "Find out where they were on Thursday night. Check out any witnesses to their whereabouts."

"Yes, ma'am." Rowley nodded. "As they've lawyered up, I won't be able to ask them direct."

Jenna rubbed her temples. "Go talk to their neighbors, call the manager of the construction site, find out where they hang out and ask around."

"Oh, sure." Rowley scribbled in his notebook.

"This leads us back to Lucas Robinson's murder." Jenna sighed. "We have no other suspects, and it will take a ton of grunt work to chase down all his enemies. He wasn't liked." She looked at Wolfe. "Have you released his body yet?"

"Yeah, I've sent Lucas Robinson's remains to the funeral parlor as we needed the space." Wolfe cleared his throat. "Is Mrs. Robinson well enough to make the arrangements?"

Jenna made more notes. "Walters, I want you to follow up with her, please. Carol Robinson seems fine to me; I visited her with Jo yesterday." She lifted her eyes to her deputies. "I'm convinced she's involved somehow. Yeah, I know she's been locked up since her husband's death, but there's something about her that sends up warning signals."

"Makes perfect sense to me." Carter barked a laugh. "I've read the file. Carol Robinson discovers her husband is having an affair and hires a hitman. This is how our killer arrived in town. Maybe he was heading out after the job and something happened on the highway. Road rage maybe, he runs the men's truck off the road and gets out his vehicle packing for bear. He guns them down and leaves."

"So why return and kill Ruby and the men at the Old Mitcham Ranch?" Jenna stood and stretched her back and then went to the coffee machine. "What would trigger him to go crazy?" She poured a cup and went back to her desk.

"A memory." Jo looked at Jenna. "Something as simple as a scent can cause an episode. If he is suffering from dissociative identity disorder, it can trigger like PTSD. Some people have blackouts, do terrible things and don't remember. Others remember it as if someone else committed the atrocities, or they see it in flashbacks."

"Yeah." Kane looked at her. "It's like another personality takes over for a time. The problem we have here is if it's one of our suspects, the other one would be aware of the sudden changes in his friend. He might be covering up for him." He sighed. "Proving it would be difficult."

A cold shiver trickled down Jenna's spine as her mind went back to her encounter with Atohi. She swallowed hard, not wanting to place the facts in order in her mind. If her assumptions were correct, it would mean her friend Atohi was lying to her, and she trusted him. She lifted her gaze from her notes. "I met Atohi and Brad Kelly yesterday. We talked about the remains of Kelly's mother, as I've mentioned. I remember he had a scratch on his jaw, which could tie in with Ruby's murder. He'd asked her out, so she'd know him and not be afraid if she ran into him. He had an abusive childhood, watched his mother and brother murdered. He arrived in town just before the killings started. We have no idea what he was doing from the time he left the res until a week ago."

"And if Carol Robinson hired him to kill her husband, when he killed the two men in Stanton Forest, it triggered the memory of his father killing his family." Kane nodded slowly. "Cold, calculating Brad steps out, and angry, murderous, out-for-revenge-on-the-world Brad comes to the front."

Jenna turned to Carter. "Is this enough to obtain a warrant for Mrs. Robinson's bank statements? The judge denied our last request. If she hired a hitman, she'd need a substantial amount of money."

"Leave that to me." Carter pushed back his Stetson with one finger. "It's only probable cause and I figure we have that in spades."

An FBI agent requesting a warrant from their local judge would carry more weight. Jenna couldn't believe her luck. "Okay, I'll leave you to handle the paperwork."

"Sure." Carter pushed another toothpick into his mouth. "When I'm done, I'll go by the other crime scenes to get a feel for this killer."

Jenna looked at the group before her. "Yes, take a look now because I need to get out a press release about the murders. As soon as it's made public, the ghouls will be out sightseeing. Once I've called it in, I'll go with Kane to speak to Atohi and see if we can find out Brad Kelly's whereabouts at the times of the murders."

"I think I'd like to sit in on the autopsies." Jo collected her things from the desk. "I'm interested to confirm the sequence of events at the Old Mitcham Ranch. It will give me a clearer picture of the killer."

Jenna closed her notebook. "Okay, we'll meet back here at five and we'll go over our findings." She glanced at Wolfe. "I know the autopsies will take a considerable amount of time. Jo will bring me up to speed if you're busy."

"I'll be working on the victims all day, so we won't be able to make it, but I'll call if I find anything significant." Wolfe tapped on her desk. "Catch you later. Jo, I'll wait for you in the van." He left the room with Emily and Webber close behind.

"I'll be right there." Jo stood.

There was a scraping of chairs as the rest of the group got to their feet, and Rowley and Walters headed out the door.

"You know something?" Jo looked at Carter. "All this is like déjà vu. Do you remember the Chameleon Killer case out of Baltimore? He left a black feather too and we had no suspects because everyone saw a different man."

"I know about the case but only read up on it last night." Carter sighed. "It's very similar to what we have now and likely the same man."

Intrigued, Jenna turned to Jo. "How come you didn't catch the killer?"

"In the end, I came to the conclusion we were either dealing with a master of disguise or a killer with multiple personalities." Jo tapped the file. "I agree with Carter. This could be the same man. He might not be aware he's dressing differently or using his left or right hand because he sees himself as whatever personality emerges. He might work for a cartel as a hitman, hence the clean kills, but then crazy Brad breaks out and goes on a killing spree as Kane described. If so, this personality is unpredictable and he can't control it. We had boots on the ground, a huge taskforce, and we couldn't catch him. If this is Brad Kelly and he's exhibiting yet a different personality, this latest one is far more dangerous than all the others put together."

CHAPTER FORTY-ONE

The wind had picked up again, piling multicolored leaves in the gutters and bringing the promise of snow. Kane stared down the street and had the strange feeling he'd stepped onto the set of a supernatural movie. The Halloween bunting on Main danced around and made strange howling noises. The plastic skeletons hanging from the streetlights appeared to be waving and grinning at the constant flow of traffic. Witches with long white hair sitting around a cauldron outside the general store seemed to come to life as their clothes flapped. Strings of plastic jack-o'-lanterns swung back and forth above the storefronts, making a clattering sound. Kane tossed his Stetson on the back seat, dug in his jacket pocket for his black woolen hat, and pulled it down over his ears. He wondered what Duke was doing all alone at home and slid behind the wheel. "Duke would've enjoyed a trip to the res."

"Maybe we won't have to go to the res." Jenna pulled out her phone. "I'll call Atohi. He might be in town."

Kane smiled at her. "Good thinking."

"Atohi, it's Jenna. We need a chat, where are you?"

"I'm close to town. Do you want me to come into the office?"

"No, how about meeting us at Aunt Betty's?"

"Sure."

"Is Brad with you?" Jenna flicked a glance at Kane.

"Nope, he's parked outside the mortician's as far as I know. I've been with the team searching the forest for Scott's remains."

"Okay, we'll see you soon." She disconnected and looked at Kane. "Do we have time to do a drive-by and see if he's there?"

Kane started the engine and backed out. "Sure. Are you planning on speaking to him?" He headed down Main toward the funeral parlor.

"No, right now all we have is suspicion. We'll need more evidence. Maybe after we've spoken to Atohi. If he can verify Brad's whereabouts and they check out, we're going to have to look elsewhere for a suspect."

The idea of seeing the funeral parlor decked out for Halloween amused Kane, and he chuckled under his breath. "I hope the mortician didn't go all out for Halloween."

"Oh…" Jenna snorted and covered her mouth but the giggle still escaped. "That would be in terribly bad taste." She gathered herself and looked at Kane. "I couldn't help picturing it… sorry. I don't know where these thoughts come from. You are such a bad influence on me, Dave."

Kane turned the corner and they slowed to drive past an old truck parked on the side of the road. Inside they could plainly see Kelly in the driver's seat, looking at his phone. "Hmm, well at least he's where he said he would be." He turned into the mortician's driveway. "Wait here, I'll go ask how long he's been out there."

He slid out the truck. Inside, it was as cold as the morgue and had the smell of embalming fluid mixed with the scent of flowers that always seemed to hang around funeral parlors. He rang the bell on the front counter and waited. A man walked through a door and closed it behind him; he looked familiar but wasn't Max Weems.

"I'm looking for Mr. Weems."

"I'm Weems, unless you want my pa, Max Weems." The young man met his gaze. "He's busy right now. How can I help you?"

Kane recalled Max Weems had a son and smiled. "Have you noticed the truck parked outside?"

"Yeah, I've seen it. It belongs to a guy by the name of Brad Kelly. He figures his mom's remains are here and he needs to be close by. My pa reckons we just let him be."

"Yeah, it would be best." Kane nodded in agreement. "How long has he been there this time?"

"I have no idea. He comes and goes." Weems shrugged. "I'm far too busy to watch his movements."

"I understand." Kane pulled a card from his pocket and handed it to him. "If he causes a problem, give me a call."

"I will." Weems glanced at the card. "Thanks, Deputy Kane."

Kane hustled back to his truck and they sped off toward Aunt Betty's Café. "We lucked out. Weems' son knows Kelly's name, but he hasn't been keeping tabs on him."

"Uh-huh." Jenna was looking at her phone. "I just ran his plates. He only purchased that truck ten days ago." She looked at him. "So, he came here by air or bus."

"Atohi will know." Kane slid his truck into a parking space outside Aunt Betty's and turned to look at her. "How do you want to play this, Jenna?"

"You talk to him, he likes you." Jenna bit her bottom lip. "It won't seem so formal either. I've always trusted him. I hope he doesn't prove me wrong."

Concerned, Kane frowned. "I like him too, he's a good guy. I'm rarely wrong about people."

Inside the café, they ordered a meal at the counter and went to their table at the back. It was cozy inside Aunt Betty's, and Kane removed his hat, gloves, and jacket before sitting down. He inhaled the delicious aroma of freshly baked pie and grinned at Jenna. "Can you smell that? Hmm, Saturday's special, peach pie."

"So I gathered when you ordered two for now and six to go." Jenna shook her head slowly. "You planning on hibernating over winter?"

Kane leaned back in his chair and flicked his gaze over her. "It wouldn't hurt you to eat more. We burn so many more calories in the cold and you're getting skinny."

"I am not!" Jenna's cheeks pinked. "I gave Jo my jeans because I've put on so much weight since I arrived here."

Kane shook his head. "Then you must have been skin and bones… Not surprising after what you went through. I've known you for a couple of years now and you've created an entirely different body shape since we started working out." He smiled up at Susie Hartwig as she arrived with their coffee. "Trust me, with our workload, not eating will make you ill."

"Ah… you wanted to see me?" Atohi Blackhawk looked from one to the other.

Astonished by his silent entrance, Kane looked up at him. No one ever managed to sneak up on him, and he'd let his guard down with a serial killer in town. He cleared his throat. "Yeah, pull up a chair. Can I get you something to eat?"

"I have a slice of peach pie coming." Atohi smiled. "Best pie in town."

"Don't start him on pie again." Jenna laughed. "All he thinks about is his next meal."

"I'm much the same." Atohi frowned. "How can I help you?"

Kane took a sip of his coffee and noticed Susie coming back with a cup and a tray. He waited for her to pass the plates around and pour Atohi's coffee before looking at him. "We've had a number of murders this week, eight so far—"

"What?" Atohi's horrified expression met his. "You're joking, right?"

Kane shook his head slowly. "Nope, and nobody knows any details, but we trust you and need some information. Can you tell me the significance of feathers in your culture?"

"Okay." Atohi's large hands slid around his coffee cup and he raised his gaze to look at Jenna. "You believe the killer is one of my people?"

"The two suspects we have are both Caucasian but the feather seems significant. One has been left at the crime scene."

"Then it is not one of my people. A feather isn't something you stuff your pillows with; to us they symbolize honor, power, and wisdom, to name a few things. If a chief gives one, it means the person is very special; it is like a medal of honor. Finding an eagle feather is an amazing gift as they have a special connection to the heavens."

Kane nodded. "So, what significance would it mean to leave one at a crime scene?"

"Let me ask you." Atohi raised one eyebrow. "If you found something precious, would you taint it with blood?"

"No, I wouldn't, but whoever is doing this is leaving a message." Kane leaned back in his chair. "The crow feathers mean something to him."

"Crow?" Atohi sipped his coffee, his pie forgotten. "Young warriors used turkey feathers in their hair; boys, not men worthy of wearing an eagle's feather. Such feathers are earned for bravery not given out like candy." He thought for a long moment. "Crows mean wisdom. They speak the truth, and some say they lead the hunter. Perhaps this killer is on a mission to find the truth, but throwing a feather on the ground is disrespectful. Feathers are displayed not hidden away." He looked at Kane with a deeply troubled expression. "This killer, if he is one of my people, is lost in his own mind."

Kane looked him straight in the eye. He hated asking the next question but he had no choice. "I have to ask you something and I don't want you to take offense because I'm asking as a deputy."

"You want to know about Brad?" Atohi sighed. "He isn't the same person as the cousin I grew up with; he's changed. He was silent for so many years, we never really understood what had happened to him. When he returned, he had so much rage inside, he blamed himself for not returning to the forest." He lifted his chin. "Honestly, I don't know him anymore, but since they took his mother's remains to the funeral home, he's calmed some."

The remorse from Atohi washed over Kane and he swallowed hard. "Could the crow feathers be significant to him?"

"Yeah, the Crow raised his mother; her father was Crow. She came back to us with her mother when he died. It is possible Brad is aware of his heritage."

Kane refilled his coffee cup from the pot on the table and then added cream and sugar. "When did Brad get to the res, and was he driving the truck then?"

"He arrived maybe a couple of weeks ago. I was away working when he showed up, and as far as I know he came in his truck." Atohi shrugged. "He's not a freeloader; he brought plenty of supplies with him and gave them to my mother, cash as well. He was grateful for all the years she cared for him."

"Okay." Kane moved to the next step. "Do you remember speaking to a waitress in here by the name of Ruby Evans?"

"Yeah, Brad asked her out for a coffee last night but she was a no-show." Atohi looked from one to the other. "How do you know about her?"

"Ruby mentioned the date to Susie Hartwig. The problem is, someone murdered her on Thursday night." Kane watched his shocked reaction. "Out at the Old Mitcham Ranch."

"What!" Atohi shook his head. "I can't believe it. She was so nice, Brad didn't think he had a chance. He was shocked when she agreed to go out with him."

Kane took a sip of his coffee. "Did Brad mention ever going out to the Old Mitcham Ranch?"

"Nope." Atohi pulled his plate close and lifted his fork. "I can only account for his whereabouts when I was with him. Outside that, I don't know where he went. Same as since we found the bones. I left him to camp in the forest on Thursday night and took food out to him on Friday around nine. We talked about his date, and he was looking forward to it." He met Kane's gaze. "He didn't sound like a person who'd just murdered her. As far as I know, he's camped out there since we found the remains and only moved when the forensic team took the remains to the funeral parlor. I can't imagine him leaving his mom alone to go off and murder people. Yeah, he's acting a little crazy right now, but everything in his past has just come crashing down on him. But killing people? I don't think so."

CHAPTER FORTY-TWO

Mind in turmoil, Jenna stared blankly out the window of Kane's truck for several minutes after taking a call from Wolfe. The trace evidence found under Ruby's fingernails was a viable sample and likely from her killer. Now all she needed was DNA from her suspects for comparison, but her chances of getting samples from lawyered-up Kyler Hall and Cliff Young would be impossible. Although, getting a visual would be better than nothing, and if either of them had scratches on their faces, she'd give their attorney, Sam Cross, the option of them giving a voluntary sample or her getting a court order. She looked over at Kane, who was watching her with interest. "I know Brad Kelly has a scratch on his chin, so we go see him first, and then we pay Kyler Hall and Cliff Young another visit."

"Whatever Hall and Young say, it won't be admissible; they've already requested a lawyer." Kane started the engine. "You'll have to go through Cross."

Jenna rolled her eyes. "That man drives me crazy." She fastened her seatbelt. "I just want to look at them and see if they have any injuries. I won't say a word."

"Okay." Kane turned onto Main Street. "I guess you want to speak to Kelly first? I have plenty of DNA collection kits in the back."

Interested to discover how Brad Kelly would react to her questions, Jenna nodded. "Yeah, let's see what he has to say. I'll question him and we'll watch his reaction. My gut tells me to haul him in for questioning, but everything we have against him is hearsay at best."

"If he is suffering from dissociative identity disorder, it may depend on which personality he is using today." Kane glanced at her and then back at the road. "He mentioned not remembering the actual murder when he arrived at the res. It all came back some years later when the cops told him his father had died."

This puzzled Jenna and it didn't explain how a person could suddenly have a split personality. "You and Jo believe he has multiple personalities, right?"

"We came to the conclusion the *killer* may have, that's why he hasn't been caught." Kane pulled over and turned to her. "Brad Kelly isn't necessarily the killer, but a lot of what happened to him could push a person into multiple personality disorder."

"How so?"

"When terrible things happen to kids, it's possible they take on safe personalities." A nerve twitched in Kane's cheek. "If a child suffers prolonged abuse, some create a different person in their mind, so the abuse isn't happening to them. When this happens, it can have a cumulative effect. So every stress that they face growing up is covered by a different personality— a front man, if you like—who can cope with the pressure. For instance, the guy who shows up for the interview may be confident, but the child who remains inside as a personality is withdrawn and can't speak." He waved a hand toward the truck parked outside the funeral parlor. "Atohi said Brad was different from when he left, angry, so get-even Brad might be out at the moment. He might be hiding savage-psychopath Brad."

Amazed by his knowledge, Jenna sucked in a breath. "So how could he be the Chameleon Killer? How do we know if this is the same man?"

"Dissociative identity disorder is categorized by a person displaying two or more distinct personalities. It's as if they carry different characters inside them and pull out the one best suited to handle the problem. Each personality often has a different name and age because they manifest at different times, so they have the age from when they emerged. They often have different characteristics, like accents and walking styles, they smoke, don't smoke, drink coffee or only drink tea. Being left- or right-handed is another possibility." He sighed. "The biggest problem is you never know who you're speaking to at any given time. Some have a dominant personality but it usually depends on the situation they're facing."

"So how many are aware of what the others are doing?" Jenna swallowed hard. "Do they know?"

"Some do and some have missing time, blackouts." Kane scratched his cheek. "Those who don't know, it's a shock because that personality is often a normal person. This isn't like a psychopath, Jenna. Most of these people are harmless and can be helped." He sighed. "On the other end of the scale, if the dominant personality is a psychopath, he'll know what everyone is doing. He controls the team and sometimes refuses to allow the normal ones to emerge."

Jenna pushed a hand through her hair, considering the implications. "So if Brad Kelly is the killer, we could trigger another episode?"

"Maybe, maybe not." Kane shrugged. "If we don't make him defensive, he'd have no reason. Hang on a minute. You're assuming he's guilty. If I remember, the other suspects became a little upset when we spoke to them."

"Okay." Jenna turned her attention to the truck parked about a hundred yards away. "Let's do this."

When Kane pulled in behind Brad Kelly's truck, Jenna noticed Brad look at them in his mirror. To her surprise, he turned, gave them a wave, and climbed out.

She walked up to him. "Afternoon."

"Sheriff Alton and Deputy Kane." Brad looked from one to the other, his strange eyes examining them closely. "Has the undertaker complained about me sitting here all day?"

Jenna shook her head. "No, we haven't had a complaint. I'm sorry but we have some bad news." She straightened. "The girl you met in Aunt Betty's Café, Ruby Evans, she's dead."

"Dead?" Brad's eyebrows crinkled into a deep frown. "When? She was supposed to meet me for a coffee last night and didn't show." He stared at Jenna. "What happened to her? Did she have an accident?"

He appeared genuinely shocked and Jenna had a pang of regret for being so blunt with him. "I'm afraid somebody murdered her."

"Who would murder her?" Brad scrubbed his hands down his face. "This town is cursed. I'm cursed. If she hadn't agreed to go out with me, she'd be okay."

"What do you mean by that?" Jenna watched him closely. "Did you have anything to do with her death?"

"Me? No!" Brad's eyes flashed with anger. "It's just everyone around me seems to die."

Another strange response. Jenna waited a beat for him to collect himself. "How did you get that scratch on your face?"

"This?" Brad touched his chin. "In the forest, why?"

"Ruby has skin under her fingernails."

"It isn't mine." Brad straightened. "You'd need to prove it with a DNA test, wouldn't you?"

Jenna nodded. "Yeah, that's the usual way."

"Well, she didn't scratch me." Brad's eyes bore into her. "I'll take a test."

Relieved, Jenna nodded to Kane, and he went to collect a sample kit from his truck. "It's the best thing to do, then there is no doubt."

"I can walk with my head held high, Sheriff." Brad stared at his boots then slowly looked at her. "Do you think after seeing my pa beat my mom to death with a shovel, I could hurt anyone?"

Jenna swallowed hard. "I don't have an opinion on this murder, Brad. I'm hunting down a list of people who last saw Ruby alive. If everyone is as helpful as you, we'll soon catch her killer." She pulled out her notebook. "Where were you Thursday night?"

"Here." Brad glanced back at the funeral parlor. "I'm making sure my mom remains here and she isn't hauled off as some exhibition for a forensic anthropology class."

"Can anyone verify that?" Jenna looked up at him. "Did you make any calls? Talk to anyone?"

"I picked up Chinese takeout around eight, I guess." Brad rubbed his chin. "I used the restrooms in the park, changed my clothes, and then came back here."

"Okay." Jenna made notes. "What about Monday night and Wednesday morning?"

"Hunting down my mother's remains or staying with them in the forest, I guess. I camped in the forest most times, and apart from Atohi dropping by, I can't prove I was there." He looked back at Kane. "Do you need to take blood for the test?"

She glanced around as Kane walked back wearing surgical gloves and carrying a DNA test kit. Turning back to Brad, she smiled. "No. It's pretty simple, just a swab from the inside of your mouth."

"How long before you know?" Brad opened his mouth for Kane to take the swab.

Jenna shrugged. "Not long. Wolfe has a superfast lab in the ME's office, with all the latest equipment."

"That's good. I don't like being a suspect." Brad wiped the back of his hand over his lips. "Is that all?"

"Not really." Kane looked at him. "Did you know about the plans for the Old Mitcham Ranch?"

"Yeah, Atohi mentioned some clown is turning it into an amusement park or something." Brad shrugged. "It might be okay for tourists, but no one in his right mind from around here will go there."

"So you know the history of the place?" Kane wasn't looking at him but writing out the paperwork for the swab.

"Yeah, everyone does, and I heard on the news about the murders. The place should be burned to the ground." Brad frowned. "Why?"

Jenna glanced at Kane, hoping her expression would prevent him from questioning Brad. She needed his signature on the paperwork.

"Ah, can you sign the consent form?" Kane rested it on the hood of Brad's truck.

As Brad scribbled his name and the date, Jenna pushed a little harder. "Have you been by there lately?"

"The Old Mitcham Ranch? No, not since I came home." Brad straightened. "I did go there once with a bunch of kids in high school one Halloween—never again. Why?"

Jenna rested one hand on her weapon in a casual stance. "That's where we found Ruby."

"Well, the test will prove I had nothing to do with hurting her." Brad glared at them. "I gotta go." He turned away and went to sit in his vehicle.

Jenna followed Kane back to his truck and they climbed inside. "What do you think?"

"He signed the paperwork with his right hand, which is a problem as we're looking for a left-handed killer." Kane stared out the window. "Dammit, he fits the profile in so many ways." He turned slowly to look at her. "Unless he has dissociative personality disorder and if so, he's hiding it well. We'd have to see the personality change to be sure."

"It's only a possibility the killer is left-handed. We're going on a hunch, based on Mrs. Robinson's statement. She could have been wrong about the time it took to kill her husband, and if you think about it, Ruby would've been dead and not struggling." Jenna shrugged. "The killer could've grabbed her by the hair with his right hand and cut with the left. If he's as smart as you think, he might have done that on purpose to confuse the investigation."

"Maybe, and if he is involved, he knows darn well, Ruby didn't scratch him." Kane started the engine. "We should drop the sample by Wolfe's office and then go see the other suspects."

"Sure." Jenna leaned back in her seat. "You know, we're only assuming the killer took Ruby to the Old Mitcham Ranch to use as bait. We haven't considered that maybe one of the guys working there met Ruby at Aunt Betty's and took her out there. Do we know if any of them have scratches?" She glanced at Kane. "Had she been sexually active? Maybe it was a rape gone wrong?"

"Then there would've been five men involved." Kane parked outside the ME's office. "Someone had to tie them up and shoot them." He shrugged. "I didn't see any evidence of a fifth man living in the trailers."

Jenna nodded. "I'll ask Wolfe about the scratches while we're here, and we'll look at the bodies of the men again." She sighed. "Right now, I feel like whoever is doing this is slipping through our fingers."

CHAPTER FORTY-THREE

Surprised to see Jenna and Kane, Wolfe turned off his microphone and peered at them over his face mask. He'd finished the preliminary examinations on all the victims and was in the middle of the autopsy on Trevor Wilson. "Please don't tell me we have another murder victim?"

"Nope." Kane held up a sealed plastic bag. "I collected a DNA sample from Brad Kelly. We thought you'd like it right away. I'm not optimistic—he's right-handed."

Wolfe stepped away from the corpse pulling off his gloves and apron. "There goes that theory, but you never know what a killer will do to throw us off his scent. Bring it to the lab. He turned to Webber and Emily. "Prepare slides of the samples I've taken while I'm gone." He looked over at Jo. "I figure Jenna will want to speak to you as well."

"Sure." Jo smiled at him and followed him from the room.

Wolfe grabbed new scrubs from a closet in the hallway, tossed his into a laundry basket, and pulled on the new ones as he walked, hopping on one foot. "The new technology I have here now will often give me a result in ninety minutes." He smiled at them. "The lab-on-a-chip is excellent for determining trace evidence at a crime scene but I prefer the Rapid DNA machine." He pulled on fresh gloves and plucked the bag from Kane's hand. "If you'll wait in there." He pointed into the lab. "We can speak while I process the sample. You can't come into the sterile area or the sample may be contaminated."

"Okay." Jenna smiled at him and led Kane and Jo through the door.

Inside the sterile room, Wolfe opened the bag and took out the sealed tube containing the sample collected from Brad Kelly. As he prepared the machine, he heard Jenna's voice come through the speaker overhead.

"Have you noticed any scratches on any of the other victims?" Jenna peered at him through the glass partition.

"Not anything notable on initial examination, but I wasn't looking for scratches." Wolfe finished preparing the sample and placed it into the machine. "If there are, I don't think they're of any consequence. I'm glad you're here because I wanted you to view Ruby Evans again so I can explain." He headed for the door and met them in the hallway. "I've also found a few inconsistencies with the guy you refer to as victim number one—Wilson."

"How so?" Jenna took face masks and gloves from the counter outside the morgue and handed a set to Kane.

"It's better if I explain when we're viewing the body." Wolfe pushed open the door to the morgue and approached the stainless-steel cabinet. "I took the temperature of all the victims at the scene and made notes on their state of rigor. The results are conflicting. Most mass murders happen within a few minutes of each other unless it's a hostage situation." He went to the drawers lining the morgue and pulled out Ruby. "What do you know about Ruby Evans' movements immediately prior to her death?"

"We have Susie Hartwig's account and the bus driver's." Kane scrolled through the files on his phone. "Rowley spoke to Susie and she said Ruby left at nine and caught the bus to Stanton Road. She said she usually walks along a trail through a wooded area to get to Elk Creek. The bus driver recalls her getting off the bus at around nine twenty."

Wolfe pulled on the fresh apron Emily handed him and pulled back the sheet on Ruby Evans. "This is where it gets confusing." He indicated to the bruises on Ruby's wrists. "This would normally indicate she was fighting to get away but she has no defense wounds."

"Are you saying her killer didn't hit her or attack her from the front?" Kane frowned. "The killer likely tied her up for the trip to the Old Mitcham Ranch. Could the injuries be due to struggling?"

Wolfe nodded. "Some of them at least." He picked up Ruby's right hand. "This is where I found the skin under her nails. Well, one nail to be exact."

"Yet her nails aren't broken." Jo held up the other hand. "She gave a swipe in protest and then was subdued."

"Yes, and if you add this to the mud I discovered on the backs of the heels of her shoes, I'd say the killer pounced on her in the alleyway and she struck out in fright. It's hard to tell from the damage, but if you look at the bruising on her neck, see here above the laceration," he pointed to two distinct thumbprints each side of her neck, "we can see the bruising clearly, made from two hands above the laceration. I think the killer subdued her by strangulation after she fainted. I believe if you go and look at that cut-through from Stanton to Elk Creek, you'll find drag marks made by her heels."

"Do you believe the marks on her wrists came from struggling when she was in the chair, not from being tied previously?" Jenna peered at the body.

Wolfe nodded. "Yeah. They're consistent with the damage caused by the tape. Here's where it gets interesting. She died first and maybe an hour or so before victim number one, Wilson. He died at least two hours before the other two."

"Which means the killer was with them for a minimum of three hours?" Kane raised both eyebrows in question. "We've assumed the killer kidnapped Ruby, took her to the ranch, set her up on the porch, and then brought her round. Her screaming alerted the sleeping men, who came to help, and the killer was waiting for them."

Wolfe looked from one to the other. "It's the only explanation I can offer you." He glanced at Jenna. "I've taken DNA samples for comparison against the men at the scene; none of them match the sample from Ruby. They all have a few scrapes, from working, but she didn't scratch any of them."

"Was she sexually assaulted?" Jenna pulled the sheet up and over Ruby's body.

"No." Wolfe pushed Ruby back into the body storage locker.

"I don't think she meant much to the killer. I agree, she was used as bait." Jo looked at Jenna. "He cut her throat post-mortem to shock the men; they probably believed she was still alive."

Wolfe nodded. "From the results I have now, it went down like this: The men came out, he made an example of Wilson, maybe because he was carrying a weapon, and shot him in the knee. From the prints on the gun, Wilson unloaded it and tossed it aside, so we can assume the killer was holding a weapon on him. He got the other men to tie each other to the chairs using the gaffer tape. I found corresponding prints on each man's tape to prove this beyond doubt."

"Who removed the hands?" Jenna looked confused.

Wolfe met her gaze. "The killer. There are no prints on the ax. He made the last man bind his own legs to the chair and one of his hands. The tape on one of his hands is clean, so our killer was wearing leather gloves, not latex or similar because they stick hard and would've left residue."

"What would induce a man to tie up his friends and then himself?" Jenna looked horrified.

"Fear." Jo walked to the body of Wilson. "The killer made an example of this man. Wolfe made the determination that someone removed his hand post-mortem. Think about the situation: a man has a gun on them. He shoots the boss in the knee and orders one of the men to tie him up, so he does it. Maybe one of the men mouthed off, so he shot Wilson. Now the others are terrified. He tells the third man, Taylor, to tie up Kenny and Skinner and then removes the dead man's hand. After that he removes Kenny's hand and so on."

"It's a power trip." Kane looked at Jenna. "He was controlling them, bending them to his will."

"All the while feeding off their pain and misery." Jo looked at Jenna. "He enjoys killing; seeing people suffer and die is like a drug to him."

"This is all the proof we need to confirm the killer planned this out." Jenna leaned against the counter. "I think he had a beef with Wilson and this is payback." She shook her head slowly. "Wilson is an out-of-towner. What the hell did he do to the killer to make him track him here, and how does this tie in with the three other homicides?"

"We've been discussing multiple personality disorder as a factor in this case." Jo leaned against the counter beside Jenna. "The mass murder could've been committed by one of several personalities."

"Yeah." Kane pulled off his gloves and mask. "This is the psychopath, leader of the pack. He is the avenger. If someone caused one of the other personalities a problem, he comes out and fixes it."

"The problem with this, Jenna." Jo raised both eyebrows. "If we're correct, we're dealing with a cold contract killer personality, responsible for Robinson and likely the Stanton Forest murders." She waved a hand toward the refrigerated cabinets. "That personality is calm and cool. He might be a really nice guy. I don't think we've met him yet because none of the men you've interviewed have been calm or cool." She looked at Kane. "How was Brad Kelly when you interviewed him today?"

"Cooperative and he denied being involved." Kane frowned. "He appeared to be quite offended that we thought he might be involved. He brought up the fact he'd seen his father kill his mother as an excuse."

"Hmm." Jo walked up and down for a few moments. "If he's our killer, he could be the personality who can handle the stress." She looked at Jenna. "The angry young man we met could've been a totally different personality."

Wolfe cleared his throat and everyone looked at him. "Whatever personality we have committing murder, as a medical examiner, the only clues I've found to indicate the murders at the Old Mitcham Ranch were committed by the same person are the black feather and the assumption he is left-handed."

"It wouldn't be unusual for a person with dissociative identity disorder to change from right- to left-handed during a switch." Jo sighed. "In fact, anything is possible. Not all are violent, some self-harm, and most have no idea the other personalities exist. If so, and Brad Kelly is our killer, he'd pass a lie detector test."

Wolfe took a breath. "One thing is for sure and that's we have a psychopath out there, and I suggest you try and stop him before he murders someone else."

CHAPTER FORTY-FOUR

It was going to be one of those awful days when they took one step forward and three back in an investigation, Jenna just knew it. The information from Jo and Kane had stymied her usual way of thinking through a case. Any of her suspects could be suffering from dissociative identity disorder and hiding a psychopath. Right now, she considered at least two of the suspects had a motive for murder. The faces of Kyler Hall and Cliff Young dropped into her mind. She pulled out her phone as she followed Kane back to his truck and contacted the site manager at the ski resort. "Hi there, it's Sheriff Alton, can you tell me if Kyler Hall and Cliff Young are working today?"

"*They were here this morning, but when they dropped by the office, they mentioned heading out to the Triple Z Bar.*"

"Okay, thanks." She disconnected and then stopped walking when Jo called her name.

"Can I come with you?" Jo hurried to her side. "Wolfe has finished the preliminary reports, and from what I can see, the cause of death of each man is obvious. I'd like to observe the behavior of the suspects if that's okay?"

Jenna nodded. "Observing is all we'll be doing. I'm looking to see if they have any visible scratches; if so, it's reasonable cause to get a court order to have them DNA-tested against the sample taken from under Ruby's nails."

"Do you want to visit the Stanton Forest crime scene? We'll be driving by it in a few minutes." Kane looked at Jo and then started the engine and they headed to Stanton Road.

"No thanks, the images were fine and your description of the crime scene summed it up well." Jo turned to look out the window. "This part of the world is incredibly beautiful; the scents and fresh air really surprised me. I'd forgotten places like this still existed. Snakeskin Gully sounded like the end of the earth, but it's much the same. It will be a good place to raise Jaime."

Jenna nodded in agreement. "There's something special about small-town life. The camaraderie is second to none and you'll both do fine. Black Rock Falls is a special place too and it's a shame we've become Psychopath Central of late."

"Hmm, I think the killers all believe they can outsmart you." Jo smiled at her. "I have an awful feeling they'll keep coming until you let one get away. One unsolved crime and they have nothing to prove."

Flashes of the recent crime scenes flooded Jenna's head in a rush so fast she gripped the seat to steady herself. "Let's hope it's not this one. With the four of us hunting down this maniac, we should get a result soon." She glanced at her watch. "Step on the gas, Dave. We have to be back at the office by five."

She leaned back in her seat watching the forest fly by in a flash of color. The sound of the engine seemed to add a sense of danger as Kane accelerated and the Beast roared in response. They sped by other vehicles, lights flashing, and she heard Jo's nervous cough from the back seat. She turned and looked at her. "Places are so far apart out here, you'll have to get used to traveling at speed."

"That's why we have a chopper." Jo gave a nervous laugh.

"ETA five minutes." Kane flashed Jenna a grin. "It's good to blow away the cobwebs from time to time."

As the truck slowed before Kane made the turn into the Triple Z's parking lot, Jenna faced Jo again. "We'll play it low-key and hope we can get close enough to them to pick up any recent injuries."

"They won't suspect me." Jo unbuckled her seatbelt as the truck came to a stop. "I know what they look like, I'll go in first."

Jenna shook her head. "I don't think that's a good idea. Like Kane said, it's not safe."

"I'll take my chances." Jo slid out the door then peered in at them. "Give me a head start." She turned and jogged across the parking lot.

"Ready?" Kane climbed out and looked at Jenna over the hood. "Is she going to be okay?"

Not overly concerned about Jo, Jenna nodded. "Yeah don't worry, she would've been trained the same as we were. I figure she can handle herself."

"If she kept up her training." Kane strode toward the bar. "It's been some years since Quantico."

As they walked into the bar, the smell of beer and sweat hit Jenna in a wall of nasty. She blinked to allow her eyes to adjust to the dim interior and spotted Jo sitting at the bar, nursing a beer. "Well, how's that?" Jenna chuckled. "She's taken a seat right next to them." She headed to the opposite end of the bar and waited for the barkeeper to walk to them. "Is that fresh coffee I smell?"

"Yeah." The barkeeper gave her a curious look. "You drove all the way out here to buy a cup of my coffee?"

Jenna met his gaze. "Nope. We've been in the mountains and I'm desperate. Give me two with cream and sugar." She sat at the bar.

"Snow's coming." Kane sat beside her and smiled at the barkeeper as he filled two cups. "There's already snow up near the new ski resort."

"Same every year." The barkeeper shrugged. "Although last year it was the coldest I remember."

As Kane made small talk with the man, Jenna's gaze slid to Jo. She'd struck up a conversation with Kyler Hall and Cliff Young. The coffee was reasonable and everything was going well, until Cliff Young placed a hand on Jo's knee.

"Hey, let go of me, lady, or I'll punch you in the face." Young's face was sheet-white.

"I wouldn't if I were you." Jo had bent his fingers back and her eyes flashed with anger.

Jenna dropped off the barstool and headed toward the argument. "Okay, what's happening here?"

"Nothing, Sheriff." Jo dropped Young's hand. "This man grabbed my thigh is all. I don't like men touching me." She placed some bills on the bar and, without a second glance, headed out the door.

Jenna stared after her and then looked at the barkeeper. "We're good here."

"I'll take care of the coffee." Kane pulled out his wallet and flicked his eyes to the door.

"Sure." Jenna walked slowly toward the door and, once outside, noticed Jo leaning against the wall. "You okay?"

"I'm fine. Hall was drinking with his left hand." Jo grinned at her. "Both men have scratches and you don't need permission for Cliff Young's DNA." She held up a finger. "I accidently caught him with my fingernail."

"Sweet." Kane had walked up beside her without a sound. "I'll grab a test kit."

Jenna hadn't taken two paces toward Kane's truck when Hall and Young walked out the door. The pair ignored them and turned toward their pickup. As they walked, Hall took a cigarette from his mouth and flicked it onto the ground. They all stood motionless as the two men drove away. "This is my lucky day." Jenna ran to the smoking cigarette and pulled a pair of gloves from her pocket. "A saliva sample and two witnesses to prove who it came from. Take that, Sam Cross."

After making sure the samples were safe, Jenna climbed back into Kane's truck. "Okay, we'll drop the samples to Wolfe and then head back to the office." She grinned at him. "Strike three."

CHAPTER FORTY-FIVE

There was one benefit of starting work at daybreak because a man got to finish early and most days he liked to be back in town before five. At this end of town, side roads led to a row of small businesses. As the need for more retail outlets grew, many houses had transformed into stores overnight. The beauty parlor, a sturdy brick dwelling, had at one time housed the local bank manager; now it spewed chemical odors in great clouds. In truth, he'd located the store by its smell. He'd been watching the movements of Ann Turner, one of the local hair stylists, for some time. It seemed she had a reputation for being manipulative. The talk around town from the womenfolk was that the small, cute, bubbly girl had a smile for any man who looked her way. She was the dangerous kind, the type that thought nothing of breaking up a happy marriage for a few nights of fun. She used her female charms like a siren and lured married men to their downfall. He chuckled, imagining his hands closing tightly around her soft, smooth neck.

Ann, like most people, followed the same daily routine to and from work. A little after five, most of the hair stylists would leave for the day, and Ann would carry the garbage to the dumpster in the back alley and then head for her car. She always parked in the same place, behind the bank in the next lot. The owner of the beauty parlor would lock up, get into her vehicle parked outside, and drive away.

The moment the owner's vehicle pulled away, he pulled on his gloves, made sure his hoodie was down over his face, and strolled along the sidewalk. The road off Main was quiet, and a swirling mist crawled across the blacktop, covering him to his knees. Dressed all in black, he could move through the fading light and blend into the shadows. It was as if he'd become the mist, sliding into spaces and then vanishing like a ghost. No traffic passed him, and one quick glance around told him that when he'd slipped into the alley, nobody had seen him. He blended into the shadows and a chilling calmness replaced the rush of anticipating a kill. In this state, he could wait here, hardly breathing for hours if necessary. He didn't have to wait long in the garbage-tainted air before she came down the steps, purse over one arm and juggling three huge black garbage bags. When she set them aside, he made out her pink leather jacket, short skirt, and black stockings disappearing into pink cowboy boots. *Dressed for me to kill.* He waited for her to open the dumpster, and as she went up on the tips of her toes to toss the bags inside, he stepped behind her. "Hello, Ann."

"Oh, you scared me." Ann's eyes widened in surprise. "Do I know you?" She turned to face him her eyes bright with expectation.

He didn't reply but grasped her by the throat, lifting her off her feet to meet his eyes. Watching their expressions was all part of the thrill. She looked startled and then alarmed as panic filled her eyes. She raked at his hands, trying to break his grip, but he had her. She wasn't getting away. Her mouth opened and closed like a fish tossed onto the riverbank but no sound came out.

It always surprised him how long it took to strangle someone. It wasn't a fast death. It was up close and personal. He could feel the life leave their bodies. Luckily, the element of surprise usually robbed people of their first instinct to survive. Most women would go for his hands in a feeble attempt to break his grasp. It was a futile move. If they dragged his pinky fingers back, maybe he'd release his grip, but he couldn't understand why they never went for his eyes or at least tried to knee him in the privates. At least Ruby had tried to attack him, lashing out with her nails before he'd subdued her.

He squeezed harder and smiled as the blood vessels exploded like little red stars in her eyes, and finally the life left her in a rush of urine. He dropped her, disgusted, and went to the faucet to wash any trace from his boots. As he walked away, he glanced behind him but all he saw in the alley was a pile of trash. He'd forgotten about her already.

CHAPTER FORTY-SIX

At last Jenna believed she'd made some headway in the case. She walked into her office and found Carter sitting opposite her desk, working on his laptop. "How did you go? Any luck with the search warrant for Mrs. Robinson's bank accounts?"

"Oh yeah." Carter grinned at her. "Obtained and served."

Jenna smiled. "Great. We're just waiting for Rowley and we can bring everyone up to speed."

"I'm here." Rowley walked into her office, followed by Kane and Jo.

Suddenly filled with a new burst of enthusiasm, Jenna dropped into her chair. "Okay, let's get the show on the road." She explained Wolfe's conclusions and what had happened at the Triple Z Bar. "We'll need statements from Kane and Jo to verify the origin of the DNA samples. Wolfe is running them now."

"I have something interesting in the Lucas Robinson case." Carter stood and went to the printer. He collected documents and handed them out. "Mrs. Robinson made two substantial withdrawals in cash about two weeks prior to her husband's death. If she can't account for the money, it's possible she paid for a hit."

Amazed, Jenna stared at the bank statement. The account was in Carol Robinson's name and the withdrawals had almost drained it. "I gather her husband was insured and she would have something to gain from his death."

"Yeah." Carter smiled. "Five million."

Kane whistled. "That's a motive, and she knew he was having an affair." He looked at Jenna. "How does someone find a hitman in Black Rock Falls?"

"Did you know she was big in IT before she married?" Carter stretched his legs out in front of him. "She probably found him on the dark web. She'll have covered up all trace on her computer as well, so we'll find nothing."

"It would've helped if the kid they'd sent me as a computer whizz had shown." Jo shook her head. "He might have been able to hunt down the hitman."

"I doubt it." Kane shrugged. "Wolfe is our go-to guy when it comes to IT, and he's found a few traces of websites in his time, but if Carol Robinson has a solid background in programming, she'll have wiped every trace clean."

"Then when we find her husband's killer, we might be able to find a money trail. If she paid him in cash and he's still in town, he'll have the money stashed somewhere." Carter looked at Jenna. "Don't you agree, Jenna?"

"Yeah, a hit is a distinct possibility, and we'll certainly be looking for a money trail." Jenna checked her notes. "Moving on. Rowley, any luck finding out where Kyler Hall and Cliff Young were at the times of the murders?"

"Only hearsay and vague memories." Rowley met her gaze. "Their neighbors recall seeing their truck outside as usual most nights. The only morning one of the neighbors noticed it missing was the morning of the Stanton Forest murders. They've already admitted to leaving early that morning." He leaned forward in his seat. "No one is prepared to give them an alibi for any of the times of death."

Glancing at the clock on the wall, Jenna frowned at him. "Oh, you had Tom Dickson cleaning out your garage today, and I've kept you back. You'd better leave now."

"It's fine." Rowley smiled at her. "I dropped by earlier and fixed him up. He's a very reliable worker. My garage is as neat as a pin."

"That's good to hear." Jenna pushed to her feet, went to the whiteboard, and brought it up to date. She turned to look at Walters. "How did you go with Mrs. Robinson?"

"I haven't gotten in to see her as yet." Walters scratched his thinning gray hair. "I went down to speak to Weems at the funeral parlor. He told me Mrs. Robinson called him and told him to cremate her husband's body the moment he arrives at the parlor. Weems showed me all the documents he'd taken to the hospital for her signature. He also told me Parker Louis and Timothy Addams, from the Stanton Forest murders, will be laid to rest next week."

"Okay, thanks."

The landline rang and Jenna held up a hand to quiet the chatter in the room. "Sheriff Alton."

It was the forensic anthropologist, Jill Bates. Her cheery voice came down the line and Jenna put the phone on speaker. "Jill, great to hear from you. Have you found anything?"

"Yeah, from the dental records, the remains we found in Stanton Forest belong to Luitl Kelly. I've finished my examination and will be passing the case to Wolfe. I've stepped up the search for her son Scott. He has to be close by but so far we've found nothing but a kid's shoe." She took a deep breath. *"Seems to me the story Brad Kelly told me about what happened is accurate. The skeletal remains we unearthed are complete. The head trauma is consistent with his memories. Another thing of note. This woman suffered constant trauma over several years. I found evidence of broken bones, in different stages of healing."*

Anger and remorse for Brad's mother swept over Jenna. "From all accounts, she tried to leave her husband. This should never have happened. I can't imagine what it would be like to live with a monster like that."

"It's more common than you think, I'm afraid." Jill cleared her throat. *"At least he's dead now and not hurting anyone else."*

Jenna's mind flashed to Brad Kelly. He'd seen and likely suffered terrible abuse as a child. *Like father, like son* played in her head like an earwig. She hoped with all her heart they'd made a mistake and Brad Kelly hadn't turned out worse than his father. She sighed and looked at the faces of the people in the room; all had expressions of concern. "Thanks, Jill, I appreciate your call. Let me know if your team finds Scott Kelly's remains. It will sure put his brother's mind at rest."

"I sure will, bye." The line went dead.

Jenna replaced the receiver and blew the bangs from her forehead. "We're at a stage in the investigation when all we can do is wait. All the evidence we have is circumstantial at best. The only thing we can do is wait for the DNA results. With luck, Wolfe will have them soon. It's after six, go home, and as it's Sunday tomorrow, stay there and I'll call if I hear any news. I'll take the 911 calls. I want everyone to rest up until needed."

She waited for her deputies to leave but Jo and Carter remained. Although she wanted to go home, soak in the hot tub and forget about mass murder for an hour or so, she had guests. "I suggest we head back to the ranch and then go out for dinner. I'm too tuckered out to cook tonight."

"Where can we get a good steak?" Carter removed his toothpick and flicked it into the trash can under Jenna's desk.

"There's a steakhouse in town, surf and turf mainly." Kane stood and looked at Jenna and Jo. "That okay with you?"

"It's fine with me and I have a generous expense account." Jo grinned. "It's one of the perks of being in charge of the field office."

Jenna smiled. "Great, I'll book a table on the way home." She stood and walked over to the pegs behind the door to grab her coat.

As they walked to the front door, Carter smiled at her. "You're sure not what I expected." He tossed another toothpick into his mouth. "I've met plenty of sheriffs in my time and not one of them could run a string of complicated investigations like you do. How do you cope with so many murders?"

Jenna gave Maggie a wave at the counter. "Go home, it's late. See you on Monday." She turned to Carter. "It's never just me, Carter, it's the team."

As they walked outside into the cold, crisp evening, Jenna inhaled the fresh pine breeze and alpine scents. A movement caught her attention and Brad Kelly, tiger eyes blazing, seemed to appear from nowhere. Caught off-guard, she instinctively took a step back. Kane and Carter must have reacted instantaneously as the next moment all she could see was Kane's wide shoulders. She glanced to her right to see Carter pushing Jo back inside the bulletproof office doors. She prodded Kane in the back. "For Heaven's sake, Kane, he's not armed."

When Kane moved slightly, Jenna stepped out from behind him and looked at Brad's angry face. "Honestly, Brad, it's not a good idea to jump out at me when we have a serial killer in town." She looked up at Kane but he had his combat face on and would not move his attention from the perceivable threat. Instead, she turned back to Brad Kelly. "Did you want to speak to me?"

"Jill Bates has confirmed the remains are my mother and now she has loaded her into a coffin and is sending her somewhere else." Brad was about to burst with rage. "Where are they taking her?" He moved closer to Jenna, looking like a trapped wild animal.

Jenna lowered her voice to just above a whisper. "I'm sorry you haven't been informed. Jill called me a few minutes ago. She is handing the case over to Wolfe. Your mother's remains will be at the morgue. Wolfe will review the findings and then release her body to you."

"I don't want her going back to the funeral parlor." Brad shook his head. "My people will take care of her now."

"You can be assured that Wolfe will treat her with the respect he gives every victim that comes into his office." Jenna could almost cut the emotionally charged air around Brad. Could the killer be standing right in front of her? Seeing him like this, it was very possible.

"Respect, huh?" Brad shook his head. "You act like you care. Nobody cared. I told my teachers when my pa bashed my mom but they did nothing. When my mom and brother went missing, did anyone care? Not one law officer came to the res looking for us. The sheriff allowed my pa to get away with murder."

Jenna gaped at him, wanting to explain. "I—"

"Save it, lady." Brad stormed off toward his truck, climbed in, and sped down Main.

"Oh, boy." Jo came out to stand beside her. "I'm sleeping with the lights on tonight."

Shaken, Jenna slid into Kane's truck. "That is one angry man."

"Yeah, he has reason, I guess." Kane started the engine and backed out onto Main.

Jenna's phone chimed and she sighed and checked the caller ID. "It's Wolfe." She answered the call. "Hi, Shane."

"I have the results of the DNA tests." Wolfe sounded bemused. *"I ran them twice to make sure, that's what caused the delay. The DNA I found under Ruby Evans' nails is a match for Brad Kelly."*

CHAPTER FORTY-SEVEN

Speechless for a moment, Jenna stared at Kane. He'd taken off with lights and sirens after Brad Kelly's truck. She took a breath. "He was just here. Are you sure?"

"Yeah, it's a match. I have no doubt." Wolfe let out a long breath. *"Unless he has an excuse for Ruby scratching him, he's our killer."*

Jenna swallowed hard. "Okay, Shane, thanks. We'll give chase and arrest him."

She disconnected but her phone rang again immediately. It was Jo. "Hi, Jo, we have a positive DNA match on Brad Kelly, we're in pursuit now."

"I guessed as much when you took off and hightailed it to the cruiser. We're right behind you." Jo was breathing heavily. *"There's no doubt?"*

Jenna shook her head and then wondered why, as Jo couldn't see her. "No, Wolfe ran the tests twice."

Ahead, the mist swirled in the headlights, blocking her view, but she could still see the taillights of Brad's old model truck. "He's heading for the morgue. No doubt he thinks he can collect his mother's remains." The back window lit up with blue and red lights as Carter raced up behind them. "I'll see you there." She disconnected and grabbed hold of the seat as Kane slid the Beast around the corner.

To her surprise, Kelly pulled over to the curb opposite the sheriff's department as if allowing them to pass by. She caught sight of his startled expression as Kane drove past and then braked hard to stop across the road in front of him. Behind them Carter had blocked any chance of retreat. She followed Kane out the truck as he advanced on Brad, and she stuck to him like glue, drawing her weapon. "Hands where we can see them."

When Kelly placed his hands on the steering wheel, Jenna nodded to Kane. She waited for him to pull open the door and drag out Kelly. He had him face down on the hood of his truck and cuffed in seconds. "Brad Kelly, you're under arrest for the murder of Ruby Evans." She read him his rights.

"Me?" Brad shook his head, almost resigned. "I knew you'd try to nail me with her murder. Found a way to fix the DNA results, huh?"

"Take him in and book him." Jenna tossed Carter the keys to the sheriff's department and turned to look at Jo. "I'll call the DA. I want Kelly in the county jail tonight."

She made the call. "My medical examiner doesn't make mistakes, and he ran the tests twice to make sure. The suspect has a scratch on his chin, the victim has his DNA under her nails. Apart from meeting once at Aunt Betty's Café, Kelly denies seeing her since. He's far too dangerous to be in my cells. He's murdered eight people." She shook her head and stared at Jo. "Yes, we have FBI agents on the case. Here, speak to Jo Blake." She thrust the phone toward her.

"Hello." Jo frowned. "I'm a behavioral analyst with the FBI field office out of Snakeskin Gully. Yes, it's new. I suggest you tell county to send a chopper and four guards. This man is capable of anything. He should be in a secure environment. I suggest you hurry." She listened for a few minutes. "Within the hour. Good." She disconnected and handed the phone back to Jenna. "It looks like we get to eat around nine."

"The steakhouse is open until midnight Saturday. I'll book a table." Jenna made the call as she walked into the sheriff's department. She found Kane on the phone to the local judge.

"Would you believe he's working at his office?" Kane smiled. "He'll wait to sign the arrest warrant."

"The prisoner is in the cells." Carter strolled up to her. "I'll write up the arrest and search warrants and run them over to the judge."

Amazed by the efficiency, Jenna smiled. "Thanks. I'm so relieved we brought him in without any problems. Has he asked for a lawyer?"

"Yeah." Kane nodded. "I'll call Sam Cross."

Jenna frowned. "Just wait until we have the arrest warrant in our hands. I don't want him to find a loophole that allows Kelly to walk."

The next moment the front door flew open and Rowley came in still dressed in uniform with Atohi close behind. Jenna shook her head. "I sent you home to rest."

"We were at Aunt Betty's." Rowley looked from her to Kane. "What happened?"

Jenna hated telling Atohi she'd charged his cousin with murder but she had no choice. "I'm sorry, Atohi, we've arrested Brad for the murder of Ruby Evans. Before you say anything, his DNA matches the skin found under her nails. He has a scratch on his face and can't verify his whereabouts during any of the murders." She sighed. "We'll call Sam Cross to represent him and he'll do it pro bono. I'll submit the evidence we have to date and leave the courts to decide."

"I don't believe it." Atohi couldn't hide the shock on his face. "Angry maybe but not a killer."

Jenna squeezed his arm. "We'll need to search his belongings. Did you see him with any large amounts of cash?"

"He had money." Atohi shook his head. "From working, he gave some to my mom. He made arrangements for his mom too and paid for them, I believe." He looked at Jenna. "You are welcome to search his room but everything he owns he carries in a backpack in his truck." He waved a hand toward the vehicle parked outside. "Can I see him?"

Jenna shook her head. "I'm sorry, no you can't."

"Then tell him I'll take care of his mom." Atohi turned and walked, shoulders slumped, out the door.

"I'll be back soon." Carter headed for the door and then turned to look at Kane. "If you're heading back to the ranch to change for dinner, can you grab me a clean shirt? I'll have a shower here while we wait for the chopper and then we won't miss our dinner reservation. Rowley will keep me company." He ran out the door, paperwork in hand.

"Sure." Kane looked after him.

Jenna turned to Rowley. "Are you okay with staying back until they pick up Kelly?"

"That's fine by me. My girl is visiting her grandma this weekend, so I've nothing better to do." Rowley looked at her. "What happens next?"

"We'll call Sam Cross the moment Carter gets back with the warrants." She leaned against the front counter, suddenly exhausted. "I've formally charged Kelly with the murder of Ruby Evans. Kane is writing up the paperwork and the DA is arranging for Kelly to go to the county jail until his hearing. He's arranging a chopper. I just hope Cross doesn't sweet talk the judge into giving him bail."

"That's unlikely to happen until at least Monday, more likely Tuesday." Kane handed Jenna the documents to sign. "We'll need to hustle if we plan on going home to feed the horses and dogs." He rubbed his belly. "We should make it back into town by nine." He looked at Rowley. "Make sure Kelly has a meal. Get something sent up from Aunt Betty's." He smiled at Jenna. "Innocent until proven guilty and duty of care, covered."

"Here comes Carter." Jo peered through the glass door. "That was fast. He drives like a madman."

"It was only two blocks away." Jenna smiled. "And as long as he flies the chopper well, you'll be fine." She zipped up her jacket and turned to Rowley. "Call me if you have any problems. We'll be at the steakhouse from nine."

"Sure." Rowley took the bunch of keys from her.

The moment Carter hurried inside with the warrants Jenna turned back to Rowley. "Call Sam Cross and then Wolfe before it gets any later and ask him what he wants to do about searching Kelly's truck." She chewed on her bottom lip. "We're looking for cash to link him to Lucas Robinson's murder but he'll want to check it for proof Ruby was inside. He'll likely have it towed to his office in the morning." She stared into space, thinking. "You'd better put out a press release. Just say we've arrested a suspect for the Old Mitcham Ranch murders. That's all, no other info."

"Okay, leave everything to me and go eat." Rowley smiled at her.

Jenna looked at Kane and Jo. "Let's go."

CHAPTER FORTY-EIGHT

The buzz of the steakhouse hummed around Jenna as she finished her meal. With the killer locked up, she could relax at last. It had been a wonderful evening, and seeing Kane and Carter in animated conversation on every topic from hunting to engines made her realize how much he must miss his friends. The coffee arrived and she chatted with Jo. It was as if she'd known her all her life and it was good to have someone with the same interests to talk to. She would miss her when she returned to Snakeskin Gully. "How was Jaime tonight?"

"She is coping better than I am." Jo smiled at her. "I've been so worried and yet she loves the house, has made friends at school already, and is talking about having a puppy."

"That's wonderful." Jenna glanced at Carter. "Do you have anyone at home, Ty?"

"Nope, it's just Zorro and me." Carter shrugged. "There's never been room for a wife in my life up to now. I like to commit one hundred percent, and being away all the time makes relationships difficult."

Jenna nodded in agreement but had noticed the admiring looks women gave him. "I'm sure there's a special someone out there for you."

"I'm not in any hurry." Carter flashed her a brilliant smile. "I'm kinda married to the job right now." He looked at Kane. "You know the feeling, right?"

"Sure." Kane leaned back in his chair and smiled. "I've only had one vacation since I arrived. The murders keep us pretty busy."

"Then let's not end the night here." Carter pushed his coffee cup to one side. "I hear there's pool and card rooms at the Cattleman's Hotel." He looked at Kane. "How long since you've had a night out with the boys?"

Jenna grinned at Kane. "Oh, go on, Dave, you know you deserve a night out." She looked at Jo. "We'll be just fine on our own."

"These things go late." Kane shook his head. "I don't like leaving you out at the ranch alone."

Jenna picked up her phone and wiggled it at him. "I have a phone and a safe room. We're both armed, plus the ranch is like Fort Knox and we have Duke and Zorro." She looked at Jo. "We'll be fine." She waved a hand at them. "Go, we'll be at home, probably soaking in the hot tub."

"You have a hot tub?" Jo's eyebrows shot up. "Count me in."

Jenna watched as Kane and Carter strolled out the door. She slipped the keys to her cruiser Carter had left on the table into her purse and returned to her coffee. "Oh, I should've asked Kane for his house key. The dogs are in the cottage, I could've brought them up to the house."

"They're probably sound asleep by now." Jo sipped her drink and sighed. "It's getting late and I'm exhausted. Ready to head home now?" She handed the waiter her credit card and waited for him to swipe and return it.

Jenna's phone chimed and she frowned at the 911 ringtone. "Dammit, it's an emergency."

"Do you want me to call Kane?" Jo pulled out her phone.

"Not yet." Jenna accepted the call. "911. What is your emergency?"

"Oh, hurry please, there's a woman out back of the beauty parlor, I think she's dead. She sure looks dead."

It was a man's voice. Jenna took a pen from her purse and wrote on a paper napkin. "Okay, what is your name and contact number?"

"Errol Stack. I was walking my dog along Alpine, and he found her. Her eyes are just staring and she has ants crawling all over." He gave her his number.

"Okay, Mr. Stack, this is Sheriff Alton. I'm in town, I'll be there in five. Wait out front in the light, don't touch anything. Stay on the line. I'll get back to you in a moment." She glanced at Jo and muted the call. "Call Wolfe. Mr. Stack has found a body out back of the beauty parlor on Alpine. I'm not spoiling Kane's night out. We'll handle this one ourselves."

"Okay." Jo made the call. "Wolfe is on his way."

"Great." Glad she'd worn her shoulder holster, Jenna stood. "The beauty parlor isn't far." She hustled out the door and ran knee deep in mist to her cruiser. "The weather is really making the town spooky this year. This mist is getting thicker by the day."

"No doubt the kids will love it when they go trick-or-treating." Jo climbed in the passenger seat. "I hope we get this case wound up in the next few days. I would love to be home with Jaime for Halloween."

Jenna started the engine and put her phone on speaker. "You okay there, Mr. Stack?"

"Yeah, waiting out front under the streetlight. I'm armed and I'll shoot if anyone jumps out at me."

Jenna shot Jo a glance. "Okay." She flicked on her wig-wag lights. "You should be seeing my cruiser soon—I'm coming down Main and will turn onto Alpine in two minutes."

The mist had gotten thicker as she turned down the side road, she spotted Mr. Stack, an elderly man with a black Boston Terrier wearing a bright red coat. She drove past, turned around, and then pulled the cruiser to the curb, but before she had the chance to get out, Jo touched her arm. Jenna disconnected the call and looked at her. "Problem?"

"If you're planning on getting out before Wolfe arrives, I'll keep the vehicle between me and Mr. Stack and watch your back." Jo pulled her weapon and slid out the cruiser, looking all around.

Fog crawled across the sidewalk toward the man and his dog. The orange glow from the streetlight and the dangling skeleton hanging from the crossbar gave the scene a spooky atmosphere. A cold breeze brushed Jenna's cheek as she stepped out of the cruiser, drawing her weapon. Apart from the light spilling across the man and his dog, and the intermittent blue and red flashes from her wig-wag lights, all around the stores and bank had vanished into darkness. She kept the open door between herself and the stranger. "Mr. Stack, please remove your weapon and lay it on the ground."

"Why?" Stack took a step closer. "I'm the one who called you. I found the body."

Jenna aimed her weapon at him, dead center of his chest. "Yes, but if you're armed, I need you to place your weapon on the ground and step away from it. This is normal procedure, Mr. Stack. Please cooperate."

"Oh, I see." Stack reached inside his coat.

"Use two fingers, take out your weapon nice and slow." Jenna held her breath and her weapon steady as he complied and placed it gently on the ground and then stepped away.

Jenna holstered her Glock and walked toward him. "I have to pat you down, Mr. Stack."

"Oh, very well." Stack turned around and placed his hands flat on the wall of the beauty parlor. "If I ever find another body, I'm walking right by."

"Clear." Jenna turned to look at Jo, who had her weapon aimed at the stranger. She cleared her throat. "Okay, Mr. Stack. Where's the body?"

"Down there." Stack pointed to an alley. "By the dumpsters out back of the beauty parlor. As we were walking by, my dog started barking and then ran off. I went to get him. I thought he was chasing rats and I nearly had a heart attack when I found the woman."

A shiver of warning went through Jenna as she peered into the darkness. She did not intend to walk into a possible trap. "How did you see her? I don't see a flashlight."

"I used the flashlight on my phone." Stack turned it on and waved it around. "See?"

At that moment, the sound of a vehicle coming down the road caught Jenna's attention. She heaved a steam-filled sigh of relief as Wolfe pulled up outside the beauty parlor. "Wait here, Mr. Stack." She picked up his weapon, slipped out the clip, and checked the chamber before placing it into her pocket.

She pulled out her phone and activated the powerful LED beam. It pierced the darkness to reveal a pair of legs sticking out from behind a stuffed garbage bag. As Wolfe came to her side, scanning the area in big sweeps, she pointed to the alley. "She's down there."

"So I see." Wolfe pulled out his flashlight and moved forward. "Webber is on his way. Cover me." He headed into the darkness.

Jenna waved Jo forward. "Let's see what we have here."

They followed Wolfe, moving their flashlights and weapons in all directions. The wall to the alley ended at the back of the beauty parlor, and a quick sweep of the area told her they were alone. Jenna turned to Wolfe. "All clear."

"Jo, give me some light." Wolfe placed his bag on the floor, pulled out gloves, and handed her a pair.

"Sure." Jo lit up the body with her phone. "Dang, she's young— what, eighteen or so?"

Jenna took in the figure, arms and legs in disarray like a rag doll tossed away by a child, and examined the horrific expression on the young woman's face. A jolt of recognition went through her and she bent closer. "I know her. This is Ann Turner. She had an affair with Lucas Robinson. I interviewed her recently. When did this happen? The beauty parlor closes at five."

"I'd say she's been dead for about four hours." Wolfe handed Jenna a pair of gloves. "I'll take some shots of the scene and then you can check her purse for ID."

As Wolfe took the shots, Jenna searched the area using a grid technique Kane had taught her. The ground was damp but no footprints led from the faucet attached to the wall. Cigarette butts littered the ground around the bottom of the steps. From the lipstick on most of them, she decided the steps must be a favorite place for the women working inside to sit and smoke. After searching the small area, she found nothing at all and returned to Wolfe and Jo. "No evidence. There's a pile of cigarette butts at the bottom of the stairs; want me to collect them?"

"Nope." Wolfe examined Ann's eyes. "I doubt this killer would've waited for her casually smoking. Criminals aren't usually that stupid." He rolled the body over and did a cursory examination. "She doesn't have a mark on her. She has something under her nails, so I'll bag them but it doesn't appear to be flesh. This looks like asphyxiation due to strangulation. There wasn't a fight. From the dropped bags and her purse, the killer surprised her, likely as she was opening the dumpster."

"This is another hit." Jo stared at the body. "Men who strangle women do so for power. It's most usual in spousal abuse. It's used to subdue a woman for rape as well. Both are acts of power over women." She pursed her lips. "I don't see that here at all. He hasn't touched her. Her clothes appear to be in order. It's as if he just walked up and killed her in the most undetectable way possible. No blood. A man of average height and weight would've been able to strangle her away from him and avoid coming into contact with her clothes, but I'd look for any trace evidence on her."

"She was a hair stylist." Wolfe frowned at her. "I can see a ton of hairs on her skirt; the likelihood of proving one of those belongs to her killer is remote. If this is a hit, he didn't leave any evidence behind." He looked at Jenna. "Brad Kelly had time to do this before you arrested him."

Footsteps running made Jenna reach for her weapon. Heart pounding, she stood her ground as Webber came into sight. "Oh, good, it's you."

"Go get my van and back it into the alley. I'm done here. I'll get her back to the morgue." Wolfe picked up the purse on the ground and tossed it to Jenna. "You'll have to contact her family." He sighed. "I'll do a preliminary tonight and leave the post until Monday. I'm pretty busy right now."

Jenna nodded. "Sure." She opened the purse and found a small amount of cash, car keys, and her driver's license. She shone her flashlight on the contents. "Ann lives out on Stoney. I'll get a statement from Stack and then we'll head out to speak to her family."

"Where's Kane?" Wolfe pulled out a body bag from his kit and gave her a curious look.

"He's at the Cattleman's Hotel with Carter." Jenna replaced the items in the purse and slid it into an evidence bag. "I have to give him time off sometimes. This can wait for the morning. I have everything under control."

"Ah, I see." Wolfe waited for his van to arrive and looked at Jenna. "We'll take it from here. If you need me, I'll be awake for some time yet."

Jenna pulled off her gloves with a snap and tossed them into the dumpster. "Thanks." She looked at Jo. "Handled many death notifications?"

"No." Jo followed her between the van and the wall. "I'm usually called in after that chore has been done. It would be one of the worst things to do, I imagine."

Jenna grimaced and headed for her cruiser to grab a statement pad. "Yeah, it is."

CHAPTER FORTY-NINE

It was close to midnight and the drive back to the ranch seemed surreal to Jenna. The homes they passed had all embraced the Halloween tradition, gearing up for a spectacular street festival the following Friday. Under a full moon the stars went on forever in a cloudless sky, but when the moonlight hit the dancing white mist sweeping across the blacktop, it seemed to create a procession of ghostly figures. With her headlights picking up the ghoulish decorations along every fence, she experienced a hint of the fear of the dark she'd had as a kid. It had been some time since she'd traveled this road without Kane by her side. She missed his solid strength and black humor; he always seemed to sense her apprehension and make her laugh.

"Anything worrying you?" Jo turned in her seat to look at her. "The notification of the next of kin was a harrowing experience. It's hard to leave work behind sometimes, isn't it?"

Jenna turned into her driveway and waited for the gate to open and the floodlights to fill the area with light. "It's not the job tonight, although I'm concerned about Ann's death. If we'd had the results of the DNA earlier, we might have saved her." She glanced around and sighed. "It just seems so strange coming home without Kane." She flicked her a glance. "He used to drive me crazy with his overprotectiveness and now I kinda miss him."

"I know what you mean." Jo chuckled. "I've worked with many Navy Seals and Marines during my time; you can make them into agents but they'll always be military. I can tell Kane was in the service just by the way he acts. They're all respectful, and putting their bodies on the line to protect people is as normal to them as breathing. Look at what happened today." She smiled. "I've only just met Ty and he had me out of danger in seconds. I noticed Kane stood in front of you, ready to take a bullet if necessary. It's not macho, it's what they're trained to do. You know, at first I found Ty arrogant, but now I'm getting to know him, he's a pretty cool guy."

Jenna pulled up to the front porch and climbed out the cruiser, back sore from a long day. Barking and the long howl from Duke echoed across the yard. "The dogs want out."

"Maybe they need to go potty?" Jo stared at Kane's dark cottage and shrugged.

"Nah." Jenna headed up the steps. "There is a fenced area out back; they can use the doggy door to get out plus there'll be plenty of food inside. I'm just glad we fed the horses before we went out. It would be a nightmare tending to them this late."

Before she had the chance to open the door, a black flash dashed across the porch. "What the—?"

"I didn't know you had a cat?" Jo bent down and picked up the purring animal. "Oh, it's lovely. Its eyes are the color of pumpkins."

Amazed to see the cat again, Jenna shook her head. "It's not mine. It showed up recently. I thought it belonged at the Old Mitcham Ranch. It showed up the day of the mass murder all covered in blood. We wouldn't have checked the place if it hadn't hightailed it in that direction. Just think, if it hadn't dropped by, the killer would still be out there, murdering people."

"Seems like it's moved in." Jo looked at her, eyes shining. "Sometimes pets choose their owners. Can she come inside?"

Jenna considered it for a minute. "I guess, but I don't have any cat things here. She'll need a litter box or whatever, won't she?"

"She'll probably tell you when she wants to go outside. She seems very intelligent." Jo rubbed the cat's head. "I wonder what her name is?"

"Pumpkin, I guess." Jenna chuckled.

She opened the front door and disarmed the alarm. "I'll find her something to eat. I have a can of tuna somewhere." She headed for the kitchen and soon had the cat settled. She turned to Jo. "That was easy enough. Now, as we don't have to go into the office in the morning, I'm going to soak in the hot tub. I have swimwear that will fit you if you want to join me." She smiled. "It's a huge tub. I'd say we'd fit ten or more Navy Seals in there with room to spare."

"I'd love to." Jo followed her to her room. "This will probably be the last night I spend here. I can't imagine the judge throwing the case out of court. You've taken a very dangerous man off the street."

"We did—the team—and I can't imagine Kelly walking with the DNA evidence." Jenna went through her drawers, searching for something suitable for Jo. She handed her a one-piece and Jo hurried off to her room to undress. She changed and stared out the window at the dark shadows surrounding Kane's cottage. She missed not having him close by. *I'm starting to rely on Kane.* She looked at her reflection in the closet mirror and shook her head. *I'm some tough sheriff, huh?*

She grabbed a pile of towels from the hall closet and met Jo as she was walking out her door. "The hot tub is down in the gym; well, in a room beside the gym." She led the way through the house and opened a door that led down a ramp into the converted basement. To her surprise the cat followed close behind, tail straight up and waving.

"Ah, so this is where you go at the crack of dawn." Jo smiled at her. "I did wonder where you and Kane disappeared to. I thought you'd gone out to the barn to feed the horses."

"We do that too. The exercise is to keep us in peak condition. In this town, you never know when you'll need to defend yourself."

Jenna led the way through the gym, opened a door, and turned on the lights to the wood-lined room that held a massive hot tub and a steam room, the latter recently installed by Kane in his downtime. "Kane did most of the work in here. The basement covers the footprint of the house, so we have tons of room. The gym I built some years ago, but he's added weight benches and a few other torture devices." She placed the towels close by and turned on the bubbles in the hot tub. "It feels decadent keeping the water hot all the time, but the solar panels keep the running costs to a minimum."

The cat jumped onto the bench and sat washing its paws. Jenna smiled. "Pumpkin has settled right in. Is the water hot enough?"

"It's wonderful." Jo slipped into the water. "I'm so going to have to get one." She looked at Jenna. "The one good thing about divorcing a prominent attorney is the settlement. Mine should be through in a couple of weeks."

Although Jo sounded okay, Jenna could hear the resentment in her voice. She wasn't sure if Jo wanted to discuss her past. "I think adultery is the hardest to forgive or get over. I can't imagine how you've coped. It must have been a shock?"

"Shock doesn't come close." Jo ran her fingers through the water. "I came home after being away for two days on a case and found my boss had moved into my house." She stared into the distance. "He'd sent Jaime to my mother's and had our things packed. It was as if we'd become nothing to him." She shook her head. "I can't forgive that, Jenna. Treating me like that is one thing but Jaime doesn't deserve it."

Seeing her pain, Jenna sighed. "Are you going to be okay?"

"Me? Yeah, I'm as tough as nails." Jo seemed to shake herself. "I know he wanted me out of the FBI but I'd never give him the satisfaction. I happen to like my job and now I have new friends." She smiled. "I'm looking forward to running the new field office, and the sheriff of Snakeskin Gully is a hunk."

Jenna laughed and then heard the cat growl. Its fur stood up all over and its tail looked like it belonged to a raccoon. It was as stiff as a board and staring at the door. "What's wrong with the cat?"

The next moment the room plunged into darkness. "Don't worry. If there's a problem with the power, the generator will kick in soon." They waited in the darkness but nothing happened. "That's unusual."

"Maybe it's a fuse or something?" Jo's voice sounded loud in the silent room.

The cat kept up a low growl punctuated by spits.

Jenna looked in its direction but the room was pitch black. "Do cats sense danger?"

"Yeah, and they have incredible hearing—maybe she was giving us a warning." Jo's voice echoed in the room.

Jenna pulled herself out the tub and felt around for the bench. "I guess we'd better find out. Dammit, I'm more tired than I thought, I've left my phone beside the bed. I never do that, not when I'm taking the 911 calls. Do you have yours with you?"

"No." Jo sounded calm. "I did the same." A splash of water and she could hear Jo walking around the tub. "I've found the towels—here, grab one. Holy shit it's dark in here."

Jenna took a towel and wrapped it around herself. "No windows. Wrap the towel around you and we'll go back upstairs. I'll get some clothes on and go see what's wrong. My Maglite is on my duty belt in my room. Place your hand on my shoulder; we need to navigate the gym to get out of here."

"Hush a minute." Jo gripped her arm. "Did you hear that?"

Above their heads the floorboards creaked as if someone was walking along the hallway and into one of the bedrooms. Heart pounding, Jenna dried off as best she could and dropped her voice to a whisper. "It should be impossible to get in here. We have military-grade security and a backup generator, but if we've been breached, it's no ordinary threat—we'll have to fight."

"The killer is locked up, so it's not him." Jo's grip intensified. "Who else would risk walking in here? You're usually armed." She moved closer. "It's probably Kane."

"No, it's not Kane." Jenna looked up at the ceiling, seeing only darkness. "He'd call out and not creep around, and he doesn't make a habit of walking into my room in the middle of the night."

Jenna's stomach turned into a ball of knots. Had she overlooked something? Did the killer have an accomplice? The idea made goosebumps rise on her bare flesh. She'd been in a psychopath's line of fire before, but she'd done nothing, said nothing to provoke an attack lately. She tried to push her concerns away and fell into her zone of professional calm, but the constant creaking above her head dragged at her nerves. Someone had trapped them in the basement without phones or weapons, and even the failsafe tracker ring she wore as a backup sat on her nightstand.

"Someone has breached your security by taking out the power." Jo's voice was barely audible, it was so low. "Your failsafe is the generator, so whoever is out there knows you have one and has disabled it. Do you have anything down here we can use as weapons?"

Jenna pictured the gym in the light. "Yeah, dumbbells. The ones I use weigh six pounds and they'll do. They're on the bench in the gym. Not that they will help much if the intruder is carrying a gun."

"I wonder if they know I'm staying here? If not, we might have an advantage." Jo's voice remained calm. "How do you want to handle this?"

"We get out of here, locate our Glocks, and call for backup." They edged toward the gym door, Jo gripping Jenna's shoulder in an elephant parade. Jenna opened the door silently and listened for any sound. Above, someone was searching the house, moving slowly from room to room. The slight creak of the floorboards gave her the impression they were dealing with one intruder. She negotiated the equipment-filled gym, and using the wall to guide her, she moved through the door to the bench, ran her fingers along the padded fabric, found what she was looking for, and handed Jo a dumbbell. She leaned against the wall. "I figure it's one man; he'll have a flashlight, so we'll be able to see him. We'll wait until he heads for the kitchen or family room. We should be able to make it to the bedrooms without him seeing us." Jenna reached back and squeezed Jo's arm. "We'll have to split up or neither of us will get to our weapons. Your room is closest. You go first and sneak inside and then I'll head for mine. If he shows, I'll charge at him, so don't look back, just get your weapon."

"Gotcha."

The hairs on Jenna's body stood to attention as a beam of light shone under the door. Footsteps creaked down the wooden ramp. Her voice seemed to stick in her throat. "Someone's coming."

CHAPTER FIFTY

The darkness closed in on Jenna in a suffocating wall. Fingers trembling with cold, she searched the door, and when her hand touched the key protruding from the lock, she turned it. The well-oiled tumblers moved without a sound. When she'd first arrived in Black Rock Falls, convinced the cartel would find her, she'd installed locks and made every door in the house secure. Her paranoia had finally paid off. She leaned against the wall, heart thundering in her chest. Whoever had breached her security was right outside.

The handle rattled and something slammed into the door. She gripped onto Jo and they waited. Two or three times the intruder tried to get inside, but then, she heard footsteps moving up the ramp. She turned to Jo, keeping her voice low. "He's sneaking around like a burglar. Although, he's gone to a ton of trouble to give up after finding the basement locked. Heaps of people lock their basements. I bet whoever is out there believes we are all out in Kane's truck. I often leave my cruiser outside the house."

"Maybe but he'd have seen our weapons and phones when he searched the house." Jo's voice was calm. "Who goes out without their phone?" She squeezed Jenna's arm. "He could be outside the door at the top of the ramp just waiting for us to come out."

Jenna thought for a moment; between the two of them, they should be able to handle an intruder even while half-naked and shivering. "I didn't hear him shut the other door. He's probably left it open."

The creaks came again. The intruder was moving away toward the family room. "Maybe he's leaving. It's now or never—coming?"

"I'm right behind you." Jo gripped her shoulder. "Go."

Jenna turned the lock and eased open the door. She waited long seconds before peeking into the hallway. The ramp ahead was seeped in darkness but dim light filtered in from the open door above. The full moon was high in the sky and would offer her enough light to see in the familiar surroundings. She moved up the ramp swiftly. At the top she looked both ways and then urged Jo to move down the hallway to her room. As she followed, cold bit into her bare flesh. Her teeth chattered. The intruder had left the front door open. She halted at Jo's door to watch her back. One weapon would be enough, two even better. No footsteps or dark shadows loomed toward her, but before she could slip past and along the hallway into her bedroom, Jo popped back out the door. In the dim light, Jenna caught the shake of her head.

"He has my weapon and phone." Jo's voice was barely a hiss.

Jenna stared at Jo. Her bare arms and legs were clearly visible in the darkness. They'd need clothes fast; damp and wearing swimwear, they wouldn't last long in the freezing wind whistling through the house.

They moved as one, reaching Jenna's bedroom a few moments later. The cat streaked past and jumped onto Jenna's bed, its silhouette a moving shadow against the light quilt. Moonlight streamed in the bedroom, and from the door Jenna could see her phone, duty belt, and backup weapon were missing from the nightstand. Once inside, she closed the door and made straight for the landline beside the bed. The line was dead.

Dropping into combat mode, she searched the room, running her hands over the few objects on the nightstand. When her fingers closed over her tracker ring, she almost whooped with joy. She depressed the stone and pushed it on her finger. It would take a few seconds for Kane to look at his phone. She dragged sweaters and jeans out her drawers. She tossed clothes to Jo, and as they dressed, she bent close to the ring. "Intruder, we are unarmed, no phones, no power. Someone is in the house." She repeated the message three times and hoped Kane could hear her. "I need you here now."

She slipped on a pair of shoes, all the better to kick with, and turned to Jo. "It will take some time for Kane and Carter to get here. We'll have to take him down alone."

"Okay, as sure as hell, I'm not sitting here waiting for him to get the drop on us." Jo moved to her side. "He's inside and we're both trained for situations like this, although strategy isn't my strength."

Jenna nodded and took control. "We have two choices. Discover his location. One of us makes a diversion and the other attacks from behind." Jenna lifted the dumbbell. "If you're not up to that, we hightail it out the window and risk running across the yard to the safe room in the barn."

"And get gunned down if he's out there waiting for us." Jo shook her head. "No, let's take him down."

"Okay." Jenna eased open the door and listened. "He's in the kitchen." She went to the window and slid it open. A blast of freezing air slammed into her as she dropped the dumbbell to the ground. "Once I'm out, count to fifty and then distract him so I can get the drop on him. Then take cover. I'll be coming through the front door."

"Okay." Jo picked up the dumbbell. "Go."

Aware that she was leaving Jo, a mother with a young child at home, in danger, Jenna hustled out the window and hung from her fingertips before dropping to the ground. Ducking to avoid detection through the windows, she bolted around the house. The dogs barking and howling had reached ballistic but the noise covered her footfalls as she ran up the steps to the porch. The front door stood wide open and she turkey-peeked around the side window to look inside. A flashlight moved from side to side, heading toward the hallway. The intruder had his back to her. Heart near bursting through her rib cage, and with her adrenalin so high her teeth chattered, she gripped the dumbbell in her right hand, slipped through the front door and hid behind the sofa.

Aware that in a flashlight beam, her breaths of steam would shine out like a beacon, she pulled the neck of her shirt over her mouth. Floorboards creaked and the footsteps came closer. Her gut tightened. He'd turned around and was heading her way. In this position, she would be an easy target, and no amount of combat training would help her against a handgun. As if he could sense her close by, he stopped walking and stood in the middle of the room. The stream of light moved from side to side, so close it passed the edge of the sofa. As he directed his flashlight away, she crawled across the small gap to the next chair. From here she could see down the passageway.

A sound as if Jo had dropped a shoe came from her bedroom. The intruder moved into the hallway. Jenna could see his outline, tall and dressed in dark colors, and wearing a balaclava. When he headed to her bedroom door, she hoped Jo had taken cover. The next second the cat shot out of the room, its feet skidding on the polished floor. It headed straight out the front door and vanished into the night.

"Damn cat." He made his way toward the door, floorboards creaking with every step.

Tense and ready to fight, Jenna got her feet under her and waited. Her heart pounded when the man shone his light into her room.

"Come out where I can see you." His voice was loud in the quiet. "Move it or die where you stand."

"Okay." Jo appeared at the door. Her voice sounded calm and in control. "What do you want?"

"I ask the questions." He motioned with the flashlight. "Get out here."

Pushing down the urgent need to charge at the intruder, Jenna duck-walked to a better position. When Jo stepped into the hallway, bathed in the intruder's flashlight, Jenna understood her motive. Jo wanted to keep him facing her to give Jenna the chance to attack from behind, but she'd put herself in danger. She might have an instant to either attack or distract the man.

Jenna pressed her ring again. The connection would be open to Kane's phone and he'd be able to hear everything. Recording the conversation would happen automatically.

"Agent Blake, so we meet at last. Just the person I'm looking for." He held the gun in his left hand and had it pointed at her head. "Where's the sheriff?"

"At the Cattleman's Hotel with Kane and Carter. It's just you and me. Do I know you?" Jo lifted her chin and blinked into the light. "Drop that light out of my eyes if you want me to talk to you."

"Oh, the demanding type. Hmm, I gathered as much." He dropped the light a fraction. "We haven't met but you've seen my work. Did you enjoy my Halloween murders?" He laughed. "Oh, I can see you're already trying to psychoanalyze me. Don't bother—better people than you have tried. I'm in the too-hard basket and you won't be living long enough to write a paper on me."

"Who am I speaking to?" Jo's confident voice didn't quiver as she stared down the muzzle of the gun. "I'm sure you hide behind many faces. Can I speak to the one who isn't a mass murderer?"

"Mass murderer?" He shook his head slowly. "I don't do mass murder. You see, blaming me for everything was your first mistake."

"So, why did you come to Black Rock Falls?" Jo hadn't moved an inch. "To kill Lucas Robinson? That was a very professional hit, much like the ones in Baltimore."

"Yeah, I did him." The man waved a hand as if encompassing the town. "I admit, coming back to Black Rock Falls unleashed the beast in me. The memories I have of living here eat me up inside. When I received a message from Robinson's wife, I asked the reason she wanted him dead. She told me he has affairs and beats her. That's two darn good reasons to kill him, I figure. When she wanted his girlfriend taken care of as well, I obliged—for a price. The bonus was killing him in her house. She had no idea I planned to blow his brains out right beside her. I stood outside the front door and watched her—man, she went crazy. It took all of my willpower not to pop her as well." He chuckled but it carried no humor. "Being paid to get rid of problems is how I survive."

"And the two men in Stanton Forest?" Jo hadn't moved an inch. "Who paid you to kill them?"

"Those smartass guys wanted to kill *me*. They tried to run me off the road." He shrugged nonchalantly. "They made me pissed so I killed them. Need any more info? Want to know how I felt killing them?"

"I wouldn't waste my time psychoanalyzing you. You're not interesting at all." Jo sounded bored and folded her arms over her chest. She was trying to make him shift personalities. "Let me speak to the man who enjoys his work. I want to know why he is killing everyone and leaving a black feather. If you're not the one in charge, who is?"

Jenna crept to within a few yards of the man. She could see him quite clearly in a shaft of moonlight. His finger was not on the trigger but resting above, and she had to make a split-second decision when to jump him before he shot Jo. She'd launch herself at him the moment she had the chance. Then a sound came from him that made her hair stand up on end. It was the voice of a child.

"Don't call him out, lady." The gun had dropped to his side. "He does terrible things and says it's payback for our mom. He won't listen to us. I've told him she wouldn't want him to be like Pa." He let out a little sob. "The feather is Mom. It's her name. He kills them for her."

The killer had shown a weakness, and without hesitation, Jenna launched herself at him, dumbbell raised. She brought it down on his head and they crashed to the floor in a pile of limbs. She looked up to see Jo dash into the cover of the bedroom, and the gun and flashlight spun away over the polished wooden floor and into her bedroom. "The gun, grab the gun."

"I can't find it." Jo scrambled around the floor. "We need him alive, Jenna."

Jenna stared after her. "Yeah, I have some questions. Why the hell is he here, for one?"

She rolled away to sit on the floor, convinced he was down for the count. To her astonishment, the man's eyes popped open and he moaned. He surged up, and turned toward her. With a roar, Jenna swung the heavy weight, striking him across his kneecaps. The man howled, spun away, and dropped heavily to his chest.

"Bitch! I'll deal with you next." He dragged himself toward the bedroom door.

Would nothing stop him? Jenna went up on her knees and took aim for the back of his head, but as if gauging her moves, he reared up and the blow grazed his shoulder.

"You're making me angry, Sheriff. I didn't come here to fight you." He pushed up from the floor and turned to look at her with a bloodstained smile.

Jenna heaved a sigh of relief as Jo appeared at the door and aimed the pistol at him. "Give it up, it's over."

"It's over when I say it's over." His confident grin sent a shiver of uncertainty through Jenna. "I came here for her." He shot a glance at Jo as if completely oblivious to the gun she held on him. "I don't like the lies you've been telling about me and it's not good for my reputation." He shook his head, sending blood spots flying, and started to crawl toward Jo again. "I need to teach you a lesson." One large hand reached for Jo's ankle.

"Touch me and I'll splatter your brains all over the wall." Jo aimed at his head.

"Go ahead. I'm the one you can't kill." He spat blood and glared at her through the skull-like sockets in his balaclava, his blood-covered lips appearing black in the moonlight.

When he suddenly laughed, Jenna reassessed the situation. Was his weapon loaded? He seemed overconfident and in control. This was one dangerous and very strong man. She shoved him hard in the back. "Stay down."

"Don't tell me what to do." He rolled to one side and grasped the front of Jenna's shirt.

Jenna jabbed him in the face with the dumbbell and sprang away. Shocked as the intruder reared up, she jumped to her feet and faced him. She had to take him down but keep him alive. As Jo took a step forward, Jenna could see the muzzle of the Glock in the moonlight. "Hold your fire."

Without hesitation, Jenna kicked out his legs and he fell hard, bouncing on the wooden floor. "Stay down."

"You're both going to die." His head whipped around to look at her. "I'm going to make you pay for this."

Jenna jumped on his back, straddling him and forcing his face into the floor. Under her, he bucked, pawing at her legs and trying to dislodge her. He had amazing strength, and the persona coming out was as mad as hell. As he pushed up, she swung the dumbbell at the back of his head, and he hit the floor hard, rattling the picture on the wall.

Sure he was out, she looked up at Jo. "Grab the flashlight. I have spare flexicuffs in my nightstand. Top drawer on the right." She dragged his arms behind him, and seconds later, Jo was thrusting the flexicuffs in her hand.

They hog-tied him, and by the time they'd finished, he was fully conscious and another personality had emerged. This one was threatening to disembowel them. Jenna sat on the floor, her back to the wall, breathing heavily.

"You should've killed me when you had the chance." The man blinked into the flashlight. "You'll never be safe again, Sheriff." He looked at Jo. "And you're already dead, lady."

"Shut up." Jenna glared at him, pushed to her feet, and went to Jo's side.

"This guy knows too many details; he has to be involved in the Chameleon Killings." Jo looked at her but the weapon remained trained on him. "Kelly must have been his accomplice."

"It's sure looking that way. DNA doesn't lie. Kelly had to be involved in at least Ruby's murder." Jenna sighed. "Is that gun loaded?"

Keeping well away from the intruder, she clung to the dumbbell as Jo checked the clip.

"Yeah. It's loaded." Jo aimed at the man's head.

Jenna spoke into her tracker ring. "Kane, the intruder is secured, we're okay." She pressed the ring again, stopping the transmission, and stared at the man. "Who the hell are you?" She cautiously leaned forward and ripped off his balaclava, and as Jo lit up his face, Jenna stared at him in disbelief. "How is this possible?" She gaped in astonishment at the wild tiger eyes of Brad Kelly.

CHAPTER FIFTY-ONE

The moment Jenna's message came through, Kane headed to his truck. His gut wrenched as he listened to the voice of a psychopath and Jenna and Jo fighting for their lives.

"What's happening?" Carter jogged to his side, pulling on his jacket.

Kane pressed his phone to his ear, not wanting to miss anything. "Someone's broken into the ranch."

"Jo and Jenna are more than capable of taking care of an intruder." Carter laughed. "I doubt anyone could get the drop on them."

Kane took long strides toward his truck. "Some crazy psychopath took out the power and has their weapons."

"What?" Carter stared at him. "Let's go, man. How come you're not barking advice?"

Kane frowned. "He got their phones as well. The audio is coming through Jenna's tracker—we all have them, they're one-way communication devices that trigger a recording on my phone."

As Jenna gave the all clear, Kane climbed behind the wheel and tossed the phone to Carter. The Cattleman's Hotel sat on the outskirts of town and they were twenty minutes away from Jenna's ranch. If the intruder broke free, he might find both women slaughtered on his arrival. He left rubber on the road as they screamed out of the parking lot.

"Who could it be?" Carter tightened his seatbelt. "Any enemies?"

Kane accelerated, pushing the pedal to the floor as they flashed alongside Stanton Forest, his headlights barely cutting through the thick swirling mist. "Too many to count. There's a bigger problem. If he cut the power, the backup generator should have kicked in in seconds. It's very reliable and I check it every Sunday like clockwork."

"With your setup, no one could get onto the ranch to cut the power." Carter looked at him. "If it were me, I'd shoot out the transformer at the end of the road. Jenna is the only occupied house along that road. She mentioned the snowplow guy had left recently for Florida. No one would be home to report the problem."

Kane flicked on the wig-wag lights and headed down the center of town. Apart from the Halloween ghosts and ghouls in a sea of white fog, not a soul loitered on Main Street, and it was just as well as he blew through town doing ninety and hit the road to Jenna's ranch in record time. They slowed and Kane hung out the window and aimed his Maglite at the ruined transformer before taking off again at speed. "You got that right, but it doesn't account for the generator."

"What about the old guy you had working there the day we arrived? Tom?" Carter hung on as the truck slid around a corner. "He could've disabled it. You said he was short of money. Maybe he decided to break in."

It seemed inconceivable to Kane that a man Jenna had helped would try to kill her at the first opportunity. He shrugged and aimed the truck along the dark highway. "He didn't act like a psychopath and has no ax to grind with Jenna. He needed work and Jenna was feeding him jobs." He glanced at Carter. "Unless he was after Jo."

"How would he know Jo? It's her first time in town." Carter rubbed his chin. "I guess we'll find out soon enough." His phone rang. "It's Jo."

"Are you okay?" Carter placed his phone on speaker.

"Yeah. Close call but all those early-morning training sessions came through for Jenna." Jo sounded bemused. *"How the hell did Sam Cross get Kelly out of custody?"*

"He what?" Carter frowned. "Beats me. Nobody informed us. As far as I know a chopper picked him up and transported him to county."

"Yeah, that's what Rowley said." It was Jenna's voice on the line. *"So how come he's hog-tied in my hallway?"*

Kane pulled up beside Jenna's cruiser and dashed inside the house. The lights were blazing. Jenna had started the generator. He stared at the prisoner in disbelief and then back at Jenna. "Carter confirmed the county jail has eyes on Brad Kelly. If he's there, who the hell is that?"

"He's not saying but from the uncanny resemblance, he has to be Brad's missing brother, Scott. Obviously, Scott Kelly didn't die in the forest after all. It would make sense as the search team haven't found a trace of his remains." Jenna looked at him. "I've read him his rights. We'll have to haul him into the office and lock him up for the night. I've arranged for deputies from Blackwater to watch him. We'll haul him downtown as soon as they're on their way. I can't send him to county without an arrest warrant, and that's going to be a problem as he refuses to give his name."

"What's your name?" Carter crouched down and looked at the prisoner.

"Take your pick." The prisoner narrowed his gaze and his voice changed to a slow drawl. "This morning I was Tom Dickson, out of Saddle Creek. Sorry about the generator, Sheriff, but I only flipped the switch to off."

"You're not Tom." Jenna stared down at him. "Tom is at least thirty years your senior and has brown eyes, gray hair, and wrinkles."

"Oh yeah, poor old Tom." He chuckled. "He never has any cash. Maybe he uses that disguise to get close to his victims. Have you never heard of contact lenses and wigs, Sheriff? The wrinkles spray on and just peel off." He smiled at her. "When I added the limp and the old coat I found in a dumpster, I had you all feeling sorry for me, huh?"

"Are you related to Brad Kelly?" Carter looked at him closely.

"What, do all us boys from the res look alike to you?" The man snorted. "Anyway, Brad is dead."

Kane leaned against the wall. "What makes you believe Brad Kelly is dead? I spoke to him not four hours ago."

"Liar." The man thrashed around. "I'd like to see you die real slow, Deputy."

"Why does speaking about Brad upset you?" Jo moved forward. "Can I speak to someone who knows?"

"Let me up from the floor and I'll let you speak to anyone you like." The prisoner's voice had changed to smooth and cajoling. "I won't hurt anyone. Promise."

Kane wanted to observe him all night. Being this close to a psychopath with dissociative identity disorder was something he'd never imagined would happen. He noticed Carter scrolling through his phone and then walk into the kitchen. He left Jo trying to get some sense out of the lunatic and followed him. "What are you looking for?"

"I'm following up on Jenna's hunch and searching for birth records." Carter smiled at him. "We know Brad Kelly's date of birth, so I've set up a search for relatives born around the same time. He looks the same age."

Kane nodded. "The eyes are unusual and the same as Brad's—they have to be related."

"Well, darn." Carter looked at him and smiled around his toothpick. "I believe we can call off the search for Scott Kelly's remains. His father didn't murder him after all. Scott and Brad Kelly are identical twins. They both escaped after their father murdered their mother." He indicated with his chin toward the hallway. "Identical twins have identical DNA. Scott is batshit crazy and admitted to killing Lucas Robinson and Ann Turner. He fits the profile and, unlike Brad, is exhibiting dissociative identity disorder. He admitted to using different disguises to get close to people. It fits in with the Baltimore murders—all the same MO but seemingly done by different people. If we search his home, I'm guessing we'll find a ton of professional disguises like contact lenses, wigs. If this guy worked alone, we've charged the wrong twin and Scott Kelly is the Chameleon Killer. It will be difficult to prove Brad isn't involved, unless this guy has scratches on him."

"It's out of our hands now." Jenna pushed both hands through her hair. "It's up to the DA to sort things out, we just catch the bad guys."

EPILOGUE

The following Friday

It was dark on Halloween night by the time Jenna finished writing the reports. She had waved goodbye to Jo and Carter on Thursday morning. Heck, she missed them already. It had been wonderful having Jo around, and she looked forward to working with her again soon.

Kane walked into her office, dressed all in black, to-go cups of coffee and a bag of takeout from Aunt Betty's Café in hand. She closed her laptop and looked up at him. "That's it, case closed."

"Not in my wildest dreams would I have figured on identical twins." Kane placed the takeout on the desk and dropped into a chair opposite her. "Not so identical... One of them was just angry and his other half turned out to be a murdering psychopath."

Jenna closed her daybook and pushed it to one side. "I'm not surprised. Brad made it to the res and they raised him in a family, but Scott lived a life of hell. What are the odds of one brother making it to safety and the other running into a pedophile in the forest?" She pulled a takeout bag toward her. "I still can't get my head around why Scott had so many personalities."

"After being held in a small room for years, his mind created different personalities to cope." Kane opened a bag containing a pie and looked at her. "His first kill was his tormentor and it gave him freedom. It opened the door to his murdering rampage, and it seems each of his tougher personalities took part. I couldn't believe the wide range of disguises we found in his home. He was a master of disguise—no wonder the FBI couldn't find anyone to match his description. If I had Tom Dickson in front of me right now, knowing he was Scott, I doubt I'd see through his disguise. Oh, he was good. I honestly believed he was an older man down on his luck. He looked nothing like Scott. I mean, with the dark brown contacts, a limp, and gray hair... he even had wrinkles."

"Yeah and he smelled pretty bad too. I think covering his unusual tiger eyes with the brown contact lenses made him generic, and the spray-on wrinkles would have fooled anyone. He even spoke differently and appeared to be an older man to everyone he met. No wonder Jo named him the Chameleon Killer. He could change into just about anyone his crazy split personality chose and no one would recognize him. To think he was working so close to people we care about." Jenna sipped her coffee. "Why didn't he try to kill any of us or Rowley?"

"It was a game to him and by fooling us, he never came into consideration as a suspect. It was a clever move." Kane rubbed his chin. "Tom was a personality he used as a front man to move around unnoticed. I guess he must have had a run-in with the workers at the Old Mitcham Ranch as Tom, and then Scott took over and decided to kill them."

"Yeah, I thought the same." Jenna nodded. "Then he turned back into Tom and calmly came to work for us the next morning. He likely burned his bloodstained clothes and disabled the generator then hightailed it in his truck up the hill overlooking the Old Mitcham Ranch to take pot-shots at us. He didn't have to leave the boundaries of my land to do that." She spun the to-go cup in her hands and looked at him. "Seems he's boasting about his crimes. Jo was able to extract tons of information from him. His story checks

out about killing his tormentor. A hunter found the bones of his
abductor long ago, and the cage in the basement, where the man
held him. It's been a cold case for years."

"I know." Kane wiped his hands on a napkin and then lifted his
coffee to his lips. "The way Jo managed to draw out his different
personalities to give their accounts of events was incredible. Listening
to his confession of the murders he committed here was intense, but
when he added a string of murders from Baltimore and other killings,
she'd been unable to solve for years, it was mind-blowing. The tape
she made of Kelly's interview will be used for teaching behavioral
analysts for years to come." He looked at her over the rim of his cup.
"I've learned a lot from her."

Jenna nodded. "I'm going to miss them but it's good to know
they're close by if we need any help."

"Yeah." Kane met her gaze. "Running through clues with other
investigators will be a bonus, and they're not likely to pull the FBI
card and take over."

"The feather was a clue we didn't understand. Not knowing the
significance slowed down the investigation." Jenna sighed. "I wish
Atohi had explained more."

"Yeah, if he'd told us Luitl regarded herself as part of the Crow
Tribe because of her father and her name means 'feather,' it would've
helped." Kane sighed. "Seems as if in Scott's deluded mind, each
time he killed, it was to avenge his mother. Atohi doesn't agree. He
believes Scott disrespected her name by dropping the feather in the
victims' blood. At least Brad is home now and was able to lay the
poor woman to rest with her people."

"It's so sad. They both thought the other twin was dead." Jenna
leaned back in her chair. "I'm glad the DA cleared Brad of all charges.
Without the scratch on Scott's wrist it would have been difficult. It's
fortunate Wolfe took another look and found soap residue in the

tissue sample from under Ruby's nails and matched it to the soap found in Scott's bathroom."

"Thank God for Wolfe." Kane raised his coffee cup in a toast.

"Amen to that." Jenna touched her cup to his. "I think the biggest shock to me was Carol Robinson getting bail. Sam Cross is going the battered-woman angle to bring down the charges." She shook her head. "At least now we know why she was so shocked at the scene."

"Yeah, she paid the hitman but had no idea when or where he'd kill her husband. She actually believed the hitman was an intruder." Kane scratched his cheek. "She's still a murderer, even if she didn't pull the trigger. She'll get life."

Jenna looked at Kane and frowned. "When you look at the cases, they can be blamed on spousal abuse. The ball started rolling with Luitl Kelly's abusive husband twenty years ago and ended with Carol Robinson."

"It's something that needs to stop." Kane's eyes flashed with anger. "Maybe we need to talk to the mayor and set up a campaign in Luitl Kelly's name. We can raise money for more safe houses for women to go to if they're in danger."

"Yeah, we'll start a campaign, now we have time on our hands. We'll call it Her Broken Wings. I'm sure the town will get behind us." Jenna indicated toward the dog. "Now it makes sense why Duke was acting strange. I put it down to the cat and now realize he probably sensed that when Scott was disguised as Tom Dickson, a killer was close by."

"I really need to learn how to speak dog." Kane bent and scratched Duke's floppy ears. "He probably thinks I'm losing my edge."

"Nah, he just thinks you're human." Jenna smiled at him. "Oh, I have some good news for you. Do you remember Mrs. Grainger? Her son held up the pharmacy for drugs for her?"

"Yeah, that case was hard to forget." Kane frowned. "Is she okay?"

Jenna nodded. "Better than okay. Since she's been under Doc Brown's care, a new specialist is on her case and she's undergoing treatment. Her son called and said she'd made a significant improvement."

"That's wonderful news." Kane cleared his throat. "Do you think now that our caseloads are clear, we could sneak off on a vacation before anything else happens? I really need a break—we all do."

He must have been reading her mind. Jenna had been thinking about making vacation time for everyone in the office. "Well, I'm hoping to get away for a couple of days to try out the ski resort before Christmas, and you did promise me a weekend."

"Sure." Kane laughed. "You're a glutton for punishment."

"Me? Why?" Jenna stared at his white grin. "Come on, what dark secret do you have now?"

"No secret but I'm one hell of a good skier." Kane chuckled.

Jenna tossed her to-go cup in the trash and laughed. "Me too."

"Oh, we're going to have fun, the slopes up there are fast." Kane balled up the paper bags and pushed them inside his cup. "I can't wait for the first snow."

"When we go, I'll have to make arrangements for Pumpkin. We can take Duke with us but she'll need someone to care for her." Jenna stared into space. "Maybe Em will take her for a couple of days. I know she likes cats."

"So, she's staying, then?" Kane raised one eyebrow. "Says the woman who doesn't like pets."

"I do so like pets, and Duke likes her too." Jenna laughed. "She's staying—she saved my life by giving me an early warning someone was in the house."

A knock came on the door and Shane Wolfe's youngest daughter, Anna, poked her head inside, although Jenna hardly recognized her in her Halloween costume. She smiled at her. "Hello, Anna, you scared me."

"Did I really?" Anna giggled. "Daddy said it's time to go get some candy." She grinned at Kane. "You look awesome."

"Thanks." Kane stood, pulled up the hood of his long black cloak, and grabbed the scythe leaning against the wall. "You look great too. Tell your dad we're on our way."

"Okay." Anna scampered off down the hallway.

Jenna stood, adjusted her demon costume, and walked around the desk. She looked at Duke, rigged out in a superhero cape and mask, and giggled. "Ready, Duke?"

The dog barked and gave her his best doggy smile and wagged his thick tail.

In the reception area, Wolfe's kids were chatting excitedly as they headed out the door. Kane and Jenna followed them into the cold, misty night and stood at the top of the steps, surveying the people moving happily along Main Street. She glanced up at Kane. In his Grim Reaper costume, he looked huge and frightening. She shivered and he turned to smile at her. "What are you grinning at, Dave?"

"Come on, my little demon." Kane took her hand with a laugh. "If we have to walk down Main Street dressed like this, let's do it like we own it."

A LETTER FROM D.K. HOOD

Dear Reader,

I am delighted you chose my novel and joined me in the exciting world of Jenna and Kane in *Her Broken Wings*. If you'd like to keep up to date with all my latest releases, just sign up at the link below. You can unsubscribe at any point and your details will not be shared.

www.bookouture.com/dk-hood

If you enjoyed my story, I would be very grateful if you could leave a review and recommend my book to your friends and family. I really enjoy hearing from readers because when I write, it's as if you are here with me, following the characters' story.

Writing a novel is a very isolated business, and I would love to hear from you—so please get in touch on my Facebook page or Twitter or through my website.

Thank you so much for your support.
D.K. Hood

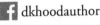 @DKHood_Author

dkhoodauthor

www.dkhood.com

dkhood-author.blogspot.com.au

ACKNOWLEDGMENTS

Where would I be without the amazing team at Bookouture, who offer support and understanding in the crazy world of publishing? Thank you so much for making me part of the family.

CPSIA information can be obtained
at www.ICGtesting.com
Printed in the USA
LVHW042246190620
658102LV00002B/145

9 781786 819024